P9-BJW-627

GANN, ERNEST KELLOGG, 1910
FIDDLER'S GREEN /

1950.
37565009117911   CENT

CLOSED STACKS

Stains
11/94
noted

CH

Gann
    Fiddler's green

CENTRAL

Fiddler's Green

ERNEST K. GANN

SANTA ROSA - SONOMA CO. LIBRARY

Fiddler's Green

SONOMA COUNTY
e.4c
FREE LIBRARY

WILLIAM SLOANE
ASSOCIATES, INC.
Publishers   New York

Copyright, MCML, by

ERNEST K. GANN

Typography and format designed by

LEONARD W. BLIZARD

Manufactured in the United States of America

To those rugged individualists,
the commercial fishermen

"FIDDLER'S GREEN" ....
. . . the imagined Elysian Field of sailors and vagabond
craftsmen—where credit is good . . . where there's many a
lass and many a glass . . . and never a stormy sea . . .

"O God, thy sea is so great, and my boat is so small . . ."
Ancient Phoenician Fisherman's prayer

Fiddler's Green

CHAPTER — — — — — — — — — — *I*

THERE WERE MANY LITTLE BOATS LIKE THE *Caledonian*, the *John Bosco*, the *Wayfarer*, the *Fred Holmes*, the *Ginger*, the *Capella*, the *Alert*, and the *Taage*. The men in these small vessels were very close to the Pacific. They lived on her abundance, for these were the fishermen.

They stood upon their dripping foredecks, sometimes leaning against the wheelhouse, sometimes sitting on a coil of anchor chain, any place where they could escape the insistent rhythm of their engines, which troubled their listening. Those who sailed alone, like Simon Lee on the *Alert*, were lonely and wet, and they listened only halfheartedly because they cared so little. If they were run down, or if they missed a bell buoy and piled on the rocks, that was just too bad. If they were to lose their boats or their lives, it would be because of a natural and annual union of elements beyond their control, and they accepted the risk. There was no arguing with the weather. A mass of warm, moist air had passed over the Pacific, brushed along the Japan Current, and, cooling, was no longer able to contain its moisture. So there was fog. The men who sailed alone smoked, rubbed their noses, watched the black Pacific for signs of tide rips, answered the lonely mews of the sea gulls with curses—and listened.

The fog lay down in the early afternoon. It was ragged at first, patches here and there along the coast, and as evening came the patches seeped into each other. Their joining hastened the night.

The fog, sliding through the Golden Gate, pushed eastward until it swallowed the city of San Francisco. It pressed upon the wharves, enveloping them and the brooding hills above them. It sank again; flowed, rose and fell, with the steep inclination of the streets. Horns on the bridges and on Lime Point, on Alcatraz Island and Mile Rock protested the intruder. They yelled separately or together, according to the whims of the light wind.

The fog rolled along the Embarcadero and Bruno Felkin was grateful for it. He gulped at it, sucking it deep into his lungs. His lungs were full of broken razor blades.

The smack of his shoes on the pavement and the whimper in his throat were the only sounds alien to the fog. Those shoes had never been designed for such a race. They were expensive shoes. The best shoes Bruno Felkin had ever owned. They were pointed, and the heels were especially high—to give a man height. They were beautiful shoes for dancing with Connie, or just standing around and looking important. No good, though, absolutely no good for running. Not when a man's whole future depended on how fast he ran. Not when his life depended on speed; on getting away from Sam's place, far away, so that at a certain time, say exactly nine o'clock, Bruno Felkin was seen somewheres else. A few minutes could make all the difference. You had to suppose they checked time carefully. A man who had just killed another man, a man who had never done any such damn foolish thing before, had to do a lot of supposing, and thinking, and running—if he didn't have a car.

But a car would have been no good anyway. Not in San Francisco. Of all the lousy cities in the world to let the mind go soft! You were a fly in a bottle in San Francisco. Smart men avoided the place. Smart men had San Francisco figured. They knew about the geography of the city. How it was all wrong: There were only four exits if you were in a hurry. The Golden Gate Bridge going north. The Bay Bridge going east. Highway 101 heading south. A single radio call could close them all. As of right now. There was always the fourth exit, only you forgot your water wings. The Pacific Ocean was so wide and wet.

Bruno ran, cursing inside as he ran. There was no breath to spare for saying it with the mouth. Not what Bruno Felkin thought of Bruno Felkin. That opinion would take a large bag of wind and much priceless time. Right now, neither was handy.

Past Pier 5. Pier 7 behind, and the cafeteria by the Bar Pilots' office. The cafeteria was closed. Past Pier 9 and now was the time to quit smoking. Right now. Instantly—when you realize what cigarettes can do to your wind. Strictly a half-horsepower engine in this Bruno Felkin. Beat up with nicotine if nothing else. Every cigarette in twenty years, every single one now gets the pay-off in a running step that hasn't got the necessary push behind it. You cheap little tinhorn.

You cheap little tinhorn. Let Sam kid around a little and you get excited. You wave the gun like a big grown-up boy, and the damn thing goes off. The fact Sam grabbed you by the neck, the self-defense angle, wasn't enough—and wouldn't be. Not for a guy who was already a three-time loser. You lost your concrete head, so now you pound the concrete for all you're worth.

Sam goes to the floor and that does for him. Obviously. What does it do for you? For Bruno Felkin? Nothing. Not one damn thing for Bruno Felkin except start you on the world's longest foot race. But Sam should never have mentioned McNeil Island. He knew you were potty about the place.

He shouldn't have said, "Bruno, this is my territory. You
and your little Western Sales Company seem to be getting some
expansive ideas. It's time we worked out some satisfactory ar-
rangement. I'll leave the details to you but be sure you include
me, and be sure you make it forty-sixty." Sam shouldn't have
said that, reaching with his big fat hand for a sixty percent slice.
Sam should have stuck to his coin machines. The diggers were
doing all right for him. He would still be able to play the horses
and the blondes if he hadn't been so unreasonable. And Bruno
Felkin could be walking instead of running. Expanding business instead of lungs. Jesus! Connie. Connie, you might be a
sharp-looking babe, but you were also sharp in the head. About
carrying the gun around—you were so right! You never liked
this rotten business. Not from the very start.

Now comes Pier 19, the Silver Java Pacific Line. You should
be in Java all right. You and Connie, making a real thing out of
some of them dreams you've had together. The dreams you always promised her would turn out all right. You both should be
anywhere but San Francisco. Some place where you'd both have
a chance to breathe like other people. Like Connie wanted.

That car coming is okay. Quit worrying about it. It doesn't
wear a siren and it's the wrong color. So what's the rush? Sam
will still be lying there and the flash-bulb boys will be taking
pictures from this angle and that angle; only missing the real
angle, as to who done it and why. The rest of the squad will be
arguing about the phone call. Or they might already be starting
out, sniffing around in likely places for a few candidates to answer their questions. They would run down the eleven-five-
hundred Health and Security file in their fat heads—and soon
enough get curious about Bruno Felkin. In fact, why kid yourself? You would be number one on their hit parade. They've
just been waiting for a chance to glom onto you. They've got
you on the other counts. Now it will be murder in the first de-

gree, or the second degree, or the third degree; what the hell difference is it going to make? You shot Sam Addleheim.

You should get a medal for shooting Sam, but they wouldn't see things quite that way. You were going to get the gas chamber for shooting Sam. Unless—

If . . . *if* you can just keep running fast enough and long enough to make Connie's place, in maybe six or seven minutes. Then they can damn well come around and you will be sitting there having coffee and doughnuts. You can be holding Connie's hand maybe, and she will look at the squad car boys with those cool eyes of hers, and you can both be all surprised. Connie's eyes could do the trick. They could make any man think about other things. You can prove you've been there all the time— well, *almost* all the time. There would be that seven or eight minutes from the phone call, maybe only six minutes if you can run faster. Connie's place is that close to Sam's, just a perch on Telegraph Hill. When you paid that first month's rent you never knew how handy it was going to be.

First you pull a stupid thing and then you have to genius the brain to get out of it. Fast. So you step over Sam, still shaking, and trying not to look at him. You're thinking smart all the time as to now what? Then comes a flash idea that should confuse anybody including J. Edgar Hoover. Eliminate a competitor, straight business protection, that's all it was, and then call up headquarters and tell them about it yourself. Who but Bruno Felkin would have the imagination to pull a thing like that?

So you hold the phone in your handkerchief, the silk one Connie gave you, and you dial that number. It only takes a few words to tell the hammerhead desk sergeant all you've got to tell, then hang up and start running. Run like hell because they already know you work alone, have no car, and couldn't get a taxi along the Embarcadero without them finding out about it.

The exact time of the phone call would be recorded. Later

you could prove you were somewheres else within a few minutes
of the call. No, *don't* be sitting there having coffee with Connie.
The two of you jump in the hay together. Let them find you
there, because that's what they would expect. Within a few
minutes of the phone call, you're in bed with your babe. Let
them figure that one out. If only you can hoof it fast enough. If
your lungs will only hold out.

Swing left now, past the Merchants' Ice and Cold Storage
Company. Pier 27 . . . up Lombard Street. Get to hell away
from the Embarcadero. Were there enough words in the phone
call to recognize the voice of Bruno Felkin? You should have
thought of that, talked higher and not so fast, not sound like
South St. Paul so much. Forget it. The idea was solid and no
tinhorn would ever think of such a thing. Not unless they were
plenty con-wise. The uniforms would have a time figuring that
one out. Then Connie, who never got excited about anything,
would be right there to back you up. Maybe Connie *would*
rather be living on some chicken farm, strictly on the level, but
she wouldn't let you down. She wasn't the kind. Think fast,
Bruno. Think as fast as your feet are going. As fast as your
breath. There are big businessmen and little businessmen. It's
smart thinking at times like this that separates the men from
the boys. You've come a long ways from South St. Paul. You and
Connie together can go lots further if you make her place in
the next four minutes.

Connie Thatcher closed the street door behind her and went
quickly down the four steps to the sidewalk. It was ten minutes
to nine and if she walked fast she would arrive at the movie before the second show started. She had been reading the paper
and discovered that the Bella Union Theatre was showing a
foreign film. They were the kind to see because they took you to
a world of strange manners, of funny-looking railroad trains,
and the printed titles at the bottom of the screen gave you the

idea you could speak a foreign language just like the players. It would be something to speak French, or Italian, say. It would be something to be proud about. Quite a step from a jerkwater town in Nebraska. Quite a ways from pearl diving across the country in one greasy spoon after the other. Getting to be a waitress in a fairly decent place . . . and then meeting Bruno Felkin really started things. There was a lot more polishing to get done, but with Bruno working you over, things were finally rolling.

"There's a lot more to it than just learning to shave your legs," Bruno said. "You got to have real class, not the showy kind, the inside kind. It don't come easy. Real class people get it thrown at them from the time they're babies, so we both got lots of time to make up. You got to read books. You got to keep your voice down. You got to wear a different kind of clothes and not have your hair look like it just come out of some plaster cast. You got real nice hair, Connie—it's blonde and fine and I love to run my fingers through it—so leave it be not too short or too long, the way the class babes wear it." The best hairdresser in San Francisco took three sessions to please Bruno. He always knew what he wanted and he wanted things just right.

"You're smart to go to the movies," Bruno said. "But don't go to movies about people like us. Stay away from them pictures . . . they always make you think you're doing all right. Like a contented cow, you get. We know all about us. Too much. So you *can* cook like somebody's mother. That don't count too much. It's more important to know how the others live. I can't explain why knowing the South of France is a swell resort makes any difference, better even than Miami which is strictly for tinhorns, but I know that it *does* make a difference. Keep your eyes open and learn. Learn twenty-four hours of the damn day because we got so much time to make up." Bruno was right, of course. But every day it was getting to be more of a question if you or anybody else could make a fancy girl out of a Nebraska

cornhusker. To change inside, you had to want something awful
bad.

Connie crossed Grant Avenue to the small grocery store on
the corner. There was one thing still to be done before she was
free to enjoy the movie. Bruno was late coming around tonight
for some reason, but he would be waiting when the movie was
over. And while he was waiting he ought to have things nice. It
was always a pleasure to have things nice for Bruno. He always
said he didn't like having a fuss made over him. He just never
had anybody try who really knew how.

The bell over the door clanged musically and summoned the
proprietor from his back room. He was a small man, as minia-
ture as his store. He had thin lips, and his smile looked tired.

"I'm in a hurry," Connie said. "Do me a favor?"

"Sure."

"I need some doughnuts and I don't want to carry them to the
movie. Would you put a dozen on my steps before you close?"

"Sure. Anything else?"

She studied a long salami that hung from the ceiling.
"That," she said. "Bruno always likes a snack. Will you put it on
the bill?"

"It goes on your bill."

She started for the door. "I'm in a hurry."

"So you said. Be careful. When you get to my age you'll know
hurrying is crazy. Nothin's worth it."

"Good night." Connie smiled and the little man winked at
her. "Thanks."

She turned down Chestnut Street lifting her face to the fog.
She enjoyed the feel of it on her cheeks. She walked with her
chin high, straight—as Bruno had explained was the way to walk.
"Little people slump because they been beat," he said. "You
got to have confidence. You got to know you're the best . . .
and so you walk proud. Sort of ease along, careless. Never get to
thinking for one second you aren't the very best."

She pushed the hood of her raincoat back from her blonde hair and pretended it was three years from now. She was in London. She was going to meet Bruno at a fancy hotel. There would be soft music and men in claw-hammer coats. They would bow when Bruno introduced her and they would know her dress came from Paris. As she walked she could almost feel the touch of the long, lovely dress against her ankles. Bruno always said, "You got to pretend the very best until it gets to be a habit. That goes for everything you do, including conversation, including you, all day long. Then it will just happen. You got to be the very best."

That's the way Bruno wanted you to think—only you still had to force it. It wasn't natural yet and there were so many times like this one, when you thought about it and it seemed it never would come natural. Golly. If Bruno would only quit that lousy business now, and the two of you could go off to some little town or even a farm and start down low where it was natural. The two of you would have something then.

Bruno ran west on Lombard, then turned to the right on Sansome Street. He passed Vince's hamburger stand at Chestnut, turned, ran west again. Damn! Chestnut was a dead end here. It banged straight into a cliff. He should know this waterfront section better, but it was too late now. He wheeled, ran around the Globe Flour Mills, crossed the railroad tracks on Francisco, and started up North Point Street. At Grant, the fog seemed suddenly heavier. It smelled of sulphur from the big chemical plant. The stink didn't make breathing any easier. Now this might be a good place to heave the gun. Get rid of it. No . . . *no!* You cheap little two-bit thinker. You iron head. Behaving just like every other punk who couldn't keep his thinking straight when the pressure was on. So some kid comes along on his way to school in the morning, or on his way home—what the hell difference where the kid is going? He finds the gun, takes it

home to play Marines, and his daddy finally turns it over to the
department—with Bruno Felkin's fingerprints decorated all
over the thing. Great. Bruno Felkin with a thumb that left a
whorl type, two deltas with the ridges revolving around the
core. As if that wasn't enough, a prominent arch in the index
fingerprint. Such a nice file they've got too. From reform school
to that grand-theft pinch for car boosting. Then the amateur
wins a ticket to McNeil Island for peddling bindles. You hang
on to that gun, putting it away of course. If you can make Connie's in three more minutes you can look real hurt when they
come around.

To the left on Stockton and beat it between the two factories
with the overhead bridge connecting them. The bridge looks
like a crazy fake hanging up there in the fog—as if it couldn't
hold anybody. Now comes the tough part. Up the hill now, up
Stockton, pushing against a twenty-degree incline which is already beginning to feel like seventy degrees. Oh, Connie! Maybe
you were right about going off to some farm! There should be a
song, my heart stopped beating on Stockton Street—because
the damn thing exploded! Only the song don't rhyme.

As he walked down Stockton Street, Corky Mullins created as
many delays as he could. It was that time of night and the longer
he could take to travel between the public baths and Fisherman's Wharf, the better and the easier. Corky was clean now.
His smell, he told himself, was favorable. Even his white cap,
his Lundberg Stetson, was washed. He had shoved it forward
and over his right eye. After the spaghetti supper and the bath
Corky was broke, but since when was that so unusual? When a
man reached sixty-four and existed without the benefit of one
of them retirement policies, the kind where like in the maga-
zines the fellow sat there in a rowboat, fishing and smoking his
pipe and smiling because he was getting paid one hundred and
fifty bucks per month for doing nothing—when a man reached

sixty-four and didn't have one of them policies, he had a problem. The problem got worse when the yearning commenced, as it always did at this time of night.

There wasn't a bar on Skid Row that didn't know Muscatel Mullins. At two bits a bottle a man really couldn't afford to stay sober. Never any trouble, just into the tank and back out of the tank next morning, the entire procedure always starting about this time of night. It went along comfortably until the time a serious mistake was made; when instead of just shoving Mullins into the regular tank until morning, they took this poor soul to the county hospital. Somebody got overhasty, and this old tired body wound up on a slab in the cool room, with a sheet over the face. That did it. The intern said it was a regular second Resurrection. He said either his apparatus was wrong or it must be Easter. Anyway it was five years ago that it happened. Now the first name had changed from Muscatel to Corky, and not one drop had wet this throat since. But it was still a problem—along about this time of night.

Corky paused to examine a telephone pole as if he had never seen one before. He read a notice tacked to the pole, from top to bottom. The notice concerned a local change of zone restriction. The language was legal and made no sense. He read the notice a second time. He blew his nose in his bandanna, sighed, and was about to turn away when he saw a man running up the hill on the opposite side of the street. Apparently the man saw Corky at almost the same moment, for his pace slowed very slightly. The man turned his head and the street light seemed to reflect against his wet face. There was a flashing impression of eyes, nose, and an open mouth, then the man turned his head away and continued running up the hill. Corky watched him until he vanished in the fog. He was a fairly small man and he was sure as hell in a hurry. The sound of his shoes hitting the pavement could be heard long after he disappeared.

At least the man was something to think about. Concentrating on him helped the problem, the yearning.

It was only about five blocks' slow amble down to Fisherman's Wharf. There would be other things besides the zoning notice; maybe a few signs to read, or a new model car to examine from bumper to bumper. Oh, there would be some things to ease the mind, there just *had* to be, but for the next block or so the running man was enough to wonder about.

Bruno stumbled over nothing. He was sure it was nothing because he had seen nothing on the sidewalk ahead of him. The sidewalk sloped to the sky, shearing upward at a crazy angle in the same damn silly way all the sidewalks in San Francisco did—without regard to a guy who had to do some running.

There were bright pin points in the fog now, swimming pin points that moved wherever they wanted to. They slid across Bruno's eyes. There was no stopping them. He closed his eyes and stumbled again, but he knew it was not because his eyes were closed. His feet just wouldn't come off the sidewalk high enough to clear a string. His ears rang. There wasn't any air left in the world. It was like running in one of those dreams or maybe on the moon. Nobody, it didn't make a damn what they were doing—nobody had ever been as tired as Bruno Felkin.

The grocery store on the corner spewed a fan of light into the fog. Just before Bruno stepped into the light, he leaned against the building which adjoined the store. From there he could see a section of Chestnut Street and Grant Avenue. He could also see the windows of Connie's apartment on the third floor of the building on the opposite side of the street. There were no lights in the windows. The place looked dead. For the love of God, Connie! Don't take me so serious about your electric bill. I was only kidding. I said I'd drop in around seven. So I am a couple of hours late. There was business to do with Sam.

Maybe she was back in the bedroom, but that didn't make

sense. Connie never turned the lights off unless she went out somewheres. Jeez Connie, you better be in the back bedroom! You better be all eager and ready or you were going to be minus a boy friend. Not for a couple of years, but forever. *Please*, Connie, switch on a light so as I can breathe again. I give in. We'll go off to your little farm.

Bruno seized his wrist and pulled it around until the light from the store shone on his watch. Five minutes exactly. Just five minutes from the time you hung up the phone and started running—some kind of a world's record. But if Connie wasn't where she ought to be, it wasn't going to be any good. The whole idea cracked open. The cops couldn't even trump up a vag charge, just because they found two people in bed together. Connie could say, sure Bruno had been out, but at the time you're talking about he was right here in bed with me. She could face right up to them with the truth, or the almost truth, and cops had one hell of a time breaking down the truth. And when it was spoken by a girl like Connie, who never had her name on a blotter any place in the whole country, they would have to start looking somewheres else. The five or six minutes that got lost somewhere, the little time you'd been running, wouldn't be enough to even hang an idea on. Being in the hay with Connie would fit in perfectly with the way your heart beat. The dumbest cop would understand that. But if Connie wasn't there?

They never would believe Bruno Felkin could run so fast. Just let one of the flatfoots try it. He'd fall on his face before he got halfway up the hill, because he wouldn't be scared and get the extra drive that made a world's champion out of Felkin. Six and a half minutes. Something had to be done, right now.

Bruno felt something warm and wet just beneath his nose. He put his finger to the place and drew it away quickly. For God's sake—his nose was bleeding! Too much running; oh, great! He blew his nose and wiped carefully around it. Looking at the

handkerchief made him dizzy. It reminded him of Sam Addleheim. He wanted to be sick. Oh, Connie, please turn on a light.
You got to—*now*. There can't be any more waiting.

He straightened his tie and blew his nose again. He lit a cigarette, taking care not to inhale as he walked into the light
from the grocery store. He pushed open the door and the bell
jingled. Somebody had to see him. *Somebody* would be able to
tell the truth and maybe Connie would turn on a light or come
back in the next few minutes.

As he walked around the stands of bread and canned vege-
tables Bruno began to feel better. He was sure his breathing
was almost normal again. When the proprietor came out of the
back room, Bruno put a half dollar on the counter.

"A pack of Camels," he said.

"All right." The little man reached to the shelf behind him
without turning. His hand went surely to the packs of cigarettes and returned to toss the proper kind on the counter.
"Anything else?"

"No. Just running low." The proprietor made change from
the cigar box and palmed the money out on the counter in an
even line.

"Don't you live across the street?" he asked. Bruno was surprised. This character's memory was *too* good. How could he
recognize anybody that had been in his store twice at the most?

Bruno's heart quickened again. It was beating as if he was
still running up the hill.

"No. I just got a friend who lives there."

"Blonde girl? Kinda tall?"

"Yeah. So what?"

"Don't get so huffy. Maybe I do like her more than lots of my
customers. She's always got a smile, for one thing, but I'm old
enough to be harmless. Anyway, she was in here a few minutes
ago. Bought some doughnuts and a salami. Wanted me to leave

them on her step. If you're going over that way I was thinking maybe you could leave them by for me. My feet hurt."

"Why didn't she take them?"

"She was off to the movies. Said she was in a hurry."

"Oh. All right, I'll take them if they're ready."

"Right here. She charged them. Now there, mister, is a girl who knows food. Not many girls do nowadays. When she picks meat or a vegetable, it's right. There's a girl knows how to buy and cook because she *likes* it, understand?"

"Yeah?" Bruno tried to laugh. But it was no time for laughing. If a man had a radio in his head he could hear them talking to the squad cars right now. The beefies from Homicide would be lifting their fat cans off their office chairs and puffing their way down the steps to their car. They would all be moving out, along the Embarcadero. Maybe making that phone call wasn't so smart after all, with Connie picking this night for the movies. The whole deal was going sour.

"Have you got the right time?" Bruno asked. The man reached in his vest and brought out a thick gold watch. There was an audible click as his fingernail snapped the cover open, and another click as he closed it. He had an air of absolute faith in his observation.

"It's nine-eight," he said.

Bruno went through the motions of resetting his own watch. "Thanks. This thing goes screwy sometimes." He turned to leave and the proprietor followed him to the door.

"I'll close up now," he said. But as he came to the door he was not looking at the lock, or the lights, or the stacks of bread, or any of the things he should have been looking at. He was looking at Bruno Felkin.

"You hurt yourself?"

"No. Why?"

"Your nose is bleeding." Bruno reached quickly for his handkerchief. Jesus! Again? Everything was going wrong. A nose that hadn't bled since a kid whacked it with a two-by-four back in South St. Paul chooses this time to start leaking, just because it had to work a little hard in a run. And this little jerk has to see it. For a moment Bruno's whole face became hot as he considered stopping the proprietor's curiosity the hard way; then he thought better of it. There was too much trouble now—even for a smart businessman.

"It happens once in a while," he said. "The doc says it's nothing serious. The fog seems to bring it on."

"Maybe you better move out of San Francisco then."

Bruno managed a smile. "Yeah. Maybe I better."

Walking down Columbus Avenue, Connie passed a dingy café. She paused for a moment to peer in the window. It was in a place just like this one that you first met Bruno, that night in Los Angeles. He came into the café just before midnight and called you by name—which was easy enough to do because "Connie" was written across the left shoulder of the waitress uniform.

"When you're through for the night, how about us two having some champagne?" he said with that nice smile. It wasn't the standard menu kind of smile, not the kind that came so often from the stew bums and operating wolves who really meant bum bourbon in some hotel room. Bruno's voice was soft and his smile was matter of fact. He *meant* champagne. So you said okay, kind of surprised at how fast you said it. Then while he finished his coffee there was a chance to watch his black eyes and be sure that he was just lonesome. He was. And it wasn't much later before you found out he had always been lonesome.

He made it easy. Just before the shift changed he went quietly outside and waited down the street. When you walked up to him he was leaning against a building, smoking.

"I'm glad you came," was all he said, and then he took your arm—not too tightly. In the street light his face looked younger than it had in the café; the deeper lines were washed away, and his mouth didn't look so much like he was mad inside about something.

It was only a few blocks to the club. He helped you up and down the curbs, and when you finally came to the table he held your chair and said again that he was really glad you came. So were you, Connie. There was a warmth about him, as if just having your company was all he wanted.

"You're taller than I am," he said.

"It's my high heels."

"If my old man and lady had fed me the right kind of food instead of feeding themselves the wrong kind of booze, it might have been different. A lot of things might have been different."

When the champagne came, he wouldn't touch it. He spun the swizzle stick in the glass for you, laughing as he did so.

"I'm thirty-two years old," he said easily. "The strongest thing I ever tasted is ginger ale. My old man probably gave me some of his bad blood, so I don't want to start any new habits. Especially not now, when I need all the brains I got."

Just why he needed his brains so much he didn't say that first night. Bruno took you back to your room and didn't even try for a good-night kiss. He just said, "I certainly like being with you." Then exit Bruno for one whole week. You thought you had said all the wrong things, telling him how you came from a farm and all you really wanted to do was get back to one, or anyway something like a farm where there would be a chance to have a few kids and run the place yourself instead of being just a poor relation. At the time you were sure everything you said was wrong. But he came back, and there was another bottle of champagne and more talk, mostly from him this time, and then began the dreaming. You found Bruno could swing wonderfully from the wildest dreaming right down to where he laid things on the line.

"Look," he said. "Look, Connie . . . I know for fairly sure

you aren't a virgin, but you're still a very nice girl . . . the kind of niceness that counts. Now I've been wanting to ask you if you could come to San Francisco with me. Don't get the wrong idea. I'm not asking you to live with me. You'd have your own place, understand—nothing fancy, but not too bad either. I'd stay right on in my hotel room, but I'd just like to have the feeling I had a place to go and always be welcome. I just have the idea we could maybe help each other. Before I ask, though, you ought to know more about me—for example, that the only school I ever graduated from was a state industrial school. Most states have these schools for kids like I was who want to smell money so bad they'll steal for it. When I got out of the school, I had a head full of dreams. I still have. I'll skip the reason but a little later they sent me to the government pen at McNeil Island for three years. I lit two for good behavior."

Bruno reached across the table then and picked up the champagne swizzle stick. He played with it for quite a while, turning the stick back and forth between his strong fingers. "Look, Connie . . . the thing I want you to understand is that I'm still doing business at the same old stand. I'm president of a little sales company, the Western Sales Company. Home office, San Francisco—in my hat. Our chief products are marijuana, heroin, and once in a while a little opium. Don't sound very nice, does it? Well, it isn't. I hate it. I hate the people who furnish it to me and I'm sorry for the people who use it. But if I don't get it for them somebody else will. Now for a guy like me who never had no real education it's the only way I can see to ever make some mark on this world. That stuff about starting out with nothing and just plain working hard is a lot of hooey unless you get some special help from somewheres. In my case I got to be extra smart to beat the strikes I had against me when I started. The things I want, and you ought to want, don't come free to people like us. We got to snatch them the hard way, especially in the beginning. Then later on you stand a chance of throwing your weight around a little, understand? So I'm quietly getting a stack and it won't be too long now before I can invest in a decent business and go see some of the things in this world I've always wanted to . . . say London or Paris . . . without giving a damn about paying the hotel bill."

That's the way it started, with Bruno going on for hours, and after a while it was easy to dream along with him. Then all of a sudden you and Bruno were like a couple of comets coming together. Bruno was a swell guy who needed taking care of, and you were just the girl to do it. Only it turned out that Bruno did most of the care-taking. He was horrified when he found out you'd run away from Nebraska after going only two years to high school.

"Twenty-three years old," he said, "and you don't know from nothin'! That we got to fix." Two days later the Grove School on Bush Street in San Francisco had a new student. It wasn't a stenographic or business school, but the real thing. Bruno said he wanted a place that could provide a sound, fundamental education. This one even gave out with homework. It was a laugh, Connie Thatcher doing homework at twenty-three; but Bruno wanted it that way and he had it that way. It was real fun pleasing Bruno.

Bruno threw the doughnuts and salami over a fence and started running again. For five precious minutes he had stood outside Connie's apartment near the steps, arguing with himself, trying to use everything he could remember, and trying to think how the Homicide Detail would proceed. Then looking down the hill, watching the golden blobs of light along the Embarcadero, he saw two things that made him give up any idea of waiting for Connie. There were two pairs of headlights poking around in the fog. The cars moved very slowly. They stopped, turned around, and retraced their paths. Then they met again, stopped once more, and huddled closely as if the

cars themselves were exchanging information. Bruno knew who
was driving the cars. They were not just citizens going home to
bed.

He ran down Chestnut and turned right on Powell, aware that
minute by minute the peculiar geography of San Francisco was
working against him. There would be a car at the end of the
Embarcadero now, the wrong end, because it was Bruno Felkin's end. He was being pushed into the bay.

ALTHOUGH THE HORNS ON THE GOLDEN GATE Bridge were enough to blast a man clean out of the wheelhouse, Barney Schriona, master and owner of the *Capella*, disliked taking his heavy dragger into San Francisco when the fog was so thick. But this was the end of a long day that had begun before the sun rose—and for the first time in a month of desultory scraping along the ocean's bottom, the combined labors of Barney and his crew had finally hit a decent reward. There were twenty boxes of sand dabs, rex sole, and English, petrale, and even some ling cod, stacked and sorted on the *Capella's* afterdeck. That was good fishing in any language—including the Yugoslavian. Barney had long since purposefully forgotten how to say it in Yugoslav, but anyhow he would be able to go home and give his wife an honest smile for a change.

The *Capella* sat upon the swirls of tide and current racing through the Golden Gate, stern down like a satisfied hen. Now that the bridge had been left behind, and the danger of running into its piers was over, Barney Schriona had comparatively little to worry about. Of course there was still the chance of ramming an anchored freighter, and reminding himself that he

was never one to like a risk, Barney changed the *Capella's* course
slightly to starboard. He kept the pilot-house windows open and
listened carefully for the horn on Alcatraz Island. When he
heard it scream just off his port bow he could confidently turn
for the glow of the city, feeling in the murk for Fisherman's
Wharf, and home.

Damn that fog horn on Alcatraz! Bruno was sure that every
stride he took made it sound more like a sick whale. It was a lot
easier running downhill now, but why did they have to go putting fog horns on pokeys? It would be worth laughing about,
things being the way they were, only the horn was inviting
Bruno Felkin in, and they hadn't even picked a jury yet. It was
one thing to keep from thinking wild, and it was another thing
to think what the hell to do now. This running couldn't go on,
breath or no breath. You could make for the Presidio, maybe
hide out in the trees—and then what? By morning there would
be a thousand soldiers who didn't have nothing else to do beating the bushes for Bruno Felkin.

Now a pair of motorcycles was snoring down Taylor Street.
They were going so slow the riders could hardly keep their
balance. They were looking, looking until their damn eyes were
falling out. And working with the cars they were pushing you
right into the bay. Only you forgot your water wings. Just wonderful.

The running was over. It was walk easily now. Make progress, but saunter along with the tourists who cluttered the sidewalk from the cable car turntable to the restaurants on Fisherman's Wharf. The Neptune, Sabella's, Sabella-Latorre, and
Alioto's—one fish joint right after another, all burning up a lot
more electricity than they had any right to be doing. Lighting
the area up like high noon. It might be good for business, but it
was no good for a man who had two motorcycles and God alone
knew how many squad cars looking for him. A man walking by

himself was all they needed for a first look; then the second look would not be exactly so much a look as a smell. A good copper could do that, and you never knew when you'd run up against a good copper. The guy could pick you right out of a crowd, half the time without being able to explain himself how the hell he did it. And so a con-wise guy never gave them the chance if he could help it.

The tourists were already thinning out. They were walking up Taylor Street to take the cable car and go back to their damn comfortable hotels and finally go back to Iowa or wherever the hell they came from. And Bruno Felkin was becoming more and more conspicuous. Jesus. Any minute now something would have to give. Back to Connie's maybe . . . wriggle, and criss-cross the streets like you used to do when you were a kid. For the birds, Bruno. It was too late for a stunt like that. Those precious five minutes were gone forever. You could have saved your breath for all of them, because now there wouldn't be any doubt about one thing. When Sam Addleheim got it, you were out on the town; wandering around. A grocery guy whose testimony would be worse than no testimony was the only proof you were a long ways from where it happened, almost when it happened. Almost, but not quite. It wasn't any good now. Going back to Connie would only get her in more trouble than she was already stuck with. She never bargained for a mess like this. She wanted things level and was willing to do a lot to make things that way. Connie was the best thing ever happened to you, Felkin. So now stay the hell away from her. She thought clean. Keep her that way, you stupid ironhead.

The motorcycles were less than a block behind now. If they were good coppers, the kind who knew what they were doing, there was still one minute, maybe two for thinking. No more. Genius the brain fast, Bruno.

Corky Mullins knew he had again defeated the yearning. For a reasonably tempting time he had stood in the saloon at the

head of Pier 43 and watched the customers play the pinball
machine. The customers were drinking blacksmiths-and-
helpers, and the smell of alcohol swallowed the stagnant air of
the place. Both the smell and the spectacle of the customers arguing over the pinball machine bored Corky. He was certain
that even if he had any money he would not have joined them.
He marched righteously out of the place after only a few minutes. It was, by God, time to retire to the *Thunder Mug.*

The *Thunder Mug* might be the most forlorn-looking boat
moored at Fisherman's Wharf, but she was a home, and that was
where a sixty-four-year-old man belonged. Home in a fairly clean
bunk, reading that copy of *Amazing Stories* for what must be
the third time.

As he passed Alioto's restaurant Corky saw a man standing
at the brilliantly lighted window. He was studying the fish in
the window as if he had never seen one before. This in itself did
not strike Corky as being unusual—the restaurants were always
lined with people who regarded a plain ordinary fish as some
sort of a miracle—but Corky had seen this man before. He
could have sworn it. He was medium sized and kind of a nice-
looking young guy, except somebody busted his nose once. His
face was kind of pinched, like he was worried or had a headache. But that was the trouble with having been drunk for
fifteen years. When you finally sobered up you were always seeing some guy you thought you had seen before and that was
because for a long time you had never really seen anybody. So
no matter how hungry for company you might be, or how much
you wanted to delay going home to the *Thunder Mug*; no matter how much it might help the yearning to maybe have the
guy share a pot of coffee; no matter—there was no use in talking
to the man at the window.

Bear down, Bruno. Bear down with some thinking about
the fourth exit from San Francisco. Figure it. Quick! So the

bridges to the east and the north were already closed? So the highway going south would be crawling with coppers? So on this night a lot of citizens were going to explain where they were going and why? But not these fish in the window. They came from San Francisco's fourth exit. They did not swim into the window of their own accord. Some wop went out through the Golden Gate without giving a damn for road blocks; and the wop came and went as he pleased. Now these fish.

Hold it! A damned squad car had stopped at the filling station across the street! One of the uniforms was getting out. Sure, Bruno, wait around to see if he's just going to fill his tank, then you won't have to worry about running. You'll have a free ride. There will be the sound of those new-type handcuffs, the kind that hiss like a rattlesnake instead of just click. Move, Bruno. Get going.

He took a few carefully controlled steps along the lighted window until he reached a narrow alleyway between Alioto's restaurant and the next one in line. He took a quick look at the filling station and the motorcycles just crossing Jefferson Street. There was no time to care where the alleyway might lead. A guy couldn't figure everything. Not when they were breathing down your neck.

Bruno took a deep breath and turned quickly into the alley. He bumped along a line of garbage cans, and started running again.

Standing on the flying bridge, Barney Schriona maneuvered his *Capella* patiently until her bow nudged the dock just astern of the *Taage*. As the deck hand ran along the dock with the bowline, Barney threw the wheel hard over and momentarily increased the power of the *Capella*'s Atlas Diesel. The stack behind him puffed softly at the fog perhaps fifty times, then Barney cut the throttle and the *Capella* swung around parallel to the dock. Barney waited a moment until the stern line was fast, then clambered down the steel ladder to the deck. It was good to be back in port—it was always wonderful.

Barney pushed the damp fedora back on his head and lit a cigarette. He blew a heavy cloud of smoke into the fog, and scratched the stubble on his chin a moment as he considered taking the next two days off entirely. He would not even come near the *Capella*. Let fellows like Hamil Linder with his *Taage* work their hearts out.

Barney yawned, and since the taste in his mouth was already bad enough he flipped his cigarette into the depths of fog and water. He had just turned to enter the wheelhouse when he saw a man walking rapidly along the dock. He was changing directions every few steps as if he didn't know where he was going. The man was almost running—also proof that he was no fisherman. Fishermen were always too tired to run, or if they weren't really tired, they thought they were. Barney yawned again. Ordinarily he would have stood waiting, to see what the man would do. He might be a thief. The wharf was lousy with them lately. But this guy wasn't even looking at the boats or their gear. Barney decided he was probably just another knucklehead tired of being a nobody and wanting to get in the papers. Okay. Let him jump in the bay. Barney Schriona was not going to stand around waiting for a splash tonight. To hell with the man. Let the Coast Guard fish him out. Barney Schriona was very, very tired, as tired as he could remember in all his fifty years, and he was going home as fast as he could get there.

As he approached the end of the dock Bruno slowed his pace. All of the boats except one seemed to be deserted. Bruno turned his face away as he passed the light from the one boat. As far as he could see the dock was deserted, and even the coffee shop, with one night light burning, was deserted. Great. Now maybe there would be a breathing spell and maybe a chance to think.

There was no use running any more—a man would obviously run out of dock before he ran out of breath. At the same time, if the coppers wanted to do any real searching of the area they were going to have to do some footwork themselves. There were nets piled on the dock, boxes, and all kinds of junk until hell wouldn't have it. There were enough places to hide a small army. And the lights along the dock wouldn't exactly put anybody's eyes out. They were just cotton balls in the fog. Very satisfactory.

He turned back a few steps, giving his mind time to slide from panic to reason. This was going to be the last chance to think and it had better be reasonable. He stood on the edge of the dock looking down at a boat. There was a closed padlock on the cabin door. There was an open hole about the middle of the boat—the hold, smart guy—where they put the cargo . . . the *fish,* by God! San Francisco's fourth exit!

Bruno snapped his fingers and looked quickly behind him. Still no coppers, but now who the hell was this coming along the dock? King Kong?

One of the biggest men Bruno had ever seen was walking slowly toward him. The night light from the coffee shop cast a huge replica of his figure on the fog. His hands were in his pockets and his head was down. Bruno was certain the man had yet to notice him. Good enough. Too many people had seen Bruno Felkin already.

Bruno slipped quickly behind a row of oil barrels and crouched down where he could safely watch the man without being seen. As he came closer his figure appeared to diminish slightly although Bruno was certain he stood a good six feet four.

The man came to within a few feet of Bruno and stopped. Bruno saw him take a heavy gold watch from his vest pocket and study it. Well, that watch was going to remain with its owner for sure. At least Bruno Felkin was having no part of a tangle with this guy. Even a bullet would probably only sting him. The man put the watch back in his pocket and called down to the one boat that had a light on.

"Hey, Barney!"

A short, heavy-set man clambered up from the boat.

"Hello, Hamil Linder," he said, reaching for the big man's hand. "When did you get in?"

"This afternoon, Barney. Vee yust beat the fog, by golly." Bruno groaned inwardly. Time, precious time a-wasting and here these two old maids had to have a gossip session on the weather and pin Bruno behind a barrel.

"Come on board the *Taage,* Barney, and vee make a cup of coffee."

"I can't do it, Hamil. Tonight I'm in a hurry." So the little guy was in a hurry? Travel with Bruno Felkin, mister, and you'll find out what a real hurry is.

"It only take a few minutes, Barney—for vun cup."

"No. Rosanna is waitin', I hope. For the first time since last month I ain't ashamed to go home to her."

"You have a good trip?"

"Twenty boxes and very little junk. Some of the best petrale and sole I ever seen. So I'm goin' home while the goin's good. If I step foot on your boat and listen to you I'll start to think again and tell myself there are more fish in the sea and I, personally, Barney Schriona, ain't forgot how to find 'em. So the two lies will make me go out again tomorrow and I'll find out they are lies. Then I will hate everything and I won't go home once more. So good night, Hamil."

They shook hands again and the big man said, "Maybe you are right, Barney. Anyvay, give my best regards to Rosanna. If I had a voman like her I vould go home too." They laughed and Bruno waited anxiously as the man called Barney moved away. Go on home to your damn Rosanna, shorty, and let's clear the population off this dock. But he turned suddenly and came back to the big man.

"I meant to ask, Hamil. How's your son comin' along?"

"Carl be quite a long-liner now. I think he come out all right. You know it's fishin' the hard vay for a young fellow, but he don't seem to mind so much."

"Good. I'm awful glad to hear it. Don't get discouraged, Hamil. All kids get in some kind of trouble before they settle down. He'll be all right. You get him all straightened out with the police?"

"Ya, Barney. The judge have a long talk vith Carl and vith me. Things be better now, I think."

"Fine. When you sailing?"

"Four in the morning."

Bruno saw them raise their hats to each other and remembered he had seen the Poles in South St. Paul do the same thing. Police? Judge? Well . . . how about this? After they said good night once more Bruno waited for the big man to leave. But he stood looking down at the boats for fully five minutes. He was almost motionless and Bruno wondered if he had gone to sleep on his feet. Go to bed, you old bastard. Get the hell out of my way. Felkin is getting housemaid's knee behind these barrels.

As if in answer to Bruno's wish, the big man sighed and lowered himself carefully down to the deserted boat. He opened the padlock and slid back the door. A light went on in the cabin.

Bruno rose stiffly from behind the barrels. He approached the edge of the dock thoughtfully and, avoiding the white shaft of fog made by the cabin light, directed his entire attention on the boat. So? Ways and means, Felkin! Now it was the *fairly* smart men who never took a chance. They never really geniused the brain, which was why they wound up in the poorhouse or the pokey. It took a really clever guy to do the unexpected— make a phone call, for instance, when a phone call wasn't neces-

sary—or when there was trouble galore, take a long, long chance.
So switching things back and forth, never letting the head
clockwork run down, kept a guy in the big leagues. This boat
was sailing for somewheres at four o'clock in the morning.
That's what the man said. This boat, that black hole; neither of
them was for tinhorns. They were for a guy with guts and imagination. For Bruno Felkin.

As Bruno waited, the light in the cabin went out. He hitched
his trousers and looked up and down the dock. No noise but the
horns and water. Bruno knelt and removed his shoes. Then he
cautiously lowered himself to the boat's deck as he had seen
the big man do. He walked silently back to the open hold.

He looked around once more, smiled at the fog, and then
lowered himself into absolute blackness.

CHAPTER — — — — — — — — — — *3*

Iₙ THE CRAMPED FORECASTLE OF THE
Taage, Hamil Linder lay in his bunk and thought about
what Barney Schriona had said to him about young people and
trouble. Of course it must be so. But his own youth had been so
different it was hard to understand why Carl acted the way he
did. There had been so many times during the last few years
when he had sought almost frantically in the depths of his memory, sounding here and there throughout his fifty years for a
true explanation of Carl.

Maybe raising the boy alone was the trouble. Perhaps when
Solveig died—let's see now, that would be eighteen years ago—
it would have been better to take another woman right away.
But it was never in your heart to do so. Never. Solveig came
with you from Norway. Her faith that you could succeed in
what seemed then like a wild adventure *let* you succeed. She
was the one who first taught you to pronounce the word "pursuit" when you studied to be a citizen and read about the pursuit of happiness. She was the one who said you would some
day have your own boat, and that it would be a beautiful boat.

And this had come to be so. It was possible that even Solveig would have trouble understanding Carl.

Trying to place himself in his son's position, Hamil thought about his own father. That seemed another life now, in Norway—it was such a long time ago. There was the North Sea . . . the weak cold light . . . and a man who fished for a full lifetime.

Hamil remembered that his father was even taller than he had grown to be, and that would better six feet three inches. His hands—Hamil could almost see them in the dark now— were exactly like his own, weathered and veined, calloused in the palms, and always red and clean when their work was done. He never became master of his own vessel, not because he lacked ambition but mainly because eight children absorbed all the money he could gather. Vessels were dear in Norway and he was always violently determined that each of his children should have more than food and clothing. It was easy to understand now why he remained a fisherman. He shared with his fellow crew members whatever they could haul from the sea, until his death. The Linders were never poor, Hamil thought . . . and they were never rich.

As he turned restlessly in the darkness the same picture Hamil had seen so many times lately returned to his mind. He was fourteen years old again. The season for the big vessels off the North Sea banks had been a dismal failure, and his father had decided to net a few herring before winter set in. He leased an oversized dory and a net that would normally need at least three full-grown men, counting on his own strength and endurance to accomplish the task. He explained to the doubters who stood along the dock, those same doubters who lounged on every dock in the world, that if a man needed to do a thing badly enough, he could do it. . . ."I will take with me only my middle son!" Hamil could almost hear his voice ringing against the stone cliffs behind the wharf. Hamil could see him pointing his finger at him and saying simply, "Get your boots, boy."

You sat side by side in the dory rowing down the fjord in the cold October twilight. The oars were of heavy ash, the thickness of your arm it seemed then, and over ten feet long. You rowed for hours without resting and when your father spoke he called you boy, though he spoke to you as another man.

"Boy, there are those who say we cannot do this thing. They say that this boat is too big and the net is too big. They say that though we find the herring we must row so far to fetch them we will not have the strength remaining to pull them in. . . . They say that if the wind sucks down the fjord as it must do this time of year, we will not on any account have the strength to row back. Boy, you should think over the things they have said."

Hamil was sure he hadn't stopped to think of the doubters just then. It seemed much more important to maintain a good stroke, and besides, if you kept quiet your father might forget himself and continue talking to you as an equal. Hamil saw his father's massive head again, sliding smoothly back and forth with each long oar stroke, framed and reframed by the cold dark mountains beyond him: the large nose almost bulbous at the end, the heavy lips and eyebrows, the eyes gray-blue in the dusk. Now, so many years later, remembering that night was like looking in a mirror. . . . "Boy, there will always be some who will say you cannot do this or you cannot do that. Everything to such people is impossible, because they have never really tried to do anything or because by leaning on someone else they find it easier to do nothing. I could be mad at those people if I was not so sorry for them. Boy, they are like sea gulls, and you know they are the most unhappy birds. I think the reason for this is that the sea gull also does nothing. A sea gull has never been heard to sing, nor does anyone care or know where they go when they die. Possibly this is because they spend their entire life standing around waiting for someone else to provide them with a free meal." He paused in his rowing then, just long enough to bounce his laughter against the fjord.

"You remember this, boy, work does something more than fill your belly. If you work well and hard, you sing inside and maybe some people will care when you die."

Thinking of the old days did more than merely ease the pain of your loneliness . . . this great loneliness that had begun when Carl laughed at you for the first time. Now loneliness seemed to be the only constant feeling in your body. You are sick with the feeling. It's the heaviest weight you ever carried. It was more than age that made your shoulders sag, more than just fifty years of living. There was always this thinking of Carl and how it might be possible to help him when every attempt at help was turned aside . . . as if help was a weak wave beating against a rock.

If it had not been for Judge Olsen you would probably never have seen Carl again. Even with the restrictions placed upon him by the court Carl did everything he could to avoid you. When Carl took the car that did not belong to him, and was found with that girl in the tourist camp, there were those terrible days when the son of Hamil Linder lived in the county jail. There was the empty waiting—almost a month while the *Taage* lay idle at the wharf. When the son of Hamil Linder was in jail there were so many other things demanding the attention . . . pleading with the police sergeant, then the captain, the lawyer—all men who spoke of things confusing to a man who seldom left the sea. Then the judge himself, who seemed to slumber as you sat talking in his chambers. And yet it was the judge who said that he did not believe Carl was all bad. He offered something not even Carl could refuse. . . . The very words were still so clear.

He said to Carl, ". . . I for one respect your father. He came to this country with nothing and he has become a fine citizen. Most of the things he struggled for, you have been given . . . and you have become a poor citizen. You seem to think that the accomplishments of a man, and his pride, can be counted in automobiles and clothes and the fawning of easy friends. You were drafted into the army and although your record shows you were never in the slightest danger, you are classified as a 'veteran.' As such you appear to think the world owes you a living. You are mistaken, because no government can support that theory for very long. I suggest you think about some of your father's standards, which you sneer at as being old-country. It's not your father who is out of key with this country, but you. Do some hard thinking about that . . . and the way your father brought you up alone though he was required to spend most of his time at sea to feed and clothe you. May I ask when you first started to work, Mr. Linder?"

"I think . . . it vas maybe nine or ten years old. Not all the time, of course."

"So, Carl, you have a lot of time to make up. Think about that and think about this. For grand theft, Carl Linder, I may sentence you to a maximum of ten years. I am sorry that it is not more. In your case it should be more because of the deliberate way you stole the car, and because of what your action has done to your father. For his sake then, and not yours, I will give you a choice. In the hope that hard work may help you—and perhaps some closer association with your father—you may elect to take my sentence of ten full years in the penitentiary at San Quentin, or you will live and work on your father's fishing vessel for a period of one year. During this time you will be on probation. Any report of laxness in your work or complaint about your sentence will immediately convince me that I have been far too lenient."

Hamil breathed slowly and heavily trying to capture sleep. But sleep refused to come. He turned on his side and listened to the wavelets brushing along the *Taage's* hull. For a while he tried to think about Barney Schriona and his wife Rosanna. Now there was a fortunate man. Barney too had migrated to

America. And the boat *Capella* which lay just behind the *Taage* was now entirely his. What's more, Barney still had the wife he had brought with him from the Dalmatian Coast. She was always there to return to, when the beating of the Pacific became almost more than a man could stand—when things on the land became confusing to a man who lived with the sea. Now if Solveig were alive she could explain this very night, the things Carl said, and maybe ease the hurt.

You docked just before the fog came in. A ton and a half of black cod wasn't bad for just you and Carl. You were pleased about it and so was he. It seemed to be a good time for understanding each other. And you had tried . . . after the decks were washed down. Hoping.

Carl had taken off his sea gear and was standing before the small metal mirror near his bunk carefully combing his blond hair. He knotted the bright tie at his throat and put on the jacket with the padded shoulders. Carl didn't need padded shoulders. His were almost as wide as your own. And besides, the jacket had cost far too much . . . or was that just an old-fashioned way of thinking?

You said to him, "I hoped maybe this night we could eat together, Carl." You said it lightly, as if making a joke—trying very hard to remove any trace of accent from your voice. "We brought in a ton and a half and so perhaps vee deserve a good steak?" There, you made a mistake, saying "vee" instead of we. No matter how careful you were it still happened and it probably always would happen.

"Vee . . . vid a dobble-yew, Pop. Just keep practicing it and you'll learn one of these days. Just keep saying dobble-yews for another twenty-seven years and maybe you'll hit one right. Now take the padlock off that coin purse of yours and give me fifty dollars."

"How can you need so much as fifty dollars?" Was that an unfair question?

"None of your damn business. That's my share of the fish and I earned it. Give it to me and skip the questions." It was true. Fifty dollars was approximately Carl's share of the past three days' catch. He had every right to demand the money, and yet—

"Carl, if you take it all you spend it. Then you have nothing but a headache in the morning. Why not I give you twenty dollars? Then maybe you vill have a smaller headache?"

He didn't return your smile. He didn't think what you said was funny, only the way you said it. His hand was extended. His feet were braced and his full mouth that sometimes looked so much like Solveig's was beginning to turn down in the way it always did before he began to say the things that hurt so much.

"Give me the dough, Pop. I want off this bucket before it stinks up my clothes. I'd just as soon a certain party didn't know I was fishing for a living." You brought out your coin purse. What else was there to do? It was the same purse your father gave you on the day of your departure for America. The fine leather had lasted a long time . . . as had the advice given with it: Fill it wisely and empty it wisely. You snapped open the ball catch and took out fifty dollars.

"I still do not unnerstan vat is so bad vith being a fisherman," you said. Carl took the money. He stuffed it carelessly into his pocket.

"Listen, Pop," Carl said, "will you for Christ's sake get wise to yourself? This is America, not the old country. You been here twenty-seven years and if you got to speak with an accent I guess nobody can ever do anything about that. But you're still *thinking* with an accent . . . like a Scandahoovian blockhead. You work your ass off and you been doin' it ever since you come here. And what have you got to show for it? A nineteen thirty-six Chevrolet, a stinking boat, and a few hundred bucks in the bank. Get wise to yourself, Pop. This is America and work is for jerks. What you want is to get yourself a forty-hour week with pay for forty-eight hours . . . and don't let them bother you on Saturdays, Sundays, or even Hallowe'en. Just get that through your thick head and remember it. Work like you do is strictly for jerks. So this is February. That leaves me eight months more to go. When September comes around I'm going ashore forever and if anybody even shoves a crabmeat cocktail in my face, I'll throw it on the floor. Times have changed. I don't care what the judge said. Eight months from now I won't have to work like a dog and then come sniveling around for a lousy fifty bucks."

For one quick moment Carl seemed to soften a little. He put his hand on your knee and the look in his eyes gave you a chance to hope. But the moment passed.

"Be a good guy, Pop. Stay out of my business and I'll stay out of yours. When you're all wound up with rheumatism I'll see what I can do to send you a few bucks to pay your doctor bills. I'm going to have money, Pop. Lots of it and fast. . . ."

"The tide starts out at four in the morning, Carl. You vill be here?"

"I won't guarantee what kind of shape I'll be in, but I'll be here. Because the judge said I *have* to be here. Enjoy your steak, Pop."

Now the evening was over and you had not enjoyed the steak because eating alone was never a pleasure. That glass of wine you ordered in the hope it would either raise your spirits or make you sleep was failing to do either one. It tasted sour. All through the meal there was the thought of Carl and of what he might be doing . . . and how pleasurable it would be if you could only sit down together at a meal that was not required by law.

There were probably other men in the city behind the fog who had also eaten alone. Empty men, comforting themselves with memories of other nights, eating as slowly as you did and lingering as long as possible over their coffee . . . trying to taste the food that had no taste . . . and feeling sorry for themselves. You must not do that, Hamil Linder. You become weaker and weaker that way. What was it Barney Schriona said? Carl would be all right? There was something in Barney's voice that said he understood. He was trying to help by saying that certainly no help was needed. So? Maybe Barney was right. If you could only be sure. Then it would be easy to lie waiting for the tide and for the memories of Solveig, for the pictures in the mind of times full of laughing and company, for the feeling of vigor and hope you have forgotten—for sleep. It was always a little easier when someone understood. . . .

Connie tried to compose herself on the couch. It was embarrassing to talk to a strange man at three-thirty in the morning if you hadn't been given a chance to fix your face or put on anything but an old bathrobe. You thought it was Bruno standing on the buzzer downstairs and the minute you switched on the bed light you knew something was wrong. Before you even unlatched the door you knew Bruno was in trouble. And when it wasn't Bruno at the door but this man with his badge—then the same curious sense told you to watch what you said. The man introduced himself as Lieutenant Kelsey and said he wanted to talk right now.

He sat down in the big corner chair and pulled a notebook from his vest pocket. After he said he didn't like being up at this hour any better than you did he began asking questions.

"How long have you known Bruno Felkin?"

"Four months."

"You been living together?"

"No."

"Have it your way, Connie. A week after Bruno brought you here we knew about it because what he does is our business."

"Bruno lives at the Granada Hotel."

"We know that too. But it so happens he didn't go home last night. Maybe you wouldn't mind telling me where he did go?"

"I don't know, *Mister* Kelsey."

"You might as well tell the truth, Connie. We'll get it sooner or later." He was looking at her steadily, taking his eyes from her face only when he wrote in his book. His hands were large and red and covered with freckles. His lined, beefy face was tired, as if whatever she said he had heard it before. Connie found it easier to keep her attention on his hands, and on the slow, even movements of his vest as he breathed. There were times when his heavy breathing was the only sound in the room.

"You ever been arrested, Connie? Now make it easier for both of us and tell me where and what for so I don't have to go dig through the files."

"I've never been arrested."

Kelsey sighed. "Have it your way. Where are you from?"

"Near Hastings. A little town called Lessing you probably never heard of."

"Nebraska?"

"Yeah."

"About twenty-five years of age?"

"Twenty-three. I can prove it."

"Ever do any hustling?"

"How would you like a slap in the face, Mr. Kelsey?"

"You're an old-looking twenty-three."

"Thanks for the flattery. . ." Connie paused and saw that he was only saying what he thought was so. She looked down at her slipper and pulled a thread from the bow. "I guess you're right," she said softly. "Things seemed to work out so I was always older than I should be."

"Ever married?"

"No. I hate to admit it but nobody ever asked me. If I knew what was wrong I'd do something about it."

"Parents alive?"

"No. I've been an orphan since I was ten."

"What do you claim for an occupation?"

Connie hesitated. "Waitress . . . I guess."

"Nice apartment for a waitress."

"I only worked in the best places. The tips were big." Connie saw the smallest of smiles appear around Kelsey's eyes. He saw a lot, this man. It was hard not to like him.

"Okay. We'll go into all those fancy places later. Now how did you get mixed up with Bruno Felkin?"

"I . . ." There was a hard question to answer exactly. It had seemed so natural after those first few meetings. Maybe it was the feeling of being needed for the first time in your own life— only how could a thing like that be explained to a stranger? "I . . . just like Bruno."

"Couldn't you find some better company?"

"He's been wonderful to me."

"Sure he has. I suppose you don't know a thing about his record?"

"He told me."

"That he's a three-time loser?"

"Yes."

"You must be in love with him," Kelsey said suddenly.

Now there, Connie, was a real question. It had come up before this man ever asked it. It had a way of coming up at odd times—in school when you looked at the other students and thought how different their reasons were for being where they were. And it came sometimes at night when Bruno left with only a quick kiss and said he was tired and was going back to the Granada Hotel. It came particularly when Bruno failed to show up for two or three nights in a row, when there would only be a phone call and you wondered if Bruno had found someone else to fill his need, and if he was ever going to come around again. It came when you wondered what Bruno could be doing without really worrying about it, or when you thought how generously Bruno had given, without once asking directly for anything.

"Would you like a cup of coffee?" Connie said.

"No thanks." Kelsey closed his book and thoughtfully stuffed it in his coat pocket. "Maybe I'm getting old and ought to retire. If I didn't know better, I might believe you were telling the truth half the time."

"What has Bruno done?"

"Killed a man."

"I don't believe it."

"Why not?"

"He couldn't . . . he's been with me all the time."

"Like for instance?"

"All day yesterday . . . a few hours ago. I *was* lying when I said I didn't know where he was. He left just before you came." Kelsey put his red hands on his knees and pushed himself up. His shoes squeaked and change jingled in his pocket as he walked toward the bedroom. He disappeared beyond the doorway, then he came back to the living room almost at once.

"You're a lousy liar, Connie. Now I believe the rest of what you said. I suppose Bruno slept on the floor."

"Of course not."

"On the chandelier maybe?"

"You're not very funny."

"Well, he didn't sleep with you."

"You're wrong." Kelsey appeared not to hear her. He crossed the room slowly, examining the furniture, and finally selected the stuffed chair in the corner near the window as a receptacle for his weight. He crossed his legs and opened the lowest three buttons on his vest. Then he twisted slightly so that his shoulder holster would not prod his side and rhythmically clinked the change in his pocket. He stared absently out the window.

"This is my eighteenth year on the force, Connie. In that time you get to see a lot of bedrooms for one reason or another.

After a while you come to understand them sort of, and without having to look for anything especially you can learn a lot, because bedrooms have a way of being great storytellers. Now yours happens to be a very good example. A blind man could see there was only one person in it last night. Chances are the person was you. It's going to be a nice morning and from now on I'd just forget any fancy stories because I'd hate to see you sent up for A. and A."

"What's that?"

"Aiding and abetting. In this state it gets you up to five years. Even a conspiracy count is good for two years, so . . ."

"You aren't scaring me."

"Think it over just the same. Now I'm going to be here until my relief comes at five o'clock. If you want to go back to bed for a while, go ahead, but if the phone rings we sort of answer it together, understand? You talk and I listen."

"I'm supposed to go to school today." Kelsey looked at her in surprise. He shook his head.

"What's this school business?"

"I thought you knew everything. It was Bruno's idea. He thinks I have a lot to learn."

"We all do." Kelsey momentarily allowed the coins to lie silent in his pocket. "For instance, I just learned you can never be sure what a smart criminal like Bruno is going to think of next."

"He *isn't* a criminal. If he ever was, he's changed."

Kelsey parted his knees and his voice took on a note of great patience. "They never change, Connie. Not the ones like Bruno Felkin. That's why I'm sorry to see you mixed up with him because sooner or later he'll sell you out. I don't have much truck with these new psychiatrists—maybe I've been in police work too long and think too much in the old-fashioned way. Also I'm a trifle short on formal education, the same as you are. But you can't knock up against men like Felkin for years without under-

standing something about them. It so happens I've never seen or
talked to him . . . but I'd be willing to bet he's really two
people. One may be a very nice guy—all the really smart ones
have that side. It's the side he shows to you, probably. He
might even *want* to be that way all the time, although I doubt
it after going through his record. Something eats away at a man
like Bruno, call it his other side if you want. It's something like
acid in a battery. The case looks fine but the plates are rotten.
Whatever it is he really wants, he knows deep inside him he'll
never get it. But he'll try, and he won't let anybody stand in his
way. It's the have-nots who fill the prisons, Connie. And a hungry man can turn into a wild animal very easy. It happens quick,
before they know it themselves. Men like Bruno get over being
hungry for food when they are kids."

"So I sit here and listen to you all day instead of going to
school?"

"That's right, Connie. You might learn something here too.
You're going to get an absent mark today because if Bruno
shows up you ought to be around to greet him. Now if you're
about to make some coffee for yourself . . . I just might
change my mind."

Without unfolding her arms, Connie pushed her feet into
her slippers and stood up. Bruno, what have you done to your
dream? You don't have to fight that hard—it was the gun I had
begged you to throw away. You put it on the dresser the first
night you stayed with me. You just said it was a good gun and
might save your neck some day. Bruno Felkin . . . doing
business just like you said, at the same old stand. Trying to
balance the strikes against you. Snatching the hard way. Oh,
Bruno. I asked you, please.

When she came to the kitchen door Connie turned and looked
at Kelsey. He was sitting so solidly in his chair—as if he had
been there forever.

"I don't feel like sleeping now. Where I come from we eat a

real breakfast, Mr. Kelsey. I'm going to have eggs and chicken livers. Like some?"

"Don't tell me you can cook."

"Back in Lessing the harvest hands seemed to think so. It's about the only thing I ever learned to do right, maybe because I like it."

"Two then. Sunny side up."

"You look like a man who'd like them easy."

"Right, Connie. Easy."

Bruno shivered. now that he was awake he wondered if he had gone blind, or maybe he was still asleep. Now wasn't this something? It just all went to show that Bruno Felkin was no tinhorn after all—when a guy could fall asleep like a baby after being chased all over hell and gone. But there were going to be some stiff joints tomorrow. . . . Hey! It *was* tomorrow. The one visible thing in this black hole was the fancy wristwatch. The watch set to a grocer's watch on Telegraph Hill. It said twenty minutes past four, and things were happening already. Wake up, smart guy, and start beating the brain again because this boat was moving. Not only was the darkness in motion, which was a crazy idea to begin with, but it was full of sound and vibration. A heavy engine was running somewhere beyond the darkness.

Bruno searched around him, then remembered the ladder he had descended. When he found it he started to climb. His head collided with something above him and he cursed softly. No wonder it was so dark. Someone had closed off the opening.

He pushed upward slowly and cautiously. The hatch gave easily at his pressure. There was a light at last, or anyway a

lighting of the darkness, the sound of the engine, and rushing
water. He opened the hatch completely and stepped out on the
deck.

Now how about this? Absolutely made to order for Bruno
Felkin and a sight to remember forever. This boat seemed to be
racing through the fog just like it was anxious to set Bruno
Felkin on his way. And you didn't have to be even a genius to
know that was the Golden Gate Bridge hanging up there in the
mist, almost overhead. San Francisco's fourth exit was opening
wide. The bridge was moving back all by itself, looking like the
gates of heaven done up with electric lights. It was a show
somebody ought to charge admission for, only they shouldn't
hold the performance at such an ungodly hour of the morning.
And they ought to heat the theater. Jesus, what a cold wind!

The *Taage* rolled and Bruno caught himself just before he
fell down. Ho, for the life of a sailor! Some sailor—Bruno Felkin. A wave sloshed through the scuppers and splattered Bruno's
shoes. It wasn't going to be easy on this crazy deck to find a place
to stand and do what had to be done right now. It seemed if a
man wanted to go bad enough he would maybe have to fall
overboard. So what? Felkin was the best swimmer ever swam
the Mississippi in St. Paul. The water was cold there too.

Bruno staggered to the mast stay, crooked his arm around it,
and braced his knees against the bulwark. This wasn't exactly
the kind of a sea voyage he had planned for so long. No orches-
tra, or bar, or deck chairs . . . no girl like Connie. The only
right thing about it was the way the boat was headed—away
from San Francisco. And one more thing could be said right
now. Bruno Felkin was a natural-born admiral with no kidding
about it. Any guy who could spend his life on the city pave-
ments and still not get even a little seasick had something extra.
The country never would know what it missed by keeping Felkin in the jug through a whole war. With Admiral Felkin in
command, the Japs would have quit long before they did.

Bruno turned around and considered the problem of the wheelhouse ahead of him. Now just to get back to the things that counted—there would be a real admiral inside that house and sooner or later he and Bruno Felkin would have to make with a staff meeting. There would have to be some fancy explanations, since it would naturally be kind of surprising to have some guy show up from nowhere, even if he was a genius. This was going to take delicate talk; the admiral and Felkin *had* to get along. This boat had to keep right on plugging out to sea.

Bruno approached the wheelhouse cautiously. He jumped back to the shadows suddenly when he found a green light shining upon him. When he saw that it was only a fixed light on the side of the wheelhouse he moved forward again until he came to a window.

It was dark inside the wheelhouse except for a thin shaft of light shining upon the face of a man just behind the wheel. Bruno examined the man carefully. Diplomacy wasn't the word for it! There was that man again. The one it wouldn't pay to argue with. He looked bigger than ever and Bruno thought he had a face like the front of a courthouse. Oh, Bruno, be nice to this guy. And hope he was all muscle and no brain. Anybody that big *couldn't* have any brains. It wouldn't be fair. Be very careful what you say to this character, Bruno. Remember, luck is like a rubber band. You can stretch it just so far.

Bruno was about to enter the wheelhouse when he saw another figure appear by the man at the wheel. He came up from somewhere below and stood rubbing his eyes and scratching his hair. He yawned and shook his head. He was almost as big as the other man but much younger. The older man smiled and they spoke a moment together.

Bruno was still creating a suitable story when the younger man turned to the door suddenly and stepped out on deck. Bruno had just time to ruffle his hair and pull his necktie halfway around his neck. Then they were standing almost face to face in the green light, this younger man and Bruno Felkin who still had only half a story.

"Who in the hell are you?"

Bruno tipped his head to one side and rubbed his hand across his mouth. "I made a mistake, I guess. Couldn't help it. Are you the boss?"

The young man measured Bruno from his shoes to his rumpled hair and he took an uncomfortably long time with his examination. Finally he called out over his shoulder to the man in the wheelhouse, "Hey, Pop! We got a passenger!"

So that was it. This would be the son who was supposed to turn out all right. With looks like his, he should worry. Bruno, your mind is still asleep. You should have been able to figure they were father and son from the looks of them. Get thinking fast now because the old man is coming to the door.

"I'm sorry, mister . . . but maybe you know how it is. I was out doing a little drinking, see . . . and I guess maybe I had too much, you know how it is. Anyway I have an idea like those ideas you get . . . well, maybe I'll take myself a little walk. So I do, and wind up down on the wharf and then all of a sudden I'm so sleepy I can't hold my eyes open. So I don't remember exactly, but your boat looks like a good place to lay down. Next thing I know, here I am."

"Come inside," Hamil Linder said. "You vill catch cold out there vith no coat."

Watch everything now, Bruno—size up the situation and be damned careful what you say. This is no time to get careless. The old man may be just a fisherman, but that's no sign he's a dumb cluck. And he's got to like you at least temporarily. Give out with the old Felkin smile that says you didn't really mean to do what you did.

"I'm sure sorry, mister. It was one of those things. I'm a salesman, see, and I had a lot of personal worries lately, see . . . and I guess I was feeling awful sorry for myself."

"I don't like to put back now," Hamil said. "Vee vould miss the tide then, and so lose a day."

"Oh, I wouldn't want you to do that. I haven't no place to go anyway . . . wouldn't miss nothing important, see?"

"But vee go to sea for maybe four or five days," Hamil explained.

Bruno, that luck of yours is better than any rubber band! It stretches forever.

"Well . . . honestly I don't care, mister. I'm fresh out of cash right now, but I could let you keep this watch or something until we get back as a guarantee I'll pay you for any food I eat."

The son was smiling and it wasn't too nice a smile. His eyes were squinting suspiciously—or was he the one who had a real hangover?

"When this bucket gets past the heads you won't be eating anything," the son said.

All right, wise guy. Right now maybe you can push Bruno Felkin around, but we'll square that away later. The first thing to do is bring the old man into line.

"Have you ever been on a boat before?" Hamil asked.

Now it was on fasties like that one where tinhorns fell down because they didn't have the brains to see what might happen even a few hours later. They always had to swing their weight around and claim to know everything, and so they hung themselves. But not Bruno Felkin. A guy is more inclined to help you if he thinks he knows more about a certain thing than you do. It makes him feel good. Remember these two had probably bounced off more waves than you ever heard of. Pull that "I'm sorry" smile again, like it was all your fault you weren't a real admiral.

"No . . . I never been on any kind of a boat. But I don't feel sick . . . not a bit, except for a hangover."

"You and me both," the son said. Bruno smiled at him. Maybe

winning the kid wasn't going to be too tough after all. You could talk about policemen and judges and the like—not that you knew any, of course.

"Why don't you just keep on going and I'll promise to stay out of your way? Maybe I could help. I'll sure be glad to do anything you say—wash dishes or anything."

"Vould you like a cup of coffee?" Hamil asked.

"Why, yeah. If it's not too much trouble."

"No trouble. Vee have coffee anyvay now." Hamil put his big hand on Bruno's shoulder and for one unexplainable moment something happened inside of Bruno Felkin. It was as if a wire snapped, or sparked; the hand was warm although its actual temperature could not be felt. The movement, simple as it was, seemed almost an embrace. It was a hell of a funny feeling.

"Come," Hamil said. "Vee do not eat until vee finish vith the baiting and that be some time. You get nice and varm from the coffee and also I have an old coat you can put on." He took a quick look at the darkness ahead and descended the ladder to the forecastle. He motioned Bruno to follow him.

It was hot in the little bright room below the foredeck. There were four bunks along the sides and Hamil indicated that Bruno should sit on a lower one.

"Vat name do they call you?" Hamil asked.

Was the old boy kidding? Bruno Felkin had been called plenty of names—a few fancy ones, in fact, by a recently deceased character named Sam. No, he wasn't kidding. You could see that by his eyes and the welcoming way he put the coffee mug on the little table. It was just the old boy's way of asking for an introduction. Now stick to the truth as close as possible, always remembering that a little lie, slipped in to cover a detail, can hang you later when least expected.

"I'm Bruno Felkin. What's your name, mister?"

"Hamil Linder. This is my son, Carl." They shook hands and

Bruno sought desperately for a joke. Get them thinking about
something else, something closely related to them. Then there
wouldn't be so much chance they might stumble onto some
embarrassing question.

"None of my business," Bruno laughed, "but just who steers
the boat while we sit here having coffee? Or is there a ghost on
board?"

"The *Taage* have an automatic pilot," Hamil said. "Funny
thing . . . I be so old-fashioned it vas a long time before I
decided to buy this vonderful thing. In the old days there alvays must be a man standing to the veel. Now it is only needed
to have a look around now and again. I suppose by and by they
vill invent some machine to make the fish yump on board. Ho,
ho! That will be a fine day. The very best day, so Carl?"

Carl ground his cigarette into a small tin can on the
table. "I don't give a damn what happens to the fish and you
know it."

Oh—oh, what gave here? The words were plain enough, but
the way this Carl was looking at his father had an angle—and it
was an angle that would have to be explored. There was a gim-
mick here, a needle. It could possibly help a man who understood it, and maybe hurt a man who didn't.

"My son is not so lucky," Hamil said quickly, and he seemed
to have suddenly become fascinated with the contents of his
coffee mug. "The *Taage* is a long-liner, as you vill see, and that
is not the easiest vay to catch a fish."

"Pop likes to do things the hard way," Carl said. "Whatever
it is, he does it the hard way."

What the hell was going on here? The kid *had* a father didn't
he? And for sure the old man wasn't a drunken bum like the
father of Bruno Felkin. He wasn't a big fat slob like your old
man who lived off everybody he could latch on to including
when he could get your ma to do somebody else's laundry. He
didn't look like a guy who would whine all the time and lie

about how his hurt back kept him from ever doing anything but lifting a bottle. He didn't appear to be the kind would kick a ten-year-old kid in the stomach because you swiped his jacket one day to keep from freezing to death. He looked like a real father—and that was something anybody was lucky to have.

"So long as you are on board and you feel all right, maybe you could help vith the baiting," Hamil said.

"Sure. Sure, anything you say."

"Can you svim?"

"Yeah. First class. When I was a kid we used to swim a lot in the Mississippi River. We could afford it because it was free. We used to have a lot of fun."

"Good. The only dangerous thing about fishing is maybe to fall overboard ven it gets rough. That is vat I keep saying to Carl. Be very careful."

"The only dangerous thing about fishing is a broken back," Carl said. "From working too hard."

Later, Bruno had cause to agree with Carl. He found himself praying for the sun to rise, for some warmth, however feeble, to touch his body. The sky, Bruno thought, is the same color as my blood—a pale frozen white. And this might be exiting from San Francisco, but Carl had something when he said it was doing things the hard way.

The *Taage* bounced on a still black sea, plunging away from the thin distant line of shore, plunging and rolling again and again in the foam of her own energy. It required considerable effort even to stand on the *Taage*'s deck and Bruno's legs already ached from the strain. The morning light which had taken forever to come revealed a pair of hands that certainly didn't belong to Bruno Felkin. They were bright red, and by now almost completely useless.

Bruno stood at a long wooden trough between Hamil and

Carl. The trough held three flat circular baskets, each of which
contained a long, carefully coiled line. According to Hamil
there were exactly two hundred and twenty-five hooks attached
to each line and these were seated in the wicker rim of its basket. A bucket of squid chopped in one-inch pieces stood beside
each basket. The squid was frozen and Bruno had long since
been unable to feel each piece as he took it from the bucket and
bent it to the hook as Hamil had shown him. Everything was
frozen, including Bruno's will when he looked at the work still
to be done. It seemed such a simple task, yet he had barely
completed a third of his first basket while Hamil and Carl each
finished two. But then neither Hamil nor his son had to stop
to blow on their hands every few minutes. They worked tirelessly, almost automatically, reaching for the bait with one hand
and then bringing their hands together in a quick rhythmic
gesture that left the bait hanging precisely just over the edge of
the basket.

"Be careful to lay the hooks side by side . . . so," Hamil
said. "If they are crossed then vee get some snarls and that is
alvays a headache."

"I'm not very fast," Bruno said. "My fingers are damn near
frozen off and they don't move just like I want them to." A
sea gull whimpered above them and Carl threw a piece of squid
at it.

"See what I mean, Felkin? Only a guy who didn't have anything else would go in for this. Hell, you ought to be out with
us some morning when it's really cold . . . when it's raining
and the wind is blowing. It's a great life—for squareheads."

Bruno wondered if he was mistaken in believing that he
sensed a touch of pride in Carl's voice. He was moving his
hands angrily, as if he hated every motion. His face was set in
what seemed to be an almost permanent sneer, and yet there
was something in the easy way he stood on the deck, his body

swaying in perfect agreement with the boat; there was something in his physical manner very opposite to the things he said.
He worked, Bruno thought, as his father worked—as if he was
born to it. It was too bad in a way, the argument between these
two, and still it was a condition that might favor Bruno Felkin
if he could ever thaw out his brain enough to fully appreciate
it. In the meantime the smart thing to do was to keep on baiting hooks, though how in God's name Hamil ever intended
to get them all down to the fish was still a mystery. He said they
would make a "small" set this morning—a mere ten baskets. By
Bruno's calculation that would be two thousand two hundred
and twenty-five hooks.

"It is not so bad," Hamil said easily. "A good man can bait
perhaps vun basket every twenty minutes. And so this morning
vee be finished some time before vee reach the hole." He
looked at Bruno and the flesh about his eyes crinkled with his
smile. "Maybe so vee even have time for another cup of coffee."

Bruno paused suddenly in his baiting. He had seen something burning on the horizon, a blood-red thing that seemed
almost within reach.

"My God! What's that!"

Hamil looked up and then roared with laughter. He stopped
in the middle of his laugh, holding his breath and looking at
Bruno as if he had seen him for the first time.

"That be the sun! Don't you know, Bruno Felkin? You
never seen the sun before?"

Bruno shook his head very slowly. He found he couldn't look
away from the spectacle. What in the hell was going on here?
Inside Felkin? What gives? A rat was a rat and he should be in
his hole when things like this took place. He shouldn't be
allowed out in the fresh air, breathing the stuff deeply, liking
the color of this ocean that just for a second was as red as Sam's
blood. A rat shouldn't ever feel lifted, or feel a part of a thing

like this. He shouldn't feel that he was a man who didn't have a thing in the world to hide. Bruno looked up at Hamil's face, now bronze in the light.

"No," he said quietly. "No . . . I never seen the sun rise just like that in my whole life. I never did."

Hamil placed his hand on Bruno's shoulder, and once more there was that strange feeling of security and warmth.

"Then I think you vill see many things, Bruno Felkin," he said simply, "many new things in the time you be at sea vith us, if you care to look for them."

The sun warmed the fog over Fisherman's Wharf and gradually dissolved its heavy content until it became a silver haze. For a time certain units of the fog resisted the attack and hung in tatters from the masts, the tops of the fish houses, and the ends of the pier fingers. It was time for basking the body, and so the members of the dock committee came out of the haze one by one and gathered in their accustomed place in the lee of the wall at Standard Fisheries.

A heavy timber stretched almost the length of the wall and the committee sat upon the timber, or put one foot on it, or disregarded its existence, according to precedent and their physical condition. It was understood among them that certain members of the committee had rights, and these were set by seniority, or oratorical ability. It had long been established that Little Bat's place along the timber was at the extreme south end, that is, as far as possible from the north end of the timber, which reached to the very edge of the dock. This precaution minimized the chances of Little Bat falling into the water when he became drunk, which he would certainly manage to arrange by noon. The members of the committee, who had far more important things to think about, were tired of retrieving Little Bat from the bay and going through the dull process of reviving him by artificial respiration.

Spade-face, who had once suffered a brain injury, and so lost his sense of smell, occupied that portion of the timber next to Little Bat. There was never any argument about his right to the position. His ability to suffer Little Bat at close quarters when he became obstreperous during the afternoon guaranteed his position. For Little Bat persisted in annoying the fish-house workers and his inevitable reward was a bombardment of fish, old eggs, boxes, and smashed crabs. No one contested Spade-face's seat on the timber, though it was recognized that he caught the sun upon his sagging shoulders perhaps five minutes before anyone else did.

Hoolihan normally took his seat on the timber next to Spade-face. It was the best seat on the timber, also held without protest, since Hoolihan was a man of means. It was well known that a sister-in-law sent him money from time to time and this sometimes allowed Hoolihan to sleep in a furnished room at night. The room was on a steep side street behind the chocolate factory and Hoolihan would descend from it each morning promptly at seven-thirty. Hoolihan claimed to have once been a sailor, but everyone knew he had never been any farther to sea than the timber. Nevertheless his opinions on boats, fish, and fishermen were listened to with respect. At some time during the day he might produce a bottle of wine from the folds of his overcoat. It was an important matter. A man who had staggered the streets the long night, a man who finally crept into a packing box, or an empty truck trailer, or a factory doorway—a man who slept outdoors or, worse yet, with the Salvation Army—could develop a powerful thirst by nine o'clock in the morning.

At the far end of the timber, nearest the water, sat Mister Fancy. He was a very small and timid man who wore a tie consistently. The tie was marked "San Francisco World's Fair, 1915." Its faded beauty was responsible for Mister Fancy's title. No one had ever been known to pay the slightest attention to him. He was merely another pair of ears to catch the wisdom of General Ball, and when he disappeared early in the afternoon his absence was seldom noticed. His situation on the timber was exposed to the harbor wind and shaded from the sun except at high noon.

General Ball was the recognized spokesman of the dock committee. He had no specific place on the timber, preferring to sit where he could find an opening for his bulk. Since his duties required him to roam the docks, the boats, and the fish houses throughout the day in search of vital information, he seldom felt it necessary to sit down anyway. He thought and talked with greater emphasis and clarity standing up. An erect posture allowed him to flay his arms against the sky as he spoke and so hold the slippery attention of his audience. General Ball wore the uniform of a regular committee member: greasy black cap, overcoat hanging almost to his ankles, and shoes with holes in both bottoms and tops. So clothed, he was immediately set apart from the irregulars who occasionally found their way to the special place of the committee—irregulars being, in General Ball's eyes, any wanderers who had no established retreat in all the city. The wanderers would come and go, standing for a few hours with their hands in their pockets, looking at their feet, listening to General Ball expound the news of the world and the wharf.

"I'll tell you," said Ball on this morning as the sun began to warm his back. "I'll tell you this, and anybody who don't listen to me is a ostrich. Now you take a farmer. Go ahead, take him. What does he do? He gets up maybe five o'clock in the morning. He goes out and milks some cows. It ain't a easy life, you understand, and sometimes the cow is sick. But sick or not, the farmer comes back to a nice hot breakfast. He eats that, then what does he do?" General Ball examined his audience for a reaction. Receiving none, he cocked his head to one side and wagged a long grimy finger at the occupants of the timber. "When a farmer gets through with his breakfast he monkeys around in the fields—"

"Jush a minute," Little Bat interrupted angrily. "Jush a mo-*ment!* Have you ever *been* on a farm?"

"No . . . no, I never been on no farm, but I say to you, a farmer's got it easy."

"Yer fruity," mumbled Little Bat. "I ain't gonna listen to you no more." As if to protect himself from further exposure to General Ball's views, Little Bat pulled his head down into the collar of his overcoat and closed his eyes. General Ball ignored him. He addressed himself to the more dependable ears of Mister Fancy and to three irregulars who had already gathered to absorb the sun. His voice assumed a tone that indicated he was prepared to be reasonable.

"A farmer now, he has his problems—sure. But after he eats his breakfast, what does he do? He goes out and climbs on a nice comfortable tractor and plows his fields, that's what he does. And all the time the gov'ment is payin' him to sit on the tractor whether he raises anything or not. Right?" General Ball did not wait for any confirmation from his audience. It was still too early in his theme to permit interruptions.

"So then this here farmer comes back home and eats a big lunch and takes a snooze afterwards—maybe even has a daytime go at his old lady. He's lyin' there thinkin' what a wonderful gov'ment we got and when he gets tired of thinkin' how swell it is, he goes out in the field and plows some more. Then he comes back home again and has a drink—"

"You gotta clock says it's time for *us* to have a drink?" asked Spade-face.

"No I ain't got a clock and I never need one because I can always tell exactly what time it is by the sun."

"Yer fruity. Yer jus' fruitier than hell," Little Bat mumbled again. One of the itinerants raised his watery eyes to blink at the sun.

"Then what time is it?" he asked.

"What difference does it make what time it is? You goin' somewhere, mister?"

"No, I ain't goin' nowhere, I just want to know what the hell makes you think you can tell time by the sun."

"I'm talkin' about farmers and if you guys will let me stick to the subject you'll learn a thing or two."

"I still want to know what the hell time you think it is," the itinerant insisted. General Ball scorched him with a look. But he held his hand toward the sun and spread his fingers slowly.

"It's ten minutes past eight," General Ball pronounced.

"That's crap," the itinerant said. General Ball at once took three pugnacious steps in his direction, paused, and then continued his approach until he was in a position to almost touch his own unshaven chin to that of his heckler.

"You callin' me a liar?"

"Yer the biggest liar I ever heerd," said the itinerant, holding his ground. "You want to make somethin' of it?"

General Ball's nose twitched suspiciously. "Where did you get the whisky?" he asked.

"How you know I got some whisky?"

"It stinks on yer breath."

"Whisky don't stink."

General Ball allowed a subtle change to come over his attitude. Then suddenly he placed a friendly hand on the itinerant's arm. He laughed hoarsely.

"Oh, pal! That's a good one, pal! That's the best one I ever heard in a long time. And now just to prove whisky don't stink, how about divvying with us. We'll conduct sort of a experiment."

"You said it was too early to have a drink."

"I never said that. Little Bat said it."

"I never did!" Little Bat almost raised himself from the timber, so violent was his protest, General Ball increased the pressure of his hand on the itinerant's arm.

"Come on, pal. Bring out the whisky. Bring it out, pal."

"What'll you pay?"

"*Pay?*" General Ball was horrified. "Listen, pal. This here is our place, see? We been comin' here every day for years and years. We like to have guests once in a while, see, but usually they got the good sense to divvy."

"This here is the end of a street but it's still a public thoroughfare. Anybody can stand here."

"Maybe so, but we share and share alike. It's a rule."

"You a Communist?"

"What's it to you?"

"I don' like Commies." Now the itinerant pushed his chin toward General Ball's.

"Then I ain't a Commie."

"And *I* ain't got no whisky left. Frisk me all you want but you won't find none at all."

"Wh' we need is no gov'ment," said Little Bat. "No gov'ment at all."

Breathing deeply to hide his disappointment, General Ball drew away from the itinerant until he again stood in a commanding position before the timber.

"Now we was talkin' about fishermen before this loud-mouth hypocrite interrupted," General Ball began.

"You was talkin' about farmers," Mister Fancy said mildly. General Ball glared at him.

"Shut up, you, and maybe you'll learn something. Now some people say fishermen are just farmers on the ocean. Get the relation? Well there ain't no comparison. In the first place the gov'ment don't give the fisherman nothin' but headaches. What they do is help out fishermen of every nation we was fightin' against in the war with money and fine boats. And as if that ain't enough, they allow their fish, these enemy fish mind you, to come into this country and flood the market. Does that make any sense?" No one challenged General Ball and so he was able to continue in a softer tone.

"As if that wasn't enough, the gov'ment throwin' the tax money in the enemies' throats, look at the life they got to lead compared to some farmer. They get up maybe at three o'clock in the mornin', the fishermen that is, and if it ain't too rough maybe they can brew a pot of coffee for breakfast—maybe. Then all day long they got to bounce around in a little boat and they don't dare even take a drink or they fall overboard and drown. So they work all day long until it gets dark, then they got to come in from wherever in the ocean they are. So if they are lucky they get in maybe at ten o'clock, or maybe not even for several days, and then what do they find? I ask you what do they find?"

Hoolihan knew his cue perfectly. "It depends," he said.

General Ball smiled upon him. "You're a hundred per cent correct. It depends on if he's got any fish or not. If he's got any fish he's got to sell 'em before they spoil. He can't be waitin' around for a decent price and the buyers know it. So they give him a first-class screwin'. And what's more, a man that can't steal his weight in fish don't stay weighin' them very long. But now suppose the fisherman don't have no luck? Does he get paid anything for his work all day? Nothin' he gets. Nothin' of course from the dealers and nothin' from the gov'ment. I feel sorry for the fishermen." General Ball reached into the pocket of his ragged overcoat and brought forth the stub of a cigar. He placed it between his yellow teeth and chewed on it reflectively. Then he studied the sun a moment and finally sighed.

"Hoolihan," he said, "have you got any money this mornin'?"

"Of course not."

"Didn't yer sister-in-law send no money at all?"

"No."

"If we could only find some guy who had a job once, we could help him collect his unemployment insurance."

"I had a job once," said the itinerant.

"When was that?" General Ball asked eagerly.

"Nineteen-thirty. I was the bes'—"

"You ain't eligible," snapped General Ball. He at once went back to his examination of the sun. "It looks to me like this is going to have to be a prospectin' day. We got to deploy. And we got to hurry because it's already gettin' late. Spade-face, you work the north side of Jefferson Street, and, Fancy, you take the south goin' the other way. Me and Hoolihan will take Bay Street and—" General Ball paused to frown at Little Bat. "He's too drunk. We may as well leave him lay because he'll never be able to pan a dime." General Ball shivered at the sun. "It looks to me like this is goin' to be a dry day. I just got a awful hunch."

"KELSEY!" CONNIE SAID. "KELSEY, ARE YOU awake?" He was slumped in the big chair and the sunlight shafting through the window made a halo of his thin gray hair. His freckled hands were folded across his stomach and his breathing had been long and even for more than an hour. Connie was fully dressed in the gray corduroy suit she normally wore to school. She had done the breakfast dishes, taken a shower, and returned to the couch . . . waiting. Waiting for what? Bruno wasn't going to call now. He *was* in trouble. If he had killed a man, as Kelsey said he did, he would never call again. But Bruno wouldn't kill . . . he might do a lot of other things, but it wasn't in him to kill. Not Bruno, who could be so gentle in the night. Not Bruno, who could understand other people's troubles and feel sorry for them—though God knows the world should feel sorry for Bruno.

Kelsey. Close your mouth. It's a nice mouth, nothing cruel about it, and yet you want to exterminate Bruno. A man who was just willing to fight for the kind of life he thinks he ought to have. You aren't just a bum with a badge, Kelsey. You came

right out and said I was a fine cook . . . but there was one
better and that was your wife who you happened to love. For
twenty-eight years you've been in love with her. That's what you
said. All right. Other people wanted a chance at the same thing,
Kelsey. Bruno, for instance . . . and me. "My wife" was a fine
phrase the way you used it, Kelsey—easy and familiar as if
it had rolled off your lips a million times, and probably it had.
"My wife . . ." this and "my wife . . ." that. And you were
still planning and hoping for things together . . . like the
transfer to the state's attorney's office you talked about. Fine,
Kelsey. Maybe Bruno and I aren't honestly in love . . . yet. It
all depends on what you mean by love, doesn't it? If it means
you can discover wonderful things together—things nobody else
would think are wonderful—then that could be love, couldn't it?
If it means you came together because you needed each other,
how about that?

Kelsey. Wake up. I want to walk in the fresh air. I'm young
and I want to be in the morning. You just think you understand
Bruno, Kelsey. You said he was a wild animal. Have you ever
heard him dream? Ever listen to him sail away on a cloud of
silken talk to times and places where nothing was impossible?
He didn't say those things just to make me feel good, Kelsey,
although they did. Bruno can make me feel like the only
woman he ever wanted to bother with. He said those things, and
he always will say them, to soothe some of the wounds he got a
long time ago. Nobody ever gave him a chance, Kelsey, everybody was too busy with themselves to give him a chance. Well,
I'm not. Little by little I'm helping him see things differently.
He's already promised to quit his business. And he will, Kelsey . . . you've got to believe that he *will*. If he's given a
chance. If somebody doesn't throw salt into those wounds again.

Look what he did for me. Took a waitress who didn't give too
much of a damn and taught me to dream. Dreaming for anyone is an important thing. And it wasn't like you think. I had

to ask for the first pass he made at me. If you exterminate
Bruno—if you cage him as you said he ought to be—then you're
exterminating a lot more than just a number on your records. I
have a lot to learn about dreaming and hoping yet. Bruno isn't
finished with his course. It takes time to get the smell of hash-
house grease out of your nose and your hair, Kelsey. I'm still
working on it . . . with Bruno's help. You don't understand
Bruno, Mr. Kelsey . . . or me. You just think you do.

Connie left the couch and went over to Kelsey's chair. She saw
the gun in his shoulder holster. His coat was turned back and it
would be so easy to reach it. For a crazy instant her hand almost
moved toward it. See, Kelsey? There's a little wild animal in all
of us. In a woman it comes out most when you're trying to protect someone who needs you. She touched his arm.

"Kelsey. Wake up." He grunted and opened his eyes. He
looked up at her face and then studied the suit she was wearing.
He yawned and rubbed his forehead.

"Was I snoring?"

"No. Not quite."

"Old men sleep in chairs, Connie."

"Maybe you better get a younger guard for me."

"You weren't going anywhere."

"How do you know?"

"I just know. What are you all dressed up for?"

"Am I under arrest or not?"

"Technically no. It's to our advantage to leave things loose for
a while. Besides, it would be a shame to let the city feed such a
good cook . . . and just to prove I have some kind of a heart
I'd like to keep your name off the blotter if it's possible."

"Thanks. But even a prisoner gets exercise. Can I go for a
walk?"

"If you don't mind taking me with you."

"Let's go."

Kelsey pushed himself up from the chair. He flexed his legs, yawned again, and searched sleepily for his hat. Connie took it off the radiator and handed it to him. Then she reached up and straightened his coat collar where it was crumpled at the back of his neck.

She led the way up the winding street that led to Coit Tower, breathing deeply of the fresh morning air. Kelsey plodded along, hands in his pockets, just a little behind her. Hill climbing, he said, was not one of his favorite sports, and why couldn't she pick some other place to walk?

They reached the little park at the top of the hill. In every direction the city spread out beneath them, the hills rising and falling until they met the sea and the streets still wet with the morning fog. The wharves fingered out at the base of the city and then there was the bay looking metallic in the sunlight. The islands in the bay still floated on a fine mist and beyond them the mountains had begun to take on depth and substance.

Connie leaned against the parapet, her chin cupped in her hands. She moved only when the wind blew her hair across her eyes, and then she swept it back patiently. She was silent for a long time. Finally, without looking at Kelsey, she spoke to him.

"Kelsey . . . do you think this is beautiful?"

"Yes. My wife and I come up here every once in a while. It's sort of a favorite place with her."

"The man you want to cage also thinks this is beautiful. Can you see him standing here, as I have . . . just looking off into the distance for hours . . . hardly saying a thing . . . can you see that same man killing somebody?"

"I told you, Connie. He's probably two people. I'm sorry."

"Bruno liked the feeling of looking down. He said once . . . it made him feel important."

"That's a feeling he's got to have, Connie. They all do. I'll tell you one thing really makes a criminal mad, and very seldom is there an exception."

"What's that?"

"If the newspapers neglect him. He doesn't like that."

"Bruno wouldn't want that kind of importance."

"When he's finally in his cell again, the first thing he'll ask for is a newspaper. You'll see."

"Who was the man who was killed?"

"Sam Addleheim. One of our lowest forms of wild animal life. The kind we knew about but could never quite pin down. Every mourner at his funeral will have at least one set of fingerprints on file with us."

"What makes you so positive Bruno did it?"

"I'm not positive. But we have to start somewhere. From all angles he's the most likely candidate. Just so you won't feel so bad, Bruno was going to get picked up soon anyway. The Vice boys have been giving him his head for a long time hoping he'd lead them to something big."

"Did he?"

"Yeah. Sam Addleheim."

Connie brought a toothpick from the pocket of her suit. She began to chew on it thoughtfully.

"No matter what you say . . . I'll stick with Bruno as long as he needs me."

Kelsey reached over and took the toothpick from Connie's lips.

"Then you better forget how to use these things, Connie. My guess is Bruno wants a lady."

Bruno and Carl sat on the *Taage's* deck with their backs against the bulwark. Hamil had said he would take this one chance to rest while the lines were soaking. According to Bruno's watch it would be another hour before any industry would be shown on the *Taage* again, and so there was plenty of time to explore an idea that had gradually risen with the sun. Like a cake, Bruno thought. Like a handsome cake, baked by Connie—a real genius.

He said to Carl, "How come you're on this boat if you hate it so much?" Sometimes if you surprised a person with a direct question right after a long silence, they gave the answer before they had a chance to think. Either way, answer or no answer, the result should provide a better line on Carl.

"I don't see where that's any of your damn business," Carl said.

Bruno smiled to himself. The difference between this punk and his father was amazing. Except for his looks there wasn't a thing to recommend him, and the easy way he stretched his long arms and legs before he bothered to return Bruno's frank examination marked him as a wise guy. Just as you thought, Bruno. One of those big outdoor kids without a brain in his head. He never knew what it was like to fight for food. The old man would have taken care of that. Look at his face. Full of color and health. Not a pock mark on it like there was on yours because he'd probably never been sick with smallpox and had to look after himself. Look at his eyes. Clear, snapping blue, in spite of his hangover. There were already wrinkles around his eyes, but that was from the sun—not from being scared half to death most of a lifetime. And his teeth were white and looked whole. They weren't yellow and rotten from bum food and knocked this way and that in one street fight after another. And he had a slow and lazy way of moving, like he was king of the heap. He wasn't bucking for anything, this Carl. He was waiting for it to come to him.

He seemed to have forgotten the question about being on the boat. Okay, wise guy. Let's go at this thing another way. Felkin has one of his hunches you could be very useful—in a temporary way.

"Your old man seems pretty swell. He's sure been nice to me."

"He's nice to everybody."

"You're lucky. My old man wasn't like that."

"Pop's all right. We just got different ideas. He's old-country."

"What's wrong with that?"

"He never gets any fun. He don't believe in it because he never took time to find what fun is. He just wants to work his dumb head off all day. Every day except Sunday."

"I see what you mean. There's no sense to it."

"If a fellow can't have a car, a few women, and the time to use 'em both, what's the use?"

"That's along my way of thinking. You in the service, Carl?"

"Yeah. I learned a lot of things in the army. One of them was not to do one damn thing you didn't have to."

"You're right, Carl. I feel the same way."

"Listen, you ever drive a Studebaker? One of the new ones?"

"No. I been pretty busy."

"They're real honeys. You can get ninety-five miles an hour out of 'em on a straight stretch. I drove one—but not for very long."

"Wreck it?"

"No. The cops came and got it."

"Oh . . ." Hold it now, Bruno. Don't rush things. Study that new light in his eyes. The kid is looking at the sky and he's seeing himself somewheres else besides on a fish boat. He is driving an all-chromium car that he's just boosted, and women are falling off curbstones watching him. "What do those cars sell for now, Carl?"

"I don't know what the down payment is exactly. It wouldn't do me any good to know now. But next year it's goin' to be different."

"How's that?"

"I'll be off the boat then and I'm gonna make some real money fast—without breaking my back."

"Why wait till next year? Maybe I could put you onto something now."

"I've got an agreement."

"With your old man?"

"No." Carl stuck his thumbs in his belt and smiled. "With a judge. I sort of borrowed that Studebaker without bothering to get the owner's permission."

"I guessed you boosted it. Mind if I give out with a little advice, Carl?"

"Stuff it. I heard it before. Stealing isn't honest."

"It's worse than that, Carl. It's dumb. Stealing is for punks who don't know their way around. No really smart man has anything to do with it in any form because it's always too complicated. If you steal things, you've got to sell the things to somebody and that's askin' for trouble. Also the somebody else is always in a position to name the sale price. If you steal money and keep it, the money gets hot. If you spend it, it runs out in a hurry. Then you've got to start all over again taking another chance. Stealing is a no-good merry-go-round."

"You seem to know a lot about it . . . for a salesman."

Now don't underestimate this kid, Bruno, just because he looks well fed and has that lazy way of moving about him. There's nothing stupid about the way he's looking at you now. There's some thinking going on behind those eyes and it's the kind of thinking that can make a monkey out of you unless you go very easy.

"I didn't exactly swallow your story about being so drunk you just fell on this boat," Carl said.

"Why not?"

"Your breath for one thing. And you don't look like the kind one glass of sherry would knock over."

Bruno laughed softly. "The funny thing is—it would."

"Then how come you're here?"

"I had a little emergency in my business and went for a walk last night to think it over. I slipped and fell off the dock."

"Is that so?"

"I've got a nice steady business, sort of a real estate business.

It requires a lot of leg work and it just happens that right now there might be a spot in it for a young fellow like you . . . providing you're willing to learn to keep your mouth shut."

"What makes you think I can't now?"

"Because you'd never have told me about the car if you had learned, Carl. Shooting off your mouth won't do in my business."

"What kind of real estate is that? Selling's not for me."

"My product sells itself. It says 'Real Estate' on the door of my office, but mostly it's a delivery service."

"Delivering what?"

"Another thing you don't do in my business is ask questions. How would you like to make maybe two hundred a week?"

"How would I like to be Rockefeller?"

"You go into port pretty often, don't you?"

"Two or three times a week."

"I might be able to figure it so you could stay right with the boat and still help me with my business. What I want you to do wouldn't take more than a few hours a day."

"And I make two hundred?"

"We might start off at that. Maybe increase it later. It depends. It's mighty nice to have something working nights for you."

"I'm your man. What's the catch?"

"You said you wanted to make money and I been thinkin' I could maybe use a little vacation. Get out in the open air and the like, more than I been. But I'm not the type to enjoy lyin' on some beach. Maybe just staying here on your old man's boat for a few weeks or longer would be just the thing for me. In the meantime somebody's got to take care of my customers. They depend on me and I'd hate to lose them. There's lots of competition in my business."

"A fish boat is a hell of a place for a vacation. Pop's is the worst of the lot."

"What's the pitch on this fish business, by the way? What makes you so sore at it?"

Carl pulled a bit of tar from a deck seam and rolled it into a ball with his fingers.

"I guess along with farming this is the oldest business in the world . . . I don't know for sure, maybe it's older. Anyway, it's run just about the same as it was a thousand years ago, and if you're a producer like pop and me are, you're holding the wrong end of the stick. You can't win against the bastards who do the buying and they make the most of it. They sit in their warm offices and wait for you to come in. Now they know damn well you're not going to haul your fish back to sea and dump 'em no matter what kind of a price they offer."

"How can they be so sure of that?"

"Does a farmer burn his crops? You'll see . . . when you work this hard for something you don't just throw it away. You can't help being proud of what you've done and the buyers know that. Once in a great while some fisherman gets heated up and tries it. He'll slap the buyer in the face with one fish and throw the rest overboard. But most of the time they put the price just above making a man quite that mad."

"What about your union?"

Carl raised his arm lazily and threw the wad of tar into the sea.

"You can't get a bunch of fishermen to decide on any one thing. They all have their own ideas . . . some of them are pretty strong in their opinions or they wouldn't be fishermen in the first place. In San Francisco, where you have to conduct half the meeting in English and half in Italian, it's just that much harder."

"Sounds to me like you're in the wrong end of this thing. Why not get smart and be a buyer? Move in?"

"You have to be related to move in and Scandahoovians aren't the merchant type. That's the trouble with us. We haven't got the nerve to make three or four hundred per cent profit."

"Three or four hundred per cent?"

"Figure it out for yourself. You go to the market to buy filet of sole. You pay at least forty cents a pound. Know what the fisherman gets for them delivered to the dock? Four cents."

"That I like, that I like very much!" Bruno looked at the sky. Well, well! The firm of Bruno and Felkin had maybe been asleep. Maybe there should be a branch office set up in this fishing business. At least it was worth a fast survey. And as for moving in without being a relative? What Carl didn't know was how you could move in on anything provided you used the old tried and true methods. A truck dumped over here, and one there. Unexplainable accidents to management personnel, a few faces rubbed up a bit . . . get one of them mixed up with a girl who knew how to follow instructions . . . ask a few questions about their life insurance . . . Hell, there were a thousand ways to move in on anybody you thought had something good.

Bruno saw that Carl was watching him closely.

"If you're thinking of making any connections in the fish business, forget it," Carl said. "They don't like outsiders, and if they have to they can be plenty rough. It's healthier to leave them be."

"You don't say, Carl? We'll have to talk some more about it sometime. Right now I want to know if your pop could be persuaded to let me stay on this boat. I'd like to live right on it—*all* the time. I might even be willing to pay him a little something."

"You sure got some screwy ideas. But pop wouldn't take paying guests. That's for party boats, puke boats we call 'em. If you stay on here, you'd work."

"I wouldn't mind. A little outdoor work would put me in condition."

"Why don't you ask him?"

"I was going to. But first I wanted to make sure I had an as-

sistant lined up for what has to be done on shore. And I want
to be sure that assistant tells nobody how much he is making or
what he's doing, understand?"

"You got him."

"Good. I happen to like you, Carl. How's your hangover?"

"I'll live. How's the one you're supposed to have?"

"A wink of sleep won't hurt it." Bruno closed his eyes and
pretended to doze. But real sleep was for punks. While you
slept, somebody got around you. Just as this Carl might do. So
far everything looked perfect. Who in the name of God would
ever suspect a husky picture of health like this Carl to be a
bindle runner? It would be a long time before even McNalley
at Vice would catch up to this one. The possibilities were big
and should have been geniused out before. Operate by remote
control and so never get picked up yourself. Pull a Sam Addleheim. You sit on what amounts to a private yacht, even if it does
smell some, and you wait for things to calm down about Sam.
You never even step on the dock. No phone calls to Connie—
no nothin'. Remote control. One thing at a time.

Corky Mullins awoke and almost instantly went back to sleep
again. He repeated the process several times and at each return
to consciousness he would estimate the progress of the morning
through the porthole near his head. He had no desire to rise
officially until every escape from the problems of the day was
brought out. There was no sense in rising at all—*ever*, by God—
with things the way they were. A man who was broke, even flat
broke, had only a single problem. A man who was in debt as
well as broke, and so in immediate danger of losing the only
thing in the world he loved, was in trouble every morning. How
bright the sun might be shining had nothing to do with it.

The *Thunder Mug* was a forty-foot piece of marine flotsam
which remained afloat only because Corky attended to her gasping bilge pump regularly. After years of pounding against the

waves and wharves of the Pacific Coast, she looked more like a
battered teakettle than a boat. Corky hid the fact from himself
but he was aware that eyes were politely averted when she
chanced to anchor with the rest of the fleet. Her topsides were
bruised and scarred until her wounds wept for paint, and her
basic lines, from her straight old stem to her drooping fantail,
were nautically hideous. She had a resigned air about her, as if
the years had slapped her unmercifully. Corky found little excuses in his heart for the *Thunder Mug's* shortcomings, as a man
might defend an ugly wife. He thought of the *Thunder Mug*
as his last love on earth. And there was always the hope she
might make his fortune.

It had been two years now since he put down his last four
hundred dollars toward their marriage. Another four hundred
dollars was supposed to be paid at the end of the first year and
the balance of four hundred more during the second year. Because of continuous bad fishing luck, not one penny of either
the second or third installments had ever been paid.

The widow of the *Thunder Mug's* former owner, Johnnie
Mae Swanson, would gladly sign the boat over as community
property if he would only abandon single status in her favor.
Boat or no boat, Corky thought, a union with Mrs. Swanson
was as dangerous an undertaking as sailing the *Thunder Mug* to
Australia via the Antarctic. Things were getting rough—very
rough. Mrs. Swanson had lost her patience. She wanted profit-
able loads of fish or a marriage license.

"Yer a good man now, Corky," he remembered Johnnie Mae
saying on one of her frequent trips to the wharf. "A man who
has the strength to forsake the bottle on his own is always a fine
man. But we can't struggle alone forever. It ain't supposed to
be that way. Me and you are not getting any younger. You
understand that, don't you, Corky?"

"I understand like a house on fire," Corky had answered. "But
I ain't about to marry you nor no other conniving battle-ax.

Leave an old man be, and look somewheres else." The exchange of opinions had taken place over a year ago, when the time limit on the payments still had a few weeks to run. Mrs. Swanson had made only two trips to the wharf since then. On the first trip she had asked Corky to give things another thought; on the last she had said the sheriff would certainly follow her.

When the slosh of water in the bilge attained a certain heavy sound, Corky knew he would have an hour at the most either to arise and work the pump or go to the bottom with the *Thunder Mug*. Not even her rotten mooring lines, these days almost permanently connected with the wharf, would hold her afloat.

"Oh God, what have I done?" Corky scratched himself from his ankles to his neck, and slowly rolled out of his bunk. Once established in a sitting position, he scratched areas of his body not already treated, put on his white cap, and concentrated furiously upon the problems of the next few hours.

There was no bread and there was no coffee and there was no money, facts which eliminated any thoughts of breakfast. There was no fuel for the make-and-break engine and the gas dock had firmly refused any further credit. Consequently there would be no fishing. The copy of *Amazing Stories* had been read so many times there could be no reading. The stove was out of oil and so there could be no warmth except what might be stolen from the sun. Other than the bilge-water pumping, it was not going to be a very busy day. Idle days were always so long, and they could get a man in trouble because they increased the yearning.

As soon as he had buttoned his long underwear securely Corky applied himself to the bilge pump. He pumped for twenty minutes and then stopped to regain his breath and examine the level of the water. He found that he was holding his own against the *Thunder Mug's* absorption of the Pacific Ocean, but not much more. Corky swore softly. It was going to be a busier day than he had supposed. For some mysterious reason

his beloved was leaking worse than ever. Maybe her worm-eaten
garboard planks had separated altogether. Or the keel had
fallen off. Corky swore again and thought how wonderful it
would be if only a man had the money to take the dear thing,
the goddamned thing, to dry dock where she might be healed.
Then he might lay his weary head on her bosom without putting on a life vest.

When he finally finished with the pump, Corky let himself
down into the cabin again, where he made preparations to shave
in cold water. Shaving with strict regularity kept a man's dignity. It was also something to do. Corky had hardly begun
when he heard steps on the deck and then voices. Few visitors
came to the *Thunder Mug*. Corky realized it was not because
the other fishermen disliked him. The boat and his appalling
bad luck with fish created an air of resignation and defeat so
powerful it could almost be inhaled. No fisherman could afford
to expose himself to such a combination. They had enough
troubles of their own, and so Corky forgave them.

He dashed water on his face and moved eagerly to the companionway hatch. Two men stood on the deck and they were
certainly not fishermen. They were large men, and from their
hats to their shoes they reminded Corky of a time he did not
like to think about.

"Hi, fella," one of them said.

"Hi. What can I do for you?"

"Can we have a little talk?"

"Sure. Come on down." The men lowered themselves carefully down the ladder and Corky motioned them to the bench
opposite his bunk. Both men displayed the inside of their wal-
lets. The sight of the gold badges confirmed Corky's worst sus-
picions.

"I suppose you're from Mrs. Swanson," he said.

"Who's Mrs. Swanson?"

"She owns this boat . . . sort of."

"We thought you were the owner." Corky waited a moment for his heart to stop pounding.

"If you're not from Mrs. Swanson that's dandy. Welcome aboard."

"We just got a couple of routine questions. Maybe you could help, or give us a lead. There don't seem to be many boats at the wharf."

"Most of them are out fishin' now."

"You just taking things easy?"

"Yeah. I caught so many fish last week I'm plannin' to retire." The men moved their heads together, examining Corky and the interior of the *Thunder Mug*.

"You keep her nice and neat."

"It gives me something to do. Also she's my baby."

"You around the wharf last night?"

"I always am. Me and cities don't get along."

"See anything unusual?"

"No. It was pretty foggy. I had a bath and went to bed early." The men looked more carefully at the cabin.

"You have a bath on this boat?"

"That depends on how you look at it. The bilge would make a fine swimming pool . . . but the water's usually so deep down there a man could drown. I favor the Salvation Army baths. Twice a week. Regular."

"What time were you up there?"

"About eight. Maybe eight-thirty. I took my time walking back. Maybe it was nine . . . I dunno. Does it make any difference?"

"It could. There was a character loose in this area we'd like to talk to." One of the men handed Corky a small pack of photographs. "Take a look at these. You ever see any one of them around here?" Corky studied the photos.

"I think I seen 'em all at one time or the other. But that's a funny thing. Since I been sober I get that feeling about damn near everyone. Man does that after he's been drunk for fifteen years." The three of them laughed together and the men stood up.

"You're a big help. But if you should see any of the mugs in those pictures, spend a nickel on a phone call to Homicide. Ask for Lieutenant Kelsey. He'll guarantee you get your nickel back."

"It so happens I don't have one of them things."

One of the men looked at Corky's face and then reached into his pocket. He put a nickel on the stove.

"Here. Be sure you dial the right number the first time."

The men climbed back up the ladder and as they disappeared Corky patted the *Thunder Mug*'s main beam just above his head.

"Just so long as they don't come from Johnnie Mae Swanson," he said, "just so long as we can manage, I'd tell 'em anything."

Corky returned to his shaving. He worked the cold lather on his face vigorously and then slowed his movements until he stopped altogether. He remembered now that he had seen a man running in the fog. Come to think of it, one of those pictures looked something like him. Maybe he ought to tell them about him. There might be at least a cup of coffee in it—and maybe some legal advice on how and when foreclosures took place.

Corky mounted the companionway ladder. He moved more quickly as he approached the deck. He looked up and down the wharf. The men were gone. Now there was the nickel on the stove. It was either a phone call or a cup of coffee. To hell with the phone call.

When Hamil came to the deck, Bruno was ready. He stood up immediately.

"Well, Skipper, I hope you got a good rest," he said. "Anybody who gets up in the morning like you do deserves same." Hamil returned his smile.

"Ya, I like to sleep more if I could, but still you die in bed and then is the time to sleep. Now I think there has been enough time for the hooks to soak. Carl, you go below and get Bruno Felkin a pair of boots. It vould be no sense to stand in the vet and fish in those shoes."

"These shoes aren't much good for anything. I think I'll throw them in the ocean." A shocked expression crossed Hamil's face and Bruno caught it instantly.

"Oh no! Those are fine shoes," Hamil said. "You should not throw them avay. You can vear them for many years, maybe."

"I was only joking. I learned when I was a kid— never throw anything away."

"Ya. That is a good vay. Now we bring aboard some fish—I hope." Hamil winked at Bruno and slapped him on the shoulder. The blow was obviously intended to be friendly, but it almost spun him around.

The *Taage* had drifted a considerable distance from the marker buoy. Hamil started the engine and returned to it, then he set a course for the first marker put down.

"If you vant, Bruno Felkin," he said, "you can stand behind me and clear the fish ven they come aboard. I vill show you how."

"Fine. It's funny but I just got a hunch this is the life for me."

"Maybe so . . . maybe so," Hamil said tolerantly. "But you perhaps change your mind by sunset tonight."

Before Bruno could detect a thing on the horizon Hamil sighted the first marker buoy, a mere black speck against the white sheet of the sun's reflection. He maneuvered the *Taage* until she came alongside and Carl caught the buoy with a swift movement of his gaff hook. Hamil helped Carl bring the buoy aboard and then put on a rubber apron. Together they heaved in the floater barrels, and finally they ran the anchor line to the gurdy.

As it began to turn Carl coiled the lines clockwise in neat piles on the deck. When some fifty fathoms were aboard, Hamil pounded it with his fist several times. The line was taut and his blows sent sprinkles of water and the leavings of jelly fish into the air. He smiled, for a taut line should mean fish—slowly being hauled from the depths.

The first anchor came aboard. Hamil stopped the gurdy and broke the jam knot which held it to the ground line.

"Now vee see how our first basket says things!"

The line passed from the water over the metal rollers projecting from the *Taage*'s rail. It then led through a narrow metal gate formed by two vertical rollers set in the deck. The rollers were barely an inch apart. Hamil said they were called the "crucifier."

The line passed from the crucifier to the gurdy, which now turned very slowly. From the gurdy it crossed the hatch to where Carl sat on a wooden stool with an empty basket held between his knees. As the gurdy revolved and the line came in, Carl reached forward the length of his arm and pulled the line to the basket. He laid it down carefully in counter-clockwise loops. Each hook was hung from the main ground line exactly the length of his reach.

Hamil stood, gaff in hand, at the projecting rollers. He anxiously watched the line emerge from the sea. When the need came, he reached across the line to the auxiliary wheel and throttle, maneuvering the *Taage* so that the line always stretched slightly away and ahead of the boat. The hooks, now baitless, were coming aboard one by one. Hamil drew down the corners of his mouth and worked his lips slowly.

"Vell . . . vell! By golly! Maybe vee draw skunk?" And then his frown softened and his eyebrows rose in the gesture of a man who was not in the least surprised. "But maybe not . . . hey? By golly? Have a look, Bruno Felkin."

A parade of white twisting bellies stretched to infinity in the liquid depths. Though the first fifty had been empty, now there was a twisting fish on every hook.

BARNEY SCHRIONA LOUNGED AROUND HIS house until past noon. After his wife Rosanna cooked a full breakfast he sat at the kitchen table for a long time, reading the newspaper with great care and attention. When his wife kissed him on the top of the head and said how nice it was to have him home for a change, he luxuriated in the unfamiliar steadiness of his chair, and the room, and the house itself. Nothing moved. When he decided to leave the kitchen and sit for a time in the living room, he negotiated the distance without banging his body against the wall, although he caught himself making a precautionary reach for a doorframe as he passed through it.

Barney always sensed small things when he returned from the sea. The silence of his home impressed him now. Very small sounds could be heard, a car passing in the street, the clink of the dishes as his wife worked about the kitchen, even the squeak of a spring as he sat down on the living-room couch. There was no continuous pounding of machinery or slosh of the ocean to blanket all other sounds; there was no smell of brine or of Diesel oil, no smell of oakum or net preservative, of cable grease, or musty blankets.

He sat on the couch smoking a cigar and watching the smoke curl upward until a thin layer of it formed above his head. The way the smoke hung there was being home—there were no cold gusts of wind to disturb it. Setting aside the possibility of an earthquake, Barney thought the home in which he sat would remain quiet for some time. Of course he was a stranger in its rooms. There were pictures on the walls to be seen as if for the first time, and there was an upright piano that had not been there the last time he had been home. The piano had been purchased by his daughter Christine from her savings as a receptionist at the telephone company, and Barney laughed quietly when he thought how many weeks her modest salary had amounted to more than the *Capella* could profit from the sea. Looking at the piano, Barney fell to thinking of his daughter and of the way she had come to him before he left his bed that morning. She had sat on the edge of the bed, combing her black hair and telling him of a world that for all of his understanding might as well have been on the star for which his boat was named.

When he finished his cigar Barney put it out carefully in the ash tray he held in his lap. Then he walked over to the piano and poked a few keys with his stubby fingers. He persevered until he could connect the first five notes of *O Sole Mio* and then suddenly abandoned the attempt. His fingers, he decided, were better suited to hauling on a drag net. But the piano was a good thing. It was also part of the land; such an instrument would soon sour at sea. Every home fortunate enough to have a daughter should have a piano. Hamil Linder, now, should have such a home, and a piano too. And a woman like Rosanna. Then perhaps he wouldn't have so much trouble with his son.

The trouble between Hamil and his son was a miserable thing to watch, and it had been ever since young Carl could be considered a man. It may have been his lack of a mother, or maybe he had just inherited an extra dose of Hamil's own strong will—it was hard to say just what the real reason was behind his behavior. And Carl wasn't the only son who behaved badly. There were at least three Italian fishermen Barney could think of who were having similar headaches with their sons. And Manuel Esforza, who had come from the Azores, had a son who refused to go near the wharves or the sea, though both had fed and clothed him since his birth.

There was no understanding these young men, Barney decided. In the old country they would have been proud of their fathers and glad to work with them. Here they seemed to feel just the opposite. Barney wished he knew some pure American families and how they worked inside, the kind of families where nobody had spoken with an accent for generations. In such families the roots must be well down by now. Everybody in the family wouldn't be excited all the time, because they wouldn't be so anxious to prove themselves. That's all Carl was doing, really. Because his father worked with his hands and didn't speak perfect American, Carl thought it made some difference in how the rest of America would look at him. Maybe it did. When Christine brought a young man around, even Rosanna went a little cuckoo. She made excuses for her home and for herself, and she spoke so carefully you could almost cut each word out with a knife. Rosanna, who ought to know better.

No, Hamil should never have tried to bring that boy up alone. It wasn't natural. It was all very well for a grown man to spend most of his life at sea, but everyone, young or old, seemed to need a quiet home. Just having one to think about was healthy. Just so there was a place where a man could stop fighting for a while. The sea was home to no one but fishes—and the damned fish could have it.

Barney went to the window and watched the street below. There was almost nothing going on there and he soon turned away to pace the living room aimlessly. He returned finally to the piano, but the first note he struck drove the tune he had been thinking of out of his mind, so he stopped and eventually wandered back to the kitchen. There he silently watched his wife knead dough for the *pasta* she had promised for lunch.

His Rosanna was a small, quiet woman and Barney thought she somehow managed to look almost exactly as she had on the day he married her. Since the ceremony had been performed some twenty-one years previously, he wondered how much his judgment might be affected by the fact he was so seldom ashore.

Let's see now . . . of the twenty-one years, he had been home, right here, less than two or three. There was still a certain stiffness between Rosanna and himself, a sort of delicate formality. It would probably always be with them. Certainly there was one very satisfactory thing about this woman, Rosanna. She had never provided the slightest doubt as to her devotion. She seemed quite content, and perhaps this was because she knew exactly where she stood. Only a mermaid could destroy her home, and he had once explained at length how seldom they were found in a dragger's net. In the old days when he had gone to Alaska for salmon, or south for tuna, Rosanna had waited months without complaint. Only once in their life together had she presumed to enter his existence at sea, and that had been something he couldn't refuse. Not for a woman like Rosanna who believed in so many things.

It happened over ten years ago when he bought the *Capella*. It was easy to remember how proud he was that day, taking Rosanna to the wharf to inspect the boat. Her interest in every little thing was surprising. Then she found the empty storage locker on the port side of the galley, and a woman's hand touched the *Capella*. The little room was the only waste space on a boat that was otherwise perfectly designed. Rosanna said it was not a mistake in design but the deliberate work of God.

"You won't use the room at all?" Rosanna asked anxiously.

"Not draggin' around here. I'll be in and out, in and out—no real long trips, you understand."

"Then please let me do something for you and for our *Capella*. This room must be a chapel—a very small one, but I will talk with the priest and everything will be here."

Rosanna had her way, and so except for the big tuna clippers down south, the *Capella* was the only boat on the Pacific Coast with her own chapel. Everything was in it although there was barely room to kneel—altar, cross, Book, and candles. Under Rosanna's direction one of the deck hands had even painted the porthole to resemble a rose window. So what if it did look funny? If it made Rosanna happy to think her husband prayed at sea, that was all right. The chapel was kept clean and that was little extra trouble because it was almost never used except for those few times when the *Capella* had been blown in at Drake's Bay over a Sunday, and the boys in the fleet had nothing else to do. Then a few, usually the older ones, would row over to the *Capella* and take five or ten minutes supposedly to make their peace with God. But the bulkhead between the galley and the chapel was very thin and more than once they had been heard to omit the more formal prayers and straightway demand that the Creator of the sea provide them immediately with better fishing.

"When do you sail again?" Rosanna asked. Barney smiled at her. He stuck his finger in the *pasta* and licked it.

"Ho, ho! I just come home and you want to get rid of me!"

"You know that's wrong, Barney. I wish you would never go." Her soft brown eyes were serious, as they always were when they spoke of the matter. Always too serious, Barney thought.

"I only clutter up the house . . . get in the way."

"The days I don't mind so much. The nights, I worry."

"About what?" Barney appeared to be astounded, although he knew exactly what she was going to say.

"The wind. I get so I hate the wind."

"Rosanna." He sighed patiently and took another dab of the

pasta. "I've told you twenty times our boat can handle the wind."

"How about the fog? How about the *Columbia?*" There Rosanna put a tough question. The drag boat *Columbia* had been run down by a steamer in the fog only a month ago, and she had sunk with all hands.

"So once in a while an accident happens. I'm careful."

"Even so—"

"What would we eat if I sat here looking out the window all day?" She laughed at him and then, as if to balance her questions, her answer became deliberately gay. She pushed his reaching hand away from her mixing bowl.

"*Pasta* cooked . . . so you don't get indigestion."

"Something has to pay for the flour and the heat."

"We could live on love."

"Ho, ho!" Barney reached across the table and touched the corner of her mischievous mouth with his finger. "At our age, then we would starve to death."

When Rosanna turned on the stove Barney had to leave the kitchen. It was just too hot. The whole house, in fact, seemed stuffy and hot. He went out the back door and stood for a time on the earth of Rosanna's modest flower garden. The feel of real earth beneath his feet surprised him. He rarely ventured into the backyard—it must have been more than a year, he supposed. Sometimes he forgot that there could be such things as earth and grass and leafed things other than seaweed. He patted his foot on the ground experimentally, as if the substance might mire him. He reached down and took a handful of earth and brought it to his nose, marveling at the smell of it. He let it dribble through his fingers and heard it peckle upon his shoes and thought again how strange it was to hear small sounds.

He strolled along the garden, uncomfortable in its strange peace. And as he moved he became a little afraid, as if he wandered in regions forbidden to him. He stooped to look more closely at a rose and sniffed its fragrance suspiciously. The thing grew, of course, but it took forever, and it could not be seen to grow. He tenderly caressed the rose and then stood up looking all about him. Of the several plants and flowers in the garden there was only one he could recognize—the rose; and that only because it was the symbol of his wife's name. He could not decide whether this was a good or a terrible thing, or if he should be ashamed, and as he walked more upon the earth he tried to discover why its power and produce interested him so little. Finally he returned to the kitchen.

"What are you thinking so hard about?" Rosanna asked the moment she saw his face. "You'll break your brain."

"How do you know I'm thinkin' about anythin' special?"

"I'm your wife. That's my business. When you frown that way, you're thinkin'. Usually it's about how to catch all the fish in the sea."

"Right now I'm not thinkin' about fish for a change. I was walkin' in your garden."

"In another month it will be pretty."

"I think it's okay now. I'm damned if it don't scare me a little. Maybe there's something wrong with me . . . I dunno . . ." Barney scratched his head.

"Of course you can't appreciate a garden."

"Why the hell not?"

"In a garden, things happen too slowly for you . . . or any other man who has been to sea . . . too long, Barney."

"It takes some knack to grow things, I guess. I don't think I could do it."

"You never tried."

"I ain't about to either, Rosanna. Much as I'd like to stay ashore, I know where I belong. It's sure one hell of a fix."

"I wish you'd stop using that word so often."

"Hell is said in the Bible all the time, left and right."

"Not by the fishermen in the Bible."

"I bet they said it. I bet they led the same hell of a life. You want at the age of fifty-six I should go wash my mouth out with soap and water?" Rosanna crossed the kitchen and kissed him on the cheek.

"Out there in your garden I am also doin' some thinkin' about Hamil."

"Haven't you got enough troubles of your own?"

"He's my friend," Barney said.

"Is he still having trouble with Carl?"

"Yeah. I'm wondering if he always will have, and why it's all the time happening. It's getting so I hate to see Hamil's face when he's thinkin' about Carl."

"Have you ever tried to talk with Carl?"

"I did once. We didn't get very far. You see, I work with my hands too. Carl don't think so much of that."

"Then he's smart. If we had a son I would want him to be something nice like a doctor or a lawyer, somebody important." Barney looked at his hands a moment, then stuffed them in his pockets and shrugged his shoulders.

"If we had a son it would be a lot more important to have him be a good man. Maybe that's one of the troubles—seems like everybody who ever came to this country in the last fifty years wants their sons to be doctors or lawyers or bank presidents so bad they get the kids thinkin' crazy. But Hamil never felt that way. He's always been a reasonable man."

"Do you want Christine to marry a fisherman?"

Barney laughed. "Let's not start that argument."

"All right then. Sit down and eat your *pasta* and forget Hamil's troubles. After you eat you can do what you want to do."

"I'm doin' it."

"No, you're not. I've been watchin' you rattle around the house. Get on down to the wharf. It might float away without you. Go get a sniff of salt air so you'll have an appetite when you come back tonight for supper."

After his meal, Barney lost no time getting to the wharf. Pulling his hat down hard against the afternoon sea wind, he marched down Hyde Street as if the success of his arrival depended upon a certain minute. On the way from his house he conceived the notion that it was absolutely necessary for him to call Hamil Linder on the radio. The fact that they were engaged in vastly different kinds of fishing had no bearing on the matter—one fisherman had to know how the other was succeeding, or he could not long remain a happy man. It was bad enough to be on the beach while another worked beyond the horizon; there was always the feeling that something would be missed, and ignorance as to how the rest of the fleet was doing always led to a strange brooding that took days to cure. Barney had seen fishermen frantically trying to fix a broken radio, half-crazy until it was working again. They had to know. Nowadays a fisherman without a radio was as incomplete as a housewife without a back fence.

Barney turned the corner at Standard Fisheries and passed expertly through the dock committee. They were all drunk now and inclined to be sociable, particularly with a man of Barney's stature on the wharf, a man who owned his own boat. Barney said hello to General Ball and to Hoolihan, but continued on his way before they had a chance to clutch his arm. He passed over the bridge between the wharf fingers, waved a hand at the coffee loungers in Castagnola's Look-Out Cafe, and, rapidly losing himself in the familiar sights and smells and sounds, he arrived at the *Capella* in high spirits. He jumped aboard eagerly and went at once to the wheelhouse, where he switched on the radio. He waited a moment for the dynamotor to warm and then brought the microphone to his lips.

"Calling the *Taage* . . . calling the *Taage* . . . the *Capella* calling the *Taage*. Do you pick me up, Hamil?" Barney waited impatiently as the radio snapped and crackled. When Hamil's deep voice finally came in, his face brightened.

"The *Taage* back to the *Capella* . . . so, vell! . . . vat do you say, there, Barney! I pick you up fine."

"The *Capella* back . . . I'm still tied to the wharf here, Hamil. How does it go? Where are you and what's the weather like?" These questions were ritual. The answers would establish certain pictures in Barney's mind so he could further relieve his intense curiosity. If the fishing was good, he would not only think but *know* he was missing something. If it was bad, he would feel slightly better lying at the wharf.

"The *Taage* back to the *Capella*. Vell, Barney, yust now vee are maybe twenty-five, thirty miles off the Gate in two hundred and sixty fathoms. There is a little breeze and slop from the west-nor'west, but nothing to bother. . . . Ven are you coming out, Barney? Over."

That squarehead rascal! He wasn't telling everything right off. He wanted to be asked, so he could come back modestly and say his boat was sinking with fish. The next question must be put as if the answer really didn't matter. That was also ritual.

"The *Capella* back. I'm gonna stay home with the wife to-night, Hamil, but we'll get out in the morning about three o'clock I hope, and maybe work out your way or up around the Cordell Bank somewhere. I haven't decided yet. By the way, Hamil, how is it going? Come back."

"Vell, so-so . . . vee put aboard one now and again. . . . Vee made a very nice set, by golly . . . right over the hole, I think!"

"The *Capella* back to the *Taage*. That's fine, Hamil. I like to see those blackies come aboard. Now maybe you wouldn't mind telling me how deep they are on deck? Come back, Hamil." There was a long pause which only increased Barney's impatience. Had the damned radio broken down? He slapped it.

"The *Taage* back to the *Capella*. Vell, Barney, like I say, vee bring one aboard venever vee can . . . not so many . . . not so few . . . but our bait vas a little soft, I think, and maybe vee lose some of it going down, hah? Over."

"How much have you got aboard, Hamil? Come back." Another long pause. The fury mounted within Barney Schriona's broad chest.

"Vell, maybe . . . it's hard to say, you know . . . yust exactly, Barney . . . could be maybe a ton, maybe a little more or less. But vee still have three baskets to pick up. And this vas a very small set . . . only ten baskets, you know. But they all pretty nice fish . . . maybe sixty per cent large."

A ton! That squarehead! He never exaggerated and was probably up to his knees in fish.

"The *Capella* back. Fine, Hamil, fine. I'm glad to hear somebody knows how to catch fish. Well, I don't want to clutter up the air any longer so I'll give you a blast tomorrow. If there's nothing further, this will be the *Capella* off and clear with the *Taage*."

"I think vee lie in the lee of the Islands tonight, Barney, and make another set tomorrow if the veather holds. So that's all from this end. Thanks for the call, Barney. The *Taage* off and clear."

Barney switched off the radio and hung up the microphone. Now it was going to be harder than ever to go home and wait quietly for supper.

When Hamil returned to the deck he started the gurdy again and once more bent to his labor with the gaff. The *Taage* was heavy with cod now, their shining black bodies pressed hard against his boots. The harvest moved together in a mass, the whole thing sliding in agreement with the *Taage*'s steady roll. And still the gurdy turned, relentlessly, holding the pace for Carl's hands as he coiled the line.

"You get what I mean?" Carl groaned. "You see, Bruno? All day long you work to get a broken back. You should be along some day when we haul up nothing but a few idiot fish. That makes you look at one of them things and wonder who is crazy."

"I never saw so many fish in my life," Bruno answered. He had fallen into the rhythm of the work, and as the fish snapped off the crucifier he reached out with a gaff and hauled them aft so Hamil would have more room. Earlier in the day he had relieved Carl at the baskets, only to find that in this one respect at least Carl spoke the full truth. After he had coiled one basket he was exhausted.

Hamil did not comment on the complaints Carl made during the long afternoon. He heard the words well enough and the sound of them before a stranger made them hurt all the more. Why did Carl have to mark their separation so plainly while this Bruno Felkin was aboard—as if he wanted all the world to know, and Bruno Felkin in particular? It became harder to understand as the day progressed, because Bruno Felkin himself was always the one to answer him.

He said, "I don't know what kind of vitamins your pop eats, Carl, but I'm goin' to get some for myself. He's a long ways from being an old man." Of course that was flattery, and untrue as well. This Bruno Felkin had a quick tongue and he wanted something. What other reason could there be for the way he sometimes almost fell overboard in his clumsy attempts to help and please? Why should he catch everything Carl had to say and turn it away as if he knew Hamil Linder longed for a shield?

There was something very strange about the fellow, concealed behind his dark eyes, and it clashed with the rest of him, for he was such an easy man to like. There was warmth in his smile and he knew how to fight. He refused to rest though he was obviously very tired. Besides clearing the fish and spelling Carl for the one basket, which was far more than any landsman could be expected to do, he had volunteered to straighten the ganging lines as they came in. He paid strict attention when he was shown how to unwind the tangles—how to let worst ones go by, and how to always be wary of the hooks. He listened carefully, but of course it happened—as it might to a man who had fished all his life.

When the two hooks caught his hand and buried deeply in his palm before the gurdy could be stopped, he did not cry out. When you turned them out of his hand with a pair of pliers he braced himself but he did not move. After it was over he simply sucked in his breath and said nothing. He squeezed out the blood until he was wet with it to his wrist, and still, when the gurdy turned again he stood straight to work. He reached for the constantly moving tangles again without fear—and even for an old-time fisherman that was not an easy thing to do.

A large ugly snarl of perhaps fifty hooks came aboard. Hamil stopped the gurdy and stood back at arm's length from it. "Yust like a coiled rattlesnake," he said to Bruno. "And the same bad disposition." Then he whacked the mess with his gaff hook while the whole line jerked and strained. The snarl partially separated with a vicious hiss. When the gurdy started again, the two entangled bunches of hooks and gangings and ground line came to Carl's reaching hands.

"Get this, Bruno?" Carl said, stuffing the snarls into the basket on his knees. "Get a good look at two extra hours' work tonight. Pretty soon you'll know what I mean. This is a union boat all right, but no fish boat ever heard of union hours." Bruno stared at the yellow sun, now just above the horizon.

"But this is the last basket," he said. "We're about through for the day, aren't we?"

"How about that, Pop? Are you goin' to tell him or should I tell him? Maybe you better. I haven't got the heart."

"Ya, Bruno Felkin, vee are almost finished vith the baskets. But vee have still to get ready for tomorrow. There be a few things to do yet."

"He means that when the last hook and anchor and buoy are aboard we're practically through for the day," Carl said. "All we got left to do then is clean about a ton and a half of fish, stow them in the hold and the livers in cans. Then we swab down the deck for exercise. All of it shouldn't take us more than three hours if we really pitch in. Then we eat supper, but don't get any ideas about hittin' the sack. After supper we straighten bent hooks, replace gangings, and remake these baskets. There aren't too many snarls so that shouldn't take us more than another two or three hours."

Hamil laughed. "Then, Bruno Felkin, you can go to a nice sleep," he said. He spoke with the words Carl had said still in his mind. Carl was showing off a little, but there was something in the tone of his voice, even as he complained, that was pleasing to hear. If he wasn't bent over the basket his chest would be out where it belonged. When he could look as he did this moment, then it was once more a pleasure to be his father.

"Sure, Bruno. You ought to be all through by midnight," Carl went on, "unless you feel like going ashore and hitting the hot spots on the Farallon Islands. We'll lie to anchor there, and if the surge don't happen to be bad, and the goddamned sea lions don't bark all night, and the wind don't make the sea gull stink too bad, you can sleep right through 'till maybe four o'clock. Or were you plannin' on an early start tomorrow, Pop?"

"No, I think four vill be early enough."

"So we beat it right back here where we are now and on the way we don't have a thing to do but bait better than two thousand hooks all over again. It's a slick life, Bruno. Just the thing for squareheads who don't know any better."

KELSEY WAS BORED ALMOST BEYOND HIS elaborate experience with boredom. For three full days now he had been sitting in Connie Thatcher's apartment from nine in the morning until five in the afternoon. Nothing had happened. Not one thing. And at last his plea that the place be only spot-checked, instead of constantly watched, had been accepted down at headquarters. Nobody was going to get anything out of this Thatcher girl. Either she didn't know and her claim of ignorance was on the level, or she was the smoothest article Kelsey had ever met.

There hadn't been a single phone call, and if Connie herself was surprised at this, she managed to hide her surprise. At the end of two or three days people usually opened up a little. It was just human, Kelsey believed, if you were careful to put them at their ease and were willing to wait. They would slip ever so slightly at first—sometimes only a word or two, words that could later be connected with other words—and then the roof would fall in. And usually when such people found out you were only trying to do a job, they opened up with little personal things that could be useful. Led along just right, they would remember some grievance against the people who had left them behind to face the music—and such mental sores could also be the beginning of the end. When a certain kind of people began to feel they were going to stand the rap, then they became confused. Then things began to move. Angles and complaints revealed themselves. But not with this Connie Thatcher. She wasn't giving out with anything useful.

Bruno was sending her to school. There should have been an angle to that, but if there was it was still a mystery. A check of the school proved a dry run. She was enrolled as a special student, had so far shown rather outstanding ability in view of her earlier education, or lack of it, and she was generally considered a quiet and well-behaved student. They explained at the school that it was a usual thing for students older than average to excel, since they attended classes with an almost desperate desire to learn.

Connie admitted Bruno was paying for the apartment, her clothes, and her food. So what? You couldn't hang either of them for that. Had the late Sam Addleheim ever been to this apartment? No. She refused to recognize the name—or had never really heard it. Who were Bruno's regular customers? Connie didn't know. Had she ever seen him carry a package anywhere? No. Why did she leave L.A.? She *liked* Felkin, which was a fine answer. Very helpful. Why did she like him so much? The answer was a composed stare from those cool, green-blue eyes. She didn't look away for a moment, which in itself was against all rules of prisoner behavior. Eyes, Kelsey thought, had always been dependable—until now. The cleverest prisoners had eye trouble, and the really intelligent ones guarded against it. Eyes were particularly reliable when dealing with women. They could never entirely control them. Now Connie Thatcher had blown the theory. Kelsey allowed his mind to drift unhappily around the fact that he would never be able to rely on eyes again.

She had a way of stepping over verbal traps in the same easy way. Wasn't she a lot taller than Felkin? No. If she wore low heels, she said, they were exactly the same height. What night clubs did they go to? None. Bruno said night clubs were for suckers and she claimed she hated them. They danced once a week at the Fairmont Hotel or the St. Francis, just like a lot of other people.

"I'm a fresh-air fiend," she said on the second day he was with her. "Some day I want a house with a lot of windows so I can open them all at once and let my nine kids out."

"You want nine kids, Connie? Tell me again what you're doing with Bruno Felkin."

"I'll settle for six kids, Kelsey." Ask her a question and you got an answer, all right, but it was always an oblique answer, a bounce-off that landed nowhere.

Who were Bruno's friends? He didn't seem to have any. Hadn't she ever met a single one? No. Didn't she want to? Not particularly. Was she going to spend the next few months or years holed up on some back street—until Bruno got tired of her and found somebody else? The answer was another look from those cool eyes.

"Could be." That was her answer to a lot of things. "Could be." Did she ever expect to see Bruno again now that he was hot on a murder charge? "Could be." Would she stick with him when he was caught? "Could be." That was the way things had gone for three days. Kelsey decided he knew her well and yet not at all. Worse yet, she was the only link with Felkin. Nothing else had shown. Not a thing.

When Kelsey, growing tired himself, allowed the pace of the questioning to lag, she would go over and reverse the stack on the record changer. She would stand there leaning upon it, as she was doing now, and hum the tunes which seemed to be her favorites. She had a nice voice, but Kelsey found her ability to sing so calmly under the circumstances very nerve-wracking. After three days he was glad his vigil was almost over.

He studied his watch and then put it back in his vest pocket.

"Connie, I have some news you'll probably be glad to hear," he said. She was changing the records again and Kelsey wondered if she was listening. She had not even bothered to turn around. She was humming with the music.

"I said I had some good news for you, Connie."

"I heard you the first time."

"You can go back to school tomorrow."

"Are you going to write an excuse for my teacher? If you just said I was detained by the police I'm sure he would raise my marks."

"Just tell them you were sick."

"That's what I was going to do. How come I can go?"

"We don't think your boy friend is going to show around here. But I wouldn't try to leave town if I were you, Connie. It wouldn't look right and you wouldn't get very far."

"I wasn't planning to leave. I like it here."

"What are you going to do?"

"Enjoy being left alone."

"We'll be around to call on you every once in a while."

"What a break. When does this happen? I want to be sure everything is nice for you."

"You never can tell. Almost any hour."

"How long does that go on?"

"Until we find Bruno Felkin." Kelsey sighed. He pushed himself to his feet, adjusted his pants, and put his hat squarely on his head. He wondered if Connie was watching him—probably not. She wouldn't let her hair down now. She would keep on pretending it meant nothing to her if he stayed or never came back again. Those steady eyes would find something else to do.

At the door he turned around to face her and found that he was right about her eyes. She was leaning against the record changer. Her eyes were closed and her whole body was immovable except for her fingers, which rose and fell lightly in time with the slow music. She was making a fool of him. Not giving a damn. Her reaction bounced strangely off the things Kelsey wanted to say.

"I hope we haven't been too much trouble . . ." he said, wondering what prompted him to say anything at all. "Most of the people I meet . . . aren't very much on the level. . . . Every once in a while I get soft in the head and start thinking you are, Connie . . . I should know better . . . but maybe that's why I like you. . . ."

"This is so sudden, Mr. Kelsey."

"You've got a lot of nerve."

"Anything so unusual about that?"

"With people like you . . . yes. They usually rat sooner or later. Connie, why don't you get yourself some nice young fellow?"

"Like who?"

"Some kid who works for an honest dollar. There's plenty of them around."

"When I need a cupid I'll call on you, Kelsey. You'd look cute in diapers."

"Have it your way, Connie. So long."

"So long."

Kelsey stood on the curbstone in front of Connie's apartment building. The people who lived on Telegraph Hill were coming home from work, panting up the steep hills, alone and in pairs. Their attention was constantly divided between the packages they carried under their arms and the effects of the strong sea breeze which tore playfully at their hats. Since the case was now his to direct more or less alone, Kelsey had already fallen into the habit of examining every face in the neighborhood. His record for breaking cases came from working beyond official hours. He was counting on his record to finally swing that appointment to the state's attorney's office. It might be five o'clock, but there was still time to fill a few gaps.

Although he had not expected anything, he was vaguely disappointed in the faces climbing the hill. They were taxpayers and there was no use in trying to imagine them as anything else. None of them would lead to the end of the broken string. When a clever man knew how to hide, he had everything in his favor, Kelsey thought sourly. And according to everything available on the Bruno Felkin case, both written and surmised, he knew his business thoroughly.

Lighting a fresh cigar, Kelsey crossed the street to the grocery store, where he waited patiently until two women had completed their purchases for the evening. When they were gone he displayed his shield to the proprietor and then took a small envelope of photographs from his pocket. Coming to the grocery store was one of those chance afterthoughts. It was probably a hopeless waste of time. It was extremely unlikely that a man like Bruno Felkin was given to shopping for food—but there was always an odd chance. Sometimes it only needed one turn of a corner to find the other end of the string. Kelsey spread the photographs on the counter.

"Have you ever seen any of these faces?" he asked. To his astonishment, the little man behind the counter picked up Bruno's photograph at once.

"I seen this fellow," he said calmly.

"When?"

"I seen him a couple of times. He has a friend across the street. A girl."

"What gives you that idea?"

"He said so."

"When was this?"

"The other night. He picked up some snacks. Boloney and eggs, I think. I was just closing shop."

Kelsey ran his finger slowly along the line of photographs, trying to hide his anxiety. This storekeeper was too positive to believe.

"Have you ever seen any of the other faces? Make sure now."

"No. I'm sure."

"What time do you close shop?"

"Nine o'clock."

"This fellow was here at *nine o'clock*? You must be wrong about the time."

"I got the best watch in the world and I don't pay myself no overtime. So when it's nine o'clock, I know damn well it's nine o'clock."

Kelsey had time to consider his disappointment while a customer came in and bought a head of lettuce and some tomatoes. Like everyone down at the department, Kelsey was dependent on informers. They were to be trusted or not trusted according to past performance. Supposing the informers had been wrong? Supposing Felkin had been in Salt Lake or Memphis or God knows where for the past month? It was said that he didn't get along with Sam Addleheim, but that was no proof he killed him. The public, the newspapers, and sometimes the bosses at City Hall had difficulty in appreciating the difference between knowing or suspecting a criminal, and proving him guilty. A half-baked case on trifles of evidence and a lot of suppositions was worse than no case against a man like Felkin. It would just give him a chance to eat three free meals in jail and then go about his business laughing his head off.

Now the phone call was recorded as received at eight fifty-one. To prove that fact was wrong, the switchboard clock would have to be wrong, and it wasn't. Felkin was in this store at nine o'clock, or so the owner said. Every informer had said Bruno Felkin was careful never to drive a car. All right? Who drove it? Connie? or did Felkin sprout wings to leap the distance from Sam's to this store?

When the customer left the store Kelsey went to the counter
again.

"What night was our friend in here?" he asked. The little
man scratched his head and took off his glasses to wipe them.

"Now I couldn't just be sure of that. It must have been either
three or four nights ago."

"That would make it Monday or Tuesday."

"It was foggy, I know."

"It was foggy on both Monday and Tuesday. Try to remember. Anything unusual that happened might help if you can
just think of something."

"You ever run a grocery store, mister?" Kelsey shook his head.
"Nothing unusual happens. This is what you call a primary business. People got to have it and I got it. Together we starve."

"You're positive it was nine o'clock?"

"You want me to swear on a Bible or somethin'?"

"No. Never mind. But do this much, will you? If you see that
man again, pick up a phone and call this number." The proprietor shrugged his shoulders and his mouth turned down at
the ends.

"The only fun I got left in life is minding my neighbor's
business," he said unhappily.

"Thanks. I'll drop around tomorrow when you aren't so busy.
In the meantime do your best to remember whether it was
Monday or Tuesday." Kelsey moved for the door.

"Would you mind telling me what the fellow done?"

"We just want to talk to him. Maybe he hasn't done anything."

"He has nose trouble of some kind, I know that. His nose was
bleeding in a funny way . . . right here at the door we talked
about it."

"What did he say?"

"He said his doctor said he ought to leave San Francisco."
Kelsey looked out at the street. Maybe Sam hit Bruno Felkin

in the scuffle and broke his nose? No, that made Bruno walking into grocery stores with a dented face. He was smarter than
that. But it might pay to check his prison medical and see if he
had ever had any nose trouble before. It wasn't much, but it
might tie in somewhere, maybe be the one blade of grass in the
desert.

"It looks like our friend took his doctor's advice."

Kelsey drove home very slowly in the last light of the day. He
was tired, partially from boredom, he told himself, and partially
because he had allowed this Felkin case to get under his skin.

When he entered the living room of his apartment on Thir-
teenth Avenue, he hung up his hat and threw his coat and
shoulder holster on the couch. His wife came out of the bedroom, moving softly in her slippers, and stood on her toes to kiss
him. He bent down and kissed her absently.

"That wasn't much of a kiss," she said, smiling. Kelsey sat
down on the couch and began to unlace his shoes.

"I know. I'm sorry. My mind just wasn't on it. I'll come in
again after a while."

She knelt in front of him and Kelsey thought for an instant
that it was rather remarkable that a woman of her age could
still kneel so gracefully. She was forty-five, a neat, plump woman
who made no attempt to disguise the gray in her hair. In the
soft light of the room she looked much younger.

"You've had a bad day," she said, reaching for his shoes.

"No, I haven't. I just sat . . . that's all." She pulled off his
shoes and they laughed quietly together.

"That's the first time you've pulled off my shoes in twenty
years," he said. "The service is improving around here."

"You just looked like you needed it. What's gone wrong?"

"Nothing. I'm still on the Addleheim case."

"No luck?"

"Not much. I'm sure this fellow's girl is the answer, or will be. In the meantime she won't talk. Sometimes I wonder if she really has anything to say."

"If you're going to sit in an apartment with her all day and night I've got a right to know what she's like."

Kelsey stretched out on the couch and put his hands behind his head. He stared at the ceiling.

"Are you interested in her looks or her personality?"

"Does she have both?"

"She does indeed, although she'd never win a beauty prize. She's a blonde, natural, I think, and inclined not to smile too often. Right now, of course, she hasn't got much to smile about. But she's not scared of me . . . or anybody else, I would guess. I would say she would make people like us a fine daughter. If . . . she wasn't a tramp."

Kelsey's wife was silent a moment. "I've never heard you talk like this before . . . about one of those people."

"I can't help liking her. She's not the regular run. But then the whole case is off center. It won't even begin to jell."

"Take a nap and forget about it. Supper won't be ready for an hour."

"All right. I'll try to forget there must be an angle . . . somewhere. But I'm so close . . . I'm so close to the answer I can almost reach out and touch it."

Simon Lee anchored his boat, the *Alert*, twenty-four miles west of the Golden Gate, where the Farallon Islands project from the sea. There was no other place to anchor and even here the shelter left much to be desired. Simon Lee hated the looks of the Islands. On foggy days the peaks and crevices were smothered in mist and the Islands seemed to be weeping. On fine evenings, such as this one, when the twilight was red, the Islands seemed to be bleeding. Simon Lee specialized in fishing for ling cod. It was a lonely enough profession without having to look at these ugly ghosts of rock.

As the sun squashed itself into a crazy oblong on the horizon, Simon stood on the foredeck of his strictly functional little boat, chewing on his pipe and studying the angle of his anchor chain. As for the weather in general and the fishing, there really wasn't too much to complain about. There were two potatoes boiling on the *Alert*'s tiny stove which would go well with one of the smaller ling cods for supper. The wind promised to behave itself and remain gentle. There was no sign of fog, so the island's horn would not wreck a night's sleep. If there was only someone to talk to besides Tunie and Turnbuckle, it wouldn't be too bad a night at all. Simon now viewed his only crew members with open distaste.

Turnbuckle was a rooster. After taking more than a year to get over constant attacks of seasickness, he had finally become invaluable. He not only saved the price of a new alarm clock, but had developed an uncanny ability to spot buoys in the fog. Long before Simon could hear their muffled clanging, Turnbuckle could be relied upon to make his way forward and point his scrawny head in the exact direction of the buoy. Thus he also saved the price of a direction finder.

Tunie was a small black dog who had become as much a part of Simon as his pipe. He was constantly at his legs, or on his lap, and spent his nights curled against Simon's shoulder. He had an exasperating habit of falling overboard at the most inconvenient times. The moment Simon dropped the *Alert*'s anchor, Tunie placed himself squarely between Simon's legs and began a verbal battle with the sea lions.

"Shut up, you stubborn little bastard, or I'll put you on the rocks forever!" Simon said. He frowned over his pipe at the dog, knowing that his words would go unheeded. Tunie was right to bark, anyway. Everyone who took a living from the ocean hated sea lions. They stole the most well-hooked fish directly before a fisherman's eyes. They fouled gear and tore nets. When at rest on the rocks they sent forth an odor that

made life peculiarly miserable for both man and dog. But the
barking contest between dog and sea lion would rob Simon of
such peace as he considered well earned at the end of the day.
There was nothing he could do about it except lay a hand to
the dog, and such a breach of respect was out of the question.

"Any man," Simon said, "would be better off with a nagging
wife!"

Simon walked aft, intending to test his boiled potatoes. He
was just about to swing down into the galley when he saw a boat
approaching from the south. She was coming up fast, her white
hull alternately hidden behind a swell and then visible in her
entirety as she foamed over a crest. A canopy of sea gulls wheeled
and cried over her stern. It was a certain sign that fish were being cleaned; the gulls had their own mysterious telegraph system and would gather just above and behind any boat within a
minute after the first knife was sharpened.

Simon recognized the boat as the *Taage* and the sight of her
cheered him. Now there would be company in the night and
some relief from the desolation of the Farallónes. And best of
all, there would be a chance to talk to Hamil Linder. Most
fishermen were at least half wild themselves, Simon thought.
Why else would they spend their lives knocking about oceans
which were out of all proportion to the size of their boats? Why
else would their every wakeful moment be concerned with the
hunt? The intensity of their thinking on the capture of fish
allowed their minds time for little else. Simon believed it must
be a very old way of thinking, a drive for survival that somehow
went beyond dollars and cents. It took a man like Hamil Linder, who thought before he spoke—a man who caught fish
instead of dreaming about catching them—to stand as visible
proof there was some reason to the business. When he could talk
to Hamil, Simon found it easier to believe he had not been
bewitched on that day ten years before, the day he traded a
secure seat as a professor of history for a bouncing deck.

Simon called to Tunie. The anger left his voice and he spoke, from long habit, as to another human.

"Hey, Tunie! Regard the horizon. Leave those sea lions be and stand by the skiff!" Simon ran down into the cabin, turned off the stove, and rushed to the deck again. He launched the skiff and, seizing the still barking dog, dropped him into it.

The *Taage*'s anchor had barely taken hold before Simon was alongside. He heaved Tunie over the bulwark and climbed aboard. Hamil extended his hand.

"Hello, Simon Lee! So! How's the professor? I have not seen you for too much time. How are the ling cod?" Simon looked at the *Taage*'s decks, still heavy with fish.

"Not as well as the blackies, Hamil. Tunie barks all the time and I think he scares every fish in the ocean. Next time he falls overboard I'm going to let him drown. Don't ever take a dog on your boat, at least not a sad and stupid hound like Tunie." Hamil bent down to pat the animal, his big fingers working around beneath Tunie's jaw.

"Ya, Simon. I think you sink your boat before you let anything happen to Tunie. I think when he looks at you like this, so sorry like . . . you take back all you say."

"All I can say for him is that he's better company than most professors. I'd sell him very reasonably."

Bruno came aft with Carl and they said hello to Simon.

"Shake hands vith Bruno Felkin," Hamil said, smiling. "By golly, he has put in a good day's work." Simon and Bruno shook hands. Carl, turning away, said there was still a pile of work to be done.

"Are you making three in your crew now, Hamil?" Simon asked.

"No . . . no. Bruno Felkin yust come along because he couldn't help it. That is one vay to tell it, so, Bruno?" Hamil laughed and left his petting of the dog to stand beside Bruno. "He yust woke up and there he vas at sea."

"Maybe I'm still dreamin'," Bruno said to Simon. "Anyway it's been good for me."

"By golly!" Hamil said. "I have a idea maybe! When are you going back to the city, Simon?"

"Tomorrow morning. I don't carry ice you know, and those ling cod won't keep forever."

"Then maybe you wouldn't mind taking Bruno vith you?"

"Of course. The *Alert* isn't very fast, but I'll be in by noon." Simon fingered his pipe while he examined Bruno. "Glad to take you."

"There you are, Bruno," Hamil said. "Special transportation. What more could you ask for?"

"You can sleep on board the *Alert* tonight and that will make it easier," Simon said. "There isn't much in the way of comfort; she's hardly a yacht, but you're welcome to what we have, including trying to sleep with this aggravating hound crawling all over you." Bruno said nothing for a moment and Simon was puzzled at his silence. What did the man expect? A real yacht complete with blondes? He should at least offer a word of thanks. He was worried about something, that was easy to see. Simon sucked air noisily through his pipe and said, "You'll really be welcome aboard. We're humble but clean."

"Sure, I'd like to make the trip in with you, and don't think I don't appreciate the offer . . . but . . . maybe it's a crazy idea and maybe I have a hell of a nerve to suggest it. . ." Bruno hesitated. He seemed to be speaking more to Hamil than to anyone else. "I was sort of wondering if Hamil could stand me around a little longer."

"Bruno is trying to say he'd like to stick aboard for a while, Pop. I told him to ask you," Carl said. Hamil studied the sky and the surge exploding against the island.

"You mean vork on the *Taage*?"

"I'd like to try."

"But how about your business?"

"I could sort of let that take care of itself for a while. A change would do me good."

"But I could not afford to pay you a full share, Bruno. A third man yust isn't worth it, no matter how good he be."

"I don't want anything. Couldn't we call it a vacation for me? If I could just stay aboard, that would be enough."

"Vell . . . ?" Hamil took Tunie's head in one hand and slowly stroked his chest with the other. He looked into the dog's eyes as if for help. "How you think of a fellow has such a idea, Tunie? Maybe he don't know vat's good for him, ya?"

"I should warn you, Mr. Felkin," Simon said, "I took a fishing vacation ten years ago and I've never returned to the land. Among other things, it cost me a nice pension."

"Come on, Pop," Carl said. "Let him stay. Then none of us will have to work so hard. You're getting decrepit and a third man always makes things easier all around."

"I tell you how vee do," Hamil said suddenly. "A man should never try to think straight on an empty belly. So? It gets him mixed up. Thinking takes fuel, yust like a engine. Come along. Vee all go below and have things to eat and some good coffee. Then after it is easier to think and talk and see vat can be done. So? That's much better."

"I have some potatoes half-boiled," Simon offered.

"No. You eat vith us . . . and little Tunie too. Maybe vee see how Bruno Felkin likes to vash dishes."

"It's an old specialty of mine," Bruno said quickly.

The night enfolded the island, and the masthead lights of the *Taage* and the *Alert* swept back and forth across the stars. The only break in the dark solitude was the hard white shaft of the Farallone Light. When the thousands of birds stopped their crying and the sea lions were finally still, Simon Lee rowed back to his boat. And except for the dog Tunie, and a sleeping rooster, he again had no one to share his thoughts. He was sorry to be alone again.

"Although I'm not so sure," he said to Tunie. "There was something about that man I can just as well leave alone. He's angry at something, Tunie . . . even when he's smiling. I hope Hamil knows what he's doing letting him stay. For no reason at all . . . I think I'd be a little afraid to have him around." Simon lit the kerosene lamp at the head of his bunk. He put on his glasses and took a worn copy of Macaulay's *Essay on Johnson* from the shelf beside him. He squirmed down beneath the blanket as Tunie found a place on his legs.

Outside the Golden Gate, the wind blew hard from the northwest. But it was only a March wind, satisfied to break itself upon the shore, content with such minor triumphs as dragging fish boats from their moorings, removing a section of the roof at Palladini's Point Reys fish house, and riling the San Francisco Bar with such energy that seventy-one crab pots were reported lost. A fall or winter Pacific wind would have been more determined.

The efforts of the outside wind were relayed through the Golden Gate by the heavy surge which pushed sullenly against the wharves within the bay. It forced the fishing boats into constant motion, though they were securely moored to the wharves. They rose and fell with the swells, sometimes separately, sometimes together. The big draggers, with their otter boards drawn up and nets hanging gracefully from their main booms, moved up and down with the dignity of dowagers at a lawn party. When an errant swell, contrary to the rest, opposed them, their cadence of movement would be rudely broken. Then they would be bounced against the wharf pilings, their wet tim-

bers would squeal in protest, and it would be some time before
their dignity could be regained. Even the big purse seiners had
trouble maintaining their stateliness. They rolled heavily with
the surge, displayed their neglected bottoms, and then rolled
them under again with hasty shame.

The inner basin, where the Italians kept their small boats,
resembled a hen house at feeding time. These boats were
largely engaged in crabbing, and their white bows with their
trim of Mediterranean blue bobbed up and down independently. They jerked at their confinement, rhyming and unrhym-
ing their motions.

The large boats, the small boats, and the surrounding
wharves were all deserted. For with the wind came frequent
spasms of driving rain. The Italians of the fleet were at home
with their wives, their sweethearts, or their thousand cousins.
They were either eating *cioppino* or making ready to eat it, and
many of them were already mildly drunk on the deep red wine
of their own manufacture.

The members of the dock committee were nowhere to be
seen. They had vanished from their timber. Where they managed to find shelter at such times no one had ever been able to
discover.

Between the outer wharf fingers and beside the pier which
supported the new ice house and the Union Diesel repair shed
lay the boats which operated more or less independently.
There were shark boats, piled high with buoys, flags, line, and
general gear. Simon Lee's *Alert* was there, and Barney Schriona's *Capella*. Corky Mullins' *Thunder Mug* wallowed with a
suspicious lack of buoyancy at the very end of the wharf. Hamil
Linder's *Taage*, her long-line baskets secured and covered with
tarpaulin, was just behind her.

In the afternoon Carl Linder mounted the *Taage's* ratlines
and stepped off to the dock. He was wearing a trench coat and a
soft green hat. He threw a mock salute to Bruno, who was

watching him through the *Taage*'s dribbling windows, and
then, as he had been instructed, he set off without apparent
haste toward the city. Bruno had said that if a man seemed in a
hurry people always wanted to know where he was going.

When he passed over the small bridge spanning the inner
basin, he paused to look at the Italian fleet. He found a great
deal of satisfaction in comparing his immediate future with the
miserable prospects of the owners and crews of the boats below
him. They could, he decided, have their life, and they knew
what they could do with it. Crabbing was really not a life, but
an existence, better fit for marine donkeys than human beings.

Bruno, now, had the right idea. He could afford to pay an
assistant two hundred dollars per week and apparently no one
strained themselves in the process. Two hundred dollars, Carl
remembered, would buy four crab pots. A man needed at least
fifty pots to work crabs. So before the season had even begun
he must lay out some twenty-five hundred dollars for gear. Then
he must set the pots at sea and immediately expose his in-
vestment to a variety of hazards. A mild storm, such as the one
now in progress, could tear the pots from their marker buoys,
or bury them in the mud and sand; or they could be stolen, or
merely pirated of their contents by other crab fishermen, who
alone among all fishermen had little feeling for mutual welfare.

Carl reminded himself to tell Bruno about the crab fishermen.
There should be some kind of an angle to work there, since
crabbers were certainly the worst suckers in the world. Carl
was just turning to leave when he felt someone tap him gently
on the shoulder. He turned quickly and saw that it was only
Corky Mullins. Poor Corky—he was an even more miserable
man than a crab fisherman. His white cap was a soggy gray from
the rain and water dribbled continuously off his large nose, now
more blue than red. For some mysterious reason Corky never
passed up a chance to attach himself to the Linders. Nothing
could be done about it. He was part of the wharf. He should

have been drawing old-age insurance or sitting in some home. He was half bum, and still it was impossible not to like him.

"You thinkin' of goin' after some crabs?" Corky said. His voice quivered a little with the cold, but there was the same enthusiasm in it there always was for anything that had to do with the sea. Carl thought again, as he had so many times before, how much Corky was like a small boy.

"Not me. I know better," Carl said.

"I'd be of a mind to go after a few . . . providing of course I could spare the time to work over some ring nets." Carl looked away from Corky's eyes, and though he wanted to smile, he nodded his head gravely. Corky had all the time in the world. As for ring nets, the price of a single one would be more than he'd had for a long time.

"Yeah," Carl said quietly, "ring nets would hardly be worth your time so late in the year, Corky. By the way, how's the *Thunder Mug*?"

"I been doin' a pile of work on her, by God, and if I do say so, there ain't a finer boat for her size in the harbor. She's practically ready for Mexico and the albacore now. Me and that boat are goin' to make a real killin' this year!"

"I bet you will, Corky." Mexico in the *Thunder Mug*? Poor dreaming Corky. With luck and a calm day his hulk might make the Golden Gate, but not much farther.

"I been to a lot of expense with her lately . . . decided there was no use in even goin' after rock cod until I had everthin' just right. Damn if the ship chandlers ain't raised their prices fer every little thing away to hell and gone out of sight."

"Yeah." Carl reached into his pocket. He knew what was coming, and the easier it could be made for Corky—somehow the better. "It's rough, I know."

"Fact of the matter is, I spent so much on my boat I ain't been feedin' too well lately. No sir, Carl."

Carl pressed a ten-dollar bill in Corky's wet hand.

"It's always tough when you're trying to outfit, Corky. Maybe this will help things along for a while." Corky looked at the bill and his white eyebrows rose and then fell slowly back into position.

"Godalmighty, Carl . . . I couldn't be just exactly sure when I could pay this much back."

"Don't worry about it. You'll make a hundred times that when the albacore come. Go get what you need."

"But you give me a five spot last week." And there had been at least four or five donations before that, Carl remembered. But Corky was Corky. Someone had to help him.

"So what? I know I'll get it back. With those new jigs Pop gave you, you'll sink the *Thunder Mug* with fish. You're the best risk in the harbor, Corky. I'm not worryin' a minute."

Corky stuffed the bill in the pocket of his ragged peajacket. He rubbed his wet nose thoughtfully.

"If I was younger—" he began to say, and then Carl poked him gently in the stomach.

"You're the youngest guy I know, Corky."

"If I can ever do—"

"I'm in a hurry, Corky. See you around." Carl walked quickly away. He forgot about Corky almost instantly. He was thinking of Bruno's instructions and how simple they would be to carry out.

Go to the post office on Mission Street—no hurry about getting there, and take your time when you do get there. Take the key he gave you and open mail box twenty-seven nine four. Remove a package the size of a cigarette carton from the box. It would be wrapped and tied with string, addressed to a Harold Sweeney. Put the box under your arm and go to a movie, any movie. Find a seat, as much alone as possible, and open the box. It would be filled with packets the size of tea bags. Take ten of the packets out of the box and wrap it up again. See the movie through, be *sure* to do that, then take the package back to the post office. Replace it in the box. Then take the packets and deliver one each to the list of addresses Bruno had provided. Explain first that you came from the Western Sales Company, and be sure to get fifty dollars in cash before you handed over the packet. Don't ask any questions and don't answer any. For all of which back-breaking labor, your share was two hundred dollars. What was in the packets?

"For two hundred dollars, you should care," was Bruno's quiet answer, and he was very right.

Next, there was an additional chore, a personal one, as Bruno had explained it. Proceed to an apartment on Telegraph Hill. A Connie Thatcher. When you get there, give her a hundred dollars first thing. Say it was from Bruno, to pay the laundry-man. She would understand. You could also tell her not to worry about anything, that Bruno was all right.

"You ought to be all finished and back on the boat by mid-night," Bruno said. "Wake me up when you get here. I'll be wanting to hear if Connie is getting along all right. She's an old friend of mine." Okay. At the salaries he paid, Bruno could explain as much or as little as he wanted to.

It didn't take too much head work to guess what was in the packages. If Bruno thought he was fooling Carl Linder, he was mistaken. It didn't make any difference one way or the other. The important thing was to pocket two hundred dollars and still have enough energy left to enjoy it. Added to the income from fishing, the total would be roughly three hundred and fifty dollars per week. Not bad for a guy twenty-five years old.

Carl passed the steel works on Francisco Street. Despite the wind and the rain the tremendous doors that formed the side of the building were open. He stood watching the men working inside at the milling machines. Their faces were dirty and pale beneath the glaring electric lights, and even the younger men, those who appeared to be about Carl's age, looked tired. They should be—the suckers. They were almost but not quite as dumb as crab fishermen. It was a cinch they would never see three hundred and fifty dollars all in one lump—free for spending. They stood all day in the midst of the damnedest clanging and banging, hunched over those machines as if they meant something to them. For the older men maybe it was all right. Like your old man, they just didn't know any better, but the young guys should have seen the light. They should know work was for dopes—and their chances of getting to be vice president or whatever the hell they thought they were accomplishing in there, their chances were the same as a private getting to be a general in the damned army. It don't work that way, hammerheads. Things are rigged so you don't have to work so hard. You can let the government take care of you, or you can get smart like Bruno Felkin—or, say, like Carl Linder.

When the afternoon was over Carl decided delivering the packages was the easiest thing he had ever done. According to the list, he called at two doctors' offices, then at four addresses on Hyde Street, where he was greeted by four middle-aged women. The rest of the addresses were closely bunched in the Negro Fillmore district. Every customer seemed happy to see the Western Sales Company man, and every one had his money ready. Five hundred dollars in less than five hours. What a business! Very easy gravy.

Now Carl stood on the corner opposite the apartment house on Chestnut and Grant for ten minutes as Bruno had instructed him to do. He was to wait until he was absolutely sure there was no one watching Connie's place.

That guy Bruno was afraid of his own shadow for some reason or other. There wasn't a soul around. And there wouldn't be on an evening like this. It was raining as it could rain only in San Francisco—like a bucket turned upside down. There was no use standing around any longer.

Carl crossed the street and ran up the apartment steps. He

pressed the buzzer marked number 3-C. Thatcher. He adjusted
his tie, pushed open the street door, and took the hall stairs two
at a time. He passed an open door and then came back to it
when he saw the number was three. He started to knock on the
door; then, changing his mind, he entered the apartment and
closed the door behind him. There was no one in the room.
This Connie was certainly not afraid of ghosts.

"Anybody home?"

"Sit down and relax." Her voice came to him from the bedroom. "I thought you were going to leave me alone for a while."

"I've got a message for you. Do you want it or don't you?"
She came out of the bedroom fastening the belt on her robe. She
took one quick look at him and turned toward the kitchen.

"Well, well, they're getting younger and younger. What are
you, a junior G-man?"

"I happen to be a fisherman—temporarily. But I'm getting
wise to a new business. Bruno's business. It seems to have quite a
future." She came out of the kitchen then. She leaned against
the doorway and folded her arms.

If she was supposed to be smiling, Carl thought, it was not
exactly a welcome-home signal. She had a full, rich, inviting
mouth, but it was turned down slightly at the ends as if its
owner refused to believe in anything. Now if that mouth could
be made to really smile, it would be a nice thing to look at. The
eyes, too, were disbelieving, and there was something about the
way she leaned against the doorway that said, Go to hell.

"Sure you have a message from Bruno. You're a regular car-
rier pigeon. And I'm supposed to send back some kind of an
answer—back to where I know he is? I'll bet you read detective
stories when you were a kid, mister." Her voice rose very
slightly. "For the fiftieth time, I *don't know* where Bruno is."

"I know where he is."

"You tell me something, handsome. Tell me the truth just for
the fun of it. Why is it that all cops are so big? Aren't there any

little cops? They might try hiring a few. Little men are smarter. It's not so far between their ears."

"I'm not a cop."

"Do you want coffee first, or do you want to start the quiz show now?" Carl smiled. Bruno did all right by himself in lots of respects. This Connie would make a nice little piece to come home to. She was fast with a comeback and had looks to make them land easy. She was the sort to be sitting beside some guy in a good-looking car—but Bruno was too old for her. She should tag along with a fellow who knew his way around at an earlier age—say Carl Linder.

Still smiling, he reached out and took her hand. She made no move to pull away as he slowly increased the pressure of his grip.

"Does it make any difference to you when we start, Connie?"

"Not a bit. I can give you my knee where it hurts the most, now or later." Carl slowly released her hand. The expression in her eyes had not changed in the slightest since he had first looked into them.

"I believe you'd try it at that."

She tilted her head slightly to one side and a question came to her eyes.

"Let me see your hand again, mister."

Carl held it open before her and she passed her fingertips across it slowly.

When she had completed the gesture, he said, "I wish you'd do that again. I like it."

"Who are you?"

"Right now—a fisherman." It was surprising how that title sounded, here in this apartment. It came so easily, for the first time—maybe it was this Connie. All of a sudden it was nothing to be ashamed of.

"I never saw a cop with hands like yours. What have you been doing, washing with sandpaper?"

"Using my back instead of my brains."

Her mouth melted a little. Watching it, Carl decided she would not be quite right in a flashy car. She was too tall, or her hair was too long, or her eyes were too wide apart—or something.

"Where's Bruno?"

"On my old man's boat."

"Is he all right?"

"He said to tell you he was fine . . . to take this." Handing her the roll of bills was a hard thing to do for some reason . . . and it was not the money itself. It was something else—an unexplainable thing. "Bruno said it was for the laundryman. He said if there was anything else you needed, tell me, and he would do something about it."

"I wish he could call off the law. This place has turned into a regular police farm. Wherever I look there's a badge."

"What did you do to attract their attention?" She took a long look at him and then backed away a little. Touching her hand to her hair, she adjusted it behind her neck as if she stood before a mirror.

"Didn't Bruno tell you?"

"No. He doesn't give out with much information."

"I missed a day at school. The truant officers think I'm a very bad girl."

"Are you?"

It was hard to tell whether she was smiling or not. She hadn't answered the question. Carl circled her slowly until he was near the bedroom door. Ignoring her, he stepped into the room. The bed looked freshly made. It was wide and that was better yet. Seeing the light from the bathroom, he went into it and wiped the rain from his face. He carefully combed his hair, took a quick look at the contents of the medicine chest, and then picked up the bottle of bath salts that stood on the end of the tub. He removed the top and inhaled deeply. He would have to give these things a try some time. Maybe Connie would be willing to show him how it was done.

He took another look in the mirror, sighed appreciatively, and swaggered easily back into the living room. It was a wonderful thing to have made two hundred dollars without really lifting a finger. And now with business out of the way, there was another small matter to be arranged. After a few days at sea, a man needed two things—food and a woman. It didn't make much difference which you had first as long as you wound up with both of them.

"Make yourself right at home," Connie said. "Don't mind me."

"Nice place . . . a very nice little place."

"So you're a fisherman? You look like one, but I can't say you act like one . . . or like I thought one would act. What did you say your name was?"

"I didn't say, but it's Carl."

"Do you know Bruno very well?"

"Not as well as I'm going to. It's too bad I don't know his girl better because I kind of like what I see. You know, Bruno's kind of on the worn-out side. If Bruno's going to take a vacation, maybe I ought to take over. I just got a hunch we'd get along . . . especially on a rainy night like this one. I wouldn't be surprised if we could find a lot to talk about. . . ."

Connie started to laugh, and then as she looked at him her laugh faded. "One thing I like is men with a new approach. Any minute now you're going to say we ought to lie down and talk things over, that you can think better in that position. Now let's just get something very clear in your head, Carl. And if you don't understand me the first time, I'll repeat for you. Bruno might not be the most respectable citizen in San Francisco, and he might not be tall and handsome. But for the time being, I'm his girl. He cares what happens to me, he pays my way, he needs me enough to make me feel important. That's quite a full bill.

Maybe I'll change my mind some day, but right now Bruno
Felkin is enough for me. Is there anything you don't understand about that?"

"I heard every word you said."

"I'll be glad to write 'em down for you just in case you forget."

"I still think we should know each other better. How about
putting on your boots and coming out for a steak. I haven't had
a chance to eat yet."

"No thanks. I'm a vegetarian this year." Carl moved toward
her again. This Connie wasn't kidding Carl Linder. She just
wanted a little urging the first time. The tramps in the bars on
North Beach were the same way. He reached again for her
hand.

"Come on, Connie. You wouldn't want me to eat alone."
She shrugged her shoulders, but she made no attempt to pull
her hand away. That was a little better. Now she was giving with
the passive resistance stuff. A little closer—now bring her close
until she could feel your strength through that thin robe—let
her feel some warmth from a first-class man, the kind she had
probably never been close to—a little kiss and then pick her up
and carry her into the bedroom.

"Rainy nights always make me sleepy, Connie."

"Run along, junior . . ." Her voice was low and without expression. It was a nice little act which didn't mean a thing because she was beginning to breathe faster.

"Go play with your knives and forks, Carl . . ." First a little
force to show who was boss and then she'd be begging. It never
failed.

"I'm warning you, junior . . ." She was just the right height.
With little girls you had to bend too far and it was hard to keep
your whole body close to them—

Carl's eyes were half-closed when she moved. He felt her
turn quickly in his arms and then saw something white flashing
toward the side of his face.

"Jesus!" Before he could raise his hand to his bleeding ear, before he entirely regained his balance, Connie swung again and her closed fist struck his stomach. Carl gasped and fell back against the wall. He shook his head to clear it, and then looked in astonishment at the blood he had wiped from his ear.

"Now, good-looking, you aren't quite so pretty. Do you want to try another round or have you had enough?" Carl smiled without enthusiasm. His wind was back, but his ear was clanging. By God, this was something new—and not very comfortable.

"If you treat all your boy friends that way you'll wind up an old maid."

"I've met enough wolves in my short time to overrun Siberia. I'm getting sick and tired of it!"

"I can see that."

"If I see you again, remember it. Now run along before I lose my temper." Carl straightened against the wall and then moved slowly toward the door. He dabbed thoughtfully at his ear. When she held the door open for him he stopped to look down at her. A little smile played around his eyes.

"You know, Connie . . . I might bleed to death."

"Go get a transfusion and come back when you grow up."

"You're quite a girl, Connie. I'll have to tell Bruno."

"He knows it. You just tell him I'll be waiting." She pushed the door shut firmly. Carl heard the lock click inside. He turned to the landing and went slowly down the steps. For some reason or other there didn't seem to be anything to get mad about. Except for this stinging ear, it was damned funny. What a haymaker! Just a little reminder that maybe Carl Linder wasn't the hottest thing that ever hit San Francisco. It was a strange feeling laughing at yourself, and cold sober at that, but Connie had sure arranged it. This girl of Bruno's was worth thinking about. She meant what she said no matter what she said. Biffo, Linder! You've had it.

So you always thought you were the big handsome guy that

no girl could resist? Have a laugh on yourself, Linder. Credit this girl of Bruno's with smashing your personal mirror. Whatever it was, he had something you didn't have . . . for one thing, a girl who was different. Meet Connie Thatcher, and next time, bonehead, bow from a distance.

In Barney Schriona's house the evening meal was finished. Hamil sat at the opposite end of the dining room table from Barney, and though the physical distance between them was great, their desire to grasp each other's beliefs was so intense they might well have been sitting side by side—drawing strength and understanding as they required it.

Haltingly, as if the exact words they wanted could not be translated into English, they admitted to each other that they were having trouble with their thinking. Something was very wrong. The spaces of silence that fell between them were sometimes more fruitful to both Hamil and Barney than the actual words which flowed back and forth the length of the cleared table. At least they enjoyed the peculiar pleasure of knowing for certain that another man was equally confused.

"We ain't so damned old . . . yet, I hope," Barney Schriona was saying. "But we will be old if we think everything that happened in the past was good and everything that goes on now is no good." Barney said this in the face of a number of things that had occurred during the evening, and Hamil understood exactly why he said it.

Barney's wife had served a fine meal of cabbage soup and *l'osso buco*, all in the best tradition. But she had hurried the last of the meal. The dishes were hardly off the table before the cheesecake and the coffee was thrust before them, and taking her own plate and coffee into the living room, Rosanna had fastened her being to the radio and become lost in the sounds that rattled from it. When she left the room, Barney shrugged his heavy shoulders uncomfortably.

"Rosanna, she is crazy for them quiz programs," he said. "She gets real sad if she misses a single one. She's after me all the time to get a telephone so it will ring and somebody at the other end will say, Missus Schriona, you just won a million bucks. I keep telling her you don't get something for nothing, but she says in America you do. I dunno . . . sometimes I think maybe Rosanna is right." Hamil laughed. He was thinking of his own wife, Solveig, and wondering if she would be doing the same thing, and if it made any difference one way or the other. During one of their silences he also wondered what it might have been like to have a daughter as well as Carl—a daughter like Barney's Christina, who at the command of a horn blown on the street ran to the window and said she would be right out.

"Even a few years ago it wasn't that way," Barney explained patiently. "Christina's fellows come to the door then. They come inside and shook my hand or said hello to Rosanna and sometimes they even sat down for a couple of minutes. But now they just sit in their car and blow the horn. The girl is supposed to come runnin'." Barney forced a laugh and again Hamil understood exactly why he felt required to make the noise.

"It might have been a good idea for us, Hamil. . . . Only thing was, at that age I could never find a horse that would whinny when I kicked him in the tail."

There was silence again as Barney examined the end of his cigar and very carefully deposited the ash in the saucer of his coffee cup. "At least one thing you can say for them kids," he went on finally. "Maybe they do have some ideas the world owes them a living, but they got a lot of guts . . . they ain't afraid. They proved that during the war. . . ."

"Ya," Hamil said. He loosened his belt and sighed. "Ya, that is so . . . but I am thinking not being afraid is a funny thing. You take a stubborn man and you make him mad. He vill not be afraid, I think. And if you tell him he is brave and tell him he vill be taken care of should he get hurt some vays . . . then maybe he is not so brave after all—*himself,* that is. The Germans found that out. So? If all of their soldiers be so brave as they vere told they be in the beginning, then maybe vee could never have won . . . but came the time they had to be brave all by themselves, ven Hitler could not hold their hands vith either vords or things . . . then suddenly they be not so brave. So? I am afraid sometimes this same thing can happen to people in America . . . even in peace. Yust like in Germany. Ven times are good it is easy to say you vill be fixed up if things go bad for you, and it can even be done . . . but then there come bad times and everyone say—take care of me—take care of me . . . and it cannot be done. Then very few people are brave suddenly, and by and by people are afraid. Then ven so many are afraid, that is the time to watch out. I am thinking it vould be much better for each vun of us to learn to be brave by ourselves . . . and that is something I am trying to teach Carl."

"Are you having any luck?"

"No . . . I don't think so anyway . . . but maybe I am wrong about the whole thing. Maybe I be thinking clumsy some more."

"You went to school, Hamil," Barney said quietly. "I didn't. I was master of a sailing vessel on the Adriatic before I could read or write. But it don't seem to make no difference. I feel the same as you. When I first come to this country I was still a young man and I thought to myself even here people has got to eat. So if I could some day have my own boat and help to feed them, then everything would be all right for Barney Schriona, as long as I was willin' to work hard. I got the *Capella* all right, but it took me a lot longer than I thought it was going to take."

Barney picked up a crumb of cheesecake from the tablecloth and swept it into his mouth. "Now I have had lots of young fellows fishing with me since the war is over. They are changing, changing all the time, first one and then the other. When the fishing is good, they stick on the job. When it's bad, you know they tell me to go to hell? Sometimes they only been fishin' two or three weeks, but they go right down to the unemployment insurance office and get in line. They say to me, 'You see, I ain't got a pension plan.' Why the hell should they work and take a chance to get their toes wet when there are so many easier ways to get money? I don't blame them . . . they are just smart. But what I want to know is does that happen just in fishin' or does it in everything else besides?"

"I don't know," Hamil said thoughtfully. "I think vee be poor judges because vee don't spend enough time on land to know vat is going on."

"Well, if it does happen in other things . . . then maybe I better think about packin' up and goin' back to Ragusa. Because if it does happen too much, this is going to be a real lousy place to live."

"You vould probably find it worse there, Barney. I don't know for sure, and it could be nobody knows, but vee are trying to say something that has to do with more than this country. Now you take my son Carl. He is big and strong and he be a good fisherman. He can handle boats and lines better than I can. All of these things I have taught him . . . but there seems to be vun thing not possible for me to teach him. He vill not be . . . proud. He vill not say to himself it is a fine thing to be a good fisherman. He vill not say it to himself because he does not *think* it is a fine thing."

"What would he like to do?"

"I don't know. He never say exactly. Vun time he thinks to run a gas station. Next time he thinks to be in some office. But to vork by his hands . . . is something to be ashamed about." Hamil put his big hands on the table and spread his clean, weathered fingers. He brought them together slowly, made two

fists, and turned them over. He studied his fists, turning his
head from one to the other as if he had never seen them before.
And when he spoke again his deep voice was almost a whisper.

"I don't know, Barney. Maybe vee are all confused because
vee are not used to this new kind of thinking yet . . . and
maybe vee don't dare be honest vith each other so much as vee
should be because there is so much that keeps us from being
honest vith ourselves. So? Maybe Carl is right. Except that I
do not feel ashamed. Before God . . . I never do."

Something was happening inside Bruno Felkin. It was inside,
in the blood, or the head. The feeling, whatever it was, refused
to be analyzed. Maybe it was just too much fresh air.

Bruno lay flat on his bunk listening to the rain peckle on the
deck a few inches above his head. His body was tired and completely at rest. He could not remember when he had ever felt
so serene in his body—it was like relaxing in a warm bath, only
now there was nothing forced about the sensation. He had not
smoked for over an hour and that in itself was an indication
something was wrong. He held his fingers up to look at them.
They were still. This had never been so before. His hands were
swollen and warm, hot, in fact; the blood could be felt throbbing
in them. And yet that too was pleasant. They were hands that
had killed a man and still they were at peace. And it was not
just because things were going right.

The *Taage* was a perfect place to hide. A man might as
well vanish into a cloud. So much was for sure. And the Western
Sales Company would continue to function, now that Carl had
taken over the leg work. Connie would be all right. She didn't
know enough, thank God, to fall into any real trouble. So what
was wrong—not with the Felkin carcass, but with the mind?
Somewhere it had jumped the trolley. It was out of hand when
it didn't have any business straying. The end of the talk with
Carl was an example. When he was told to keep his mouth
shut to everybody.

". . . including your father. No use in his knowin' you're making money working for me, understand?"

"Pop and me don't get along. I'll tell him nothing," Carl said. Right then the Felkin mind slipped a cog. And Felkin climbed on a soap box. The words snapped out before the Felkin mind could catch them. And the Felkin fists were closed, ready to swing at that too good-looking face and a few other places that would cut him down to Felkin size.

"I don't happen to like the way you treat your pop. As of now, you're going to change it, understand?"

For why say a thing like that? Felkin was suddenly twice as mad as he had ever been at Sam Addleheim. You almost put yourself out of business before things got rolling. Who cared if Carl wanted to call his father a dumb bastard? Felkin? It must have been another Felkin—maybe leading some boy scout troop. It took a good five minutes to calm down and get squared around with the world again. It was punk thinking. You were going to give the world another chance to kick you in the teeth. Maybe the feeling started when Hamil came to you after the cod were unloaded and banged you on the back with that ham fist of his. He shoved twenty-six dollars at you.

"Your share, Bruno Felkin. I vas thinking and thinking how to be fair because you vorked so hard as I vould let you." When you handed the money back to him, he pushed it away again, laughing.

"No, this is the best vay and really I am cheating you, maybe. The first day you don't know much, so? And the second day yust a little better help. So ven a thing like this happens it is proper to give one-quarter share. By and by, maybe, you deserve a full share."

By and by? How about that? By and by, Bruno Felkin a fisherman! Working for a living just like everybody else! Not while you are still in your right mind. As soon as things eased off about Sam Addleheim then Felkin had other things to do.

That rest cure with Connie, the trip to Europe, big style. Why
have a dream if you never took time out to make it work? Only
damn this Carl and his father. Carl because he was for sure the
worst excuse for a man you ever met. And damn Carl's father
for being as he was, mixing up your thinking every time you
looked at him, making Bruno Felkin want to break his own
neck to please the guy. Damn all people like Hamil and Connie . . . being around such people knocked you off balance.

There was a heavy thump on the deck just above Bruno's
head. He raised himself on his elbow quickly. This would be
Carl returning. Things must have gone along all right; he was
just about on schedule.

Bruno heard the wheelhouse door slide open, and a pair of
wet boots appeared on the first step of the ladder beside his
head. The boots paused and then descended the ladder, and
after them the legs, the body, and finally the wet bald head of
a man Bruno had never seen before.

"Waddya say there . . . ?" the man said.

"Hello." The man took a dishrag from the rod near the
stove and mopped the droplets of water from his red face and
the top of his head.

"Hamil's not aboard, huh?"

"No. Some old friend of his—Barney somethin' or other—
come along and they went off together."

"Oh." Without trying to hide his disappointment, the man
looked at Bruno and then at the stove. "I saw your light and
thought I'd come over for a cup of coffee and maybe some talk.
I guess you don't know me. I'm Corky Mullins." He held his
hand up to Bruno. "Nights like this get pretty lonesome over
on the *Thunder Mug.* Mind if I make some coffee? I make the
best goddamned coffee you ever tasted . . . blacker than a
whore's heart . . . with a real boost in it."

Without waiting for Bruno's approval Corky filled the pot
and turned up the stove. And as he measured and poured, mak-

ing an elaborate ceremony of the process, words flowed from
him in such volume Bruno found it almost impossible to follow
him.

"I take it you're the new man," Corky said. "I heard Hamil
had a new fellow on board, but I couldn't believe it at the time
since everybody has tried to fish with Hamil so they can really
learn their business the right way, but he's not much for takin'
them along. You're a lucky bastard, Mr. . . . what did you
say your name was . . . well, it don't matter, so long as you
have a pair of ears to bend. Anyway, you're sonsobitchin' lucky
to be with Hamil Linder because he's not only got a fine boat
but knows the names and addresses of every fish in the Pacific
Ocean. Now it's March and you're long-linin', and maybe that
don't seem too good for all the work involved . . . but come
the first run of salmon in April or so, and Hamil will be out
there draggin' them silver beauties in so fast the gurdies will be
smokin'. And this year with salmon maybe startin' out at
twenty-eight cents a pound dressed or maybe better, God only
knows how much money you'll make . . . then along come
August and a few albacore off shore and Hamil will be right
after them gorgeous bastards, just pullin' in one slug after the
other while the rest of us is scratchin' for a few lousy here-and-
there stragglers.

"Myself now, I do my best to tag on to the *Taage* and fish
where she fishes, just knowin' that ways I can't miss, but the
goddamned *Thunder Mug* likes to play submarine the minute
she roughs up outside and there I am tryin' to bail and fish at
the same time which of course won't work . . . and pretty
soon I'm all alone in the middle of nowhere standing on top
the cabin and wavin' my pants for a tow or the goddamned Coast
Guard—" Corky paused to regain his breath and then, as if
ashamed, he again looked up at Bruno. "I talk too much, I
guess . . . don't I, mister?"

"Well . . . you seem to have a lot on your mind."

"A man gets that way when he's alone too much, I'll be god-damned if he don't. You just run off at the mouth until hell won't have it you want to talk so bad. I'll tell you how bad it gets and then maybe you won't mind so much. It gets so bad that a man even considers marryin', like in my case with this Johnnie Mae Swanson, and anybody who would marry that battle-ax is real hard up. . . . But the day will come when I might do it, just some day when I'm not thinkin' too clear . . . some day when I just got to talk so bad I can't stand it no more. Of course I'd rather talk about fish than anything in the world which is hard to do with a woman, and it's extra hard for me because I don't catch much except skunk, scrap, and idiot fish. I know I make you laugh because you must be an old-timer if you're fishin' with Hamil. You don't look much like one, but you must be one of them Seattle Scandahoovian high-liners if I'm guessin' right . . . down here to show us poor boys how to fish?"

"I don't know one end of a fish from the other," Bruno said, wishing Corky Mullins would have his coffee and go. Carl was due back any minute and they would need to go over some things alone.

Corky looked up in disbelief. "You mean to tell me you never fished before?" he said.

"No. Hamil just sort of inherited me."

"Well, now I *will* be goddamned. Carl didn't tell me nothin' about that. It's peculiar because Carl is the best friend I got in the whole wide world."

"Is that so?"

"Why a fella would have to go a couple a million miles to find a better man than that Carl for his age. He takes right after his old man, only naturally he's more full of hell, you know . . . opens up more than his pop."

"Mind if I ask what Carl ever did for you?"

"Mind? Why goddamnit, man, I'd be glad to tell anybody.

Carl, he's the only one on this wharf don't laugh at me and my boat. He knows I'm gonna make out all right, he knows it so well he's always come through if I happen to be a little short."

"If he's such a wonderful kid, how come he don't behave better to Hamil?"

Corky scratched his head and then his chest. He avoided looking at Bruno and his words slowed for the first time.

"Many a time I wondered that myself, mister. Carl, he's free and easy like and Hamil ain't. It's just a natural shame they can't see eye to eye. For instance Hamil ain't really tight, but he sure don't go throwin' his money around which is why I can't figure you bein' here as third man. Is he givn' you a share?"

"A quarter of a share, I think it is." Corky was looking at Bruno with new interest. He took a step closer to the bunk, and though his smile was friendly, Bruno saw suspicion behind his eyes.

"I've seen you somewheres before," Corky said. "I could swear to God I seen you before. Now let me think where we could've met—"

"I spent lots of time on the East Coast. Maybe it was there . . . around New York maybe."

"No. I never been to New York. You're too young to have been a vino . . . so it couldn't have been when I was drunk those years, like happens so much to me . . . thinkin' I seen guys before. No sir, I seen you when I was sober. Now let me just see if I can guess. Christ, but I'm sure gettin' old when I can't remember where I seen a face as plain as I seen yours." Corky scratched his bald head anxiously.

"You're mixed up unless you've been up in Canada recently. I spend most of my time in Canada."

"No . . . I never been to Canada. Now where in the hell could we have met . . . just where in the almighty hell—?" Bruno swung down from his bunk. Move, you knucklehead! Get a different light on your face. Do anything to distract this old jerk's attention.

"That's the best coffee I ever smelled," Bruno said.

"Say . . . you wasn't the fellow I seen runnin' up Stockton Street the other night, was you? Like you was runnin' from some woman?"

Bruno pointed a finger at his chest. "Me?" he said in amazement. "Corky, you're sure mixed up. If you had seen a woman running ahead of a man, then maybe that would be me hot after her . . . but not running away from one. I guess there's nothing I'd rather not do than run."

"Whoever this was must've been your twin brother." Corky's voice was full of disappointment. "It sure nettles my head when I get to thinkin' I seen somebody and it comes out I never did. It's the result of seepage into the brain . . . combination of alcohol and salt water, both of which I've had too much of . . . they say it corrodes the brain. Rust all over my head where there ought to be hair. Reminds me of a phrase from the Bible which goes as follows . . ." Corky took a pose beside the stove, swung his arm out and looked up at the deck beams. " 'Woe unto them that rise up early in the mornin' that they may follow strong drink . . . that continue till night till wine inflames them. . . .' "

Without changing the tilt of his head, his eyes returned to examine Bruno's face. "There was another thing we had to learn before the Salvation Army would give us any breakfast in them days," he said. " 'Wine is a mocker, strong drink is raging . . . and whosoever is deceived thereby is not wise.' "

"Those are fancy words," Bruno said quietly.

"Them words always got us breakfast. I'll never forget them words so long as I live. If I was only as good at faces as I am at words I could be damn sure where it was I seen you, mister."

CHAPTER — — — — — — — — — — — *9*

THE YEARLY APPROACH OF THE SALMON TO known waters was forecast in the gradual quickening of human tempo along the coast from Monterey north to Alaska. Those fishermen who had beached themselves for the winter straggled down to the docks and the boat yards, and stood in damp groups as they calculated the cost of fitting out once more against the few dollars remaining in their pockets. There were trolling poles to be bought, and new boots; spoons, wire, leads, leaders, nylon line, insulators, clips, salmon rubbers, hooks, swivels, gaffs, and gurdies. Supplies of food were the last thing to be considered.

The boats, whether used during the winter or not, required labor and careful attention. For this was the beginning of the fisherman's chance at survival.

The *Taage* made one more trip for black cod before Hamil decided the time had come to prepare his vessel for the salmon. He took the *Taage* across the bay to Sausalito. In a small ship-yard he had her hauled at a modest fee. Aside from the actual hauling up the marine railway, Hamil, along with the other fishermen, intended to perform the necessary work of fitting out himself. The *Taage*'s bottom was covered with slime, barnacles, and here and there fine whiskers of sea grass hung from her seams. Working with a fresh-water hose and stiff brushes, Hamil, Bruno, and Carl soon had her bottom clean. She would be allowed to dry, and then a coat of anti-fouling paint would be applied to her underbody just before she slid back in the water.

In the shipyard Bruno slowly became aware that working on the *Taage* was something more than the simple maintenance of a wooden structure. He saw Hamil walk away from the wooden cradle which held her mass, and he saw him stand silently for a long time studying her sheer and flare and dead rise as if he had never seen them before. He was surprised to find himself standing silently beside Hamil, and he wondered why it was such a satisfactory moment.

"A boat be a funny thing," Hamil finally said, and watching his eyes Bruno knew that he was speaking more to himself than to him. "A boat can receive the love of a man and hold it yust like a voman. So? A boat lives . . . it is natural to stand here and admire her. I think that is why men stand on docks all over the world . . . looking at the boats. They become young again . . . you could say there is some magic about boats. . . ."

"Yeah, I kind of feel that way myself," Bruno said. "I can't figure it. A couple of weeks ago I didn't know one end of a boat from the other." That was sure the truth, only whatever magic there might be in a boat like the *Taage* didn't explain this screwy feeling about Hamil. Or the way Felkin was getting soft in the head. Why, you were just walking around bare-faced in the world like anybody else . . . like there never was a Sam Addleheim. Like the only business you had was to stand around and listen while an old squarehead ran off at the mouth about boats. For a fact you been spending more time lately thinking about Hamil's opinion of you than you have remembering what the San Francisco Police Department thinks of you. Time is wasting, Felkin. Just keep this up and you'll wake up some day with a fine view of salt water all right—or don't they have any windows in the San Quentin gas chamber? Quit dreaming this way, Felkin! You *got* to stop it.

"Ya . . ." Hamil said softly, "it be fine to stand here and look at a good boat. But vee don't get much vork done this vay."

"I'm just about done with the winch," Bruno said as they walked toward the *Taage*.

"You be a pretty good machinist, Bruno."

"Yeah. I like it. We had a machine shop where I went to school." They sure did. The best machine shop the state of Minnesota could provide its juvenile prisoners. Keep on pretending it was a real school, Felkin, and after a while you'll believe it yourself.

Just after the regular shipyard workers stopped for the day, it began to rain. The water poured steadily from the low clouds that seemed to have draped themselves permanently over the Sausalito hills. Overhauling the anchor winch on the *Taage*'s foredeck was a miserable job but Bruno continued to concentrate intensely on it despite the rivulets of cold water running down the back of his neck. He had already scraped all the grease and paint from the drum and now he had contrived an invention he was sure would please Hamil. What an inventor, this Felkin! By tripping this little spring, the anchor chain could be released with a mere twist of the wrist.

After he had worked the spring release a number of times and was certain the adjustment was just right, Bruno went to the ladder which had been placed against the *Taage*'s side. If Hamil would have a look at his invention and approve, it would be the end of a damn fine day's work.

He was halfway down the ladder when he saw something that made him forget his pleasure. Carl was standing near the cutwater, where he had been the better part of the afternoon. He was supposed to be recaulking two seams in the bow planks but he had spent most of his time avoiding the heavier rain squalls, or finding other excuses to drop his iron and hammer. Now Hamil was standing behind his son, his big frame straight and angry although his voice remained reasonable.

"Vell, Carl," he was saying, "I don' think you do so good today, so? You spend the whole damn afternoon and not two seams caulked? You been daydreaming, maybe?"

Carl took a vicious swing at the cotton, so hard he drove the iron deep into the seam. Hamil's voice lost its calm.

"Carl! Vat you *do*! That is no vay to treat a ship!"

Carl yanked out the iron, and just as he started to swing again Hamil caught his arm. Carl wheeled on his father.

"If you don't like the way I caulk your bucket get some other guy!" He dropped the iron and hammer at his feet. "Take your hands off me, Pop!"

"You been loafing all day, Carl, and you hurt the boat that vay . . ."

Bruno could hardly believe what he saw. Carl's fist flew up and struck his father squarely on the chin. Hamil grunted and sank to his knees. He caught feebly at Carl's boot tops and finally his face made a little splash as it hit a puddle of water.

Suddenly Bruno's face flamed. He forgot everything as the blood pounded through his whole body. Crazy. Crazy! He left the ladder in a long dive before Carl had a chance to move.

Carl should have collapsed beneath Bruno's weight, but instead he managed to stay on his feet. Twisting his powerful shoulders, he spun and shook Bruno off. Bruno landed hard on a pile of boards ten feet away.

"What the hell's got into *you*?" Carl demanded.

"I been puttin' this off too long!" Not so crazy now. Think! Remember if Carl once hits you squarely, it's Felkin who will be taught a lesson—to stay out of other people's business. Go back to the streets of South St. Paul—keep the old tricks going fast!

Make those rotten years pay off. But don't kill him. No edge of your hand across his throat and no kicks in the groin—unless you have to.

Before Carl could take a step toward him, Bruno charged. He butted Carl with his head, square at his belt line. Carl gasped and staggered back, his arms spread wide. Bruno closed in immediately, not even trying to hit with his fists. Fists were for amateurs and sportsmen. Use the stunning power of your elbows back and forth across his ribs and belly. Give him another elbow flashing up against the jaw—now! Follow it with your open palm, the butt of the palm, smashing up against his face. Now! Don't spar. Don't wait for breath. This fight can't last that long.

Carl went down flat on his back, and almost before he struck the ground Bruno was on top of him with all the speed he could gather. The force of his knees hitting Carl's stomach should have knocked the wind from him, but Bruno knew instantly he had underestimated Carl's condition. Before he could twist away, Carl's long arms were around him and his enormous strength took over. Soundless except for their panting, they lay locked. As Carl slowly tightened his grip, Bruno felt his own breath going. Break away! Right now! Remember this second how you did it in South St. Paul.

His head was just a little below Carl's. Suddenly Bruno snapped his head upward against Carl's jaw with all the strength in his neck. The blow broke Carl's grip and Bruno rolled free. But a precious second was gone. Carl was over his surprise, and he was on his feet. He might be bleeding at the mouth, but he was coming fast—a heavy board in his hand. Now was the time to close with Carl, and it had to be done just right.

Bruno heard the brush of air as the board swept just over his head, then he was in tight against Carl, working with his elbows again, working back and forth, weaving his body with every vicious hit. And his feet were going now in the old way, the

South St. Paul way, kicking at Carl's kneecaps—anything to make him drop the board.

Carl backed away, wiping his mouth. He threw the board at Bruno and rushed again, swinging his big fists wildly. But he moved uncertainly and Bruno was ready. The elbows had done it. All right, wise guy. Keep slipping fast.

As Carl lunged toward him Bruno feinted, ducked, and reached up for his hair. He seized Carl's head with both hands and, yanking down with all his might, raised one knee at the same time. His knee met Carl's face and it should have finished things. It always did in South St. Paul. But Carl kept his feet. Though he was half blind when he raised his head, he struck out and hit Bruno so hard he seemed to bounce from his feet. Bruno knocked down a sawhorse as he reeled away. He fell on a stack of iron piping.

Carl followed him as swiftly as he could move. Bruno had just time to twist on his side and catch Carl's advance. He hooked his toe behind Carl's ankle and with his other foot kicked Carl above the knee. Carl yelled with pain, but the trick didn't quite work. He was off balance, but he failed to go down.

Get on your feet, Bruno! It's all you need now you're really in business.

His hand had found a rudder pinion and he could not have ordered a handier thing. It was a heavy metal rivet. It fits so nice inside your fist, just like a roll of nickels did in South St. Paul, and Los Angeles, and Cleveland, and everywhere else Felkin had fought to live. A roll of nickels—nothing like them. Every kid who knew his way around carried one handy in his pocket, just in case. No cop could hang a concealed-weapon charge on you for a roll of nickels and they made a hammer out of a fist. And so would a rivet.

Bruno stood with his hands at his side waiting for Carl to come to him. He swayed a little, pretending he was almost out. When Carl took the bait, he still waited until the last possible second. Then, twisting to one side, he swung.

Carl's head snapped back. His arms went out and then fell uselessly to his sides. He fell back one step and hit the ground with a thud. All right, big stuff. You're out. But in South St. Paul there was only one sure way to finish a fight. It made sure a guy stayed down. Bruno kicked Carl twice in the head.

And then Bruno sat down. He was still burning hot. He could feel his heart pounding blood through the veins in his neck. Felkin—you're boss. But you've made another mistake. You're a goddamned crazy fool!

Head down on his arms, Bruno had rested only a moment before he heard a step behind him. Still tense, he turned and was almost instantly on his feet. It was Hamil. He was looking at Bruno questioningly, as if trying to see beyond his eyes.

"Get some vater," Hamil said quietly, and then he knelt beside his son.

When Bruno came back with sea water in a can, Hamil took it from him and wiped Carl's face with his wet handkerchief. They said nothing until Carl moved his legs and groaned.

"You could have killed him," Hamil said without anger. His big hands were shaking as he wiped Carl's face.

"Yeah—"

"You don't fight like a man, Bruno Felkin. You fight like a animal."

"No fights are nice. Not if you got to win."

"Why did you do it?" Bruno looked down at Carl, and then he looked away toward the *Taage*.

"I dunno . . ." he said. "I don't know why the hell I did it."

Together they lifted Carl to his feet and supported him until his balance returned. And as they stood together holding him, Hamil said, "Thanks . . . Bruno Felkin."

Now it might be the spring of the year all right, but there were certain things about women, Kelsey decided, spring could not be blamed for. The easing of the rains might have something to do with their behavior, or perhaps the old saw about the phase of the moon. Or it could be that in his fifty-four years Kelsey had lost rather than gained in his understanding of the feminine character. Connie Thatcher had become a sharp pain in his head, and in what remained of his heart. Here was a girl who had managed to revive some hope for the human race in him, and then having done so, she promptly pushed that hope into the gutter—where he should have left it in the first place. For being so foolish as to tolerate hope after such long absence, Kelsey pitied himself.

Since Bruno Felkin's disappearance over a month ago, the girl had behaved herself strictly not according to Hoyle. That was when the hope started. A careful shadowing of her movements and activities, even a few talks with her, revealed nothing. She had certainly not seen Bruno Felkin and it was extremely doubtful if she had communicated with him. But at last a new angle had evidenced itself. "So now *I'm* up all night," Kelsey mused. "With my age and seniority, I still miss my sleep because human beings are untrustworthy, insincere, conniving, corrupt, dangerous . . . and bastards and bitches without any exception." Kelsey's opinion now included Connie Thatcher. She was no longer set aside from other women.

His memory advised him that invariably the kind of girls who shared the life of men like Bruno Felkin remained reasonably faithful to them for at least a week. Then it would always begin. A new man would appear on the scene, and if he was not quite as handsome, he was at least further along in the world. The "bounce-off," as Kelsey called it, was as predictable as the stars. Then as soon as the first man was safely in exile, either out of the state or in prison, the new man moved in officially. Since the nature of their business made the Brunos poor security risks, a smart girl always tried to have at least one prospect in reserve. Connie hadn't seemed to be quite that way, but at last she was running true to form. You do not learn something new every

day, Kelsey thought. You learn something once and then are
damn silly enough to forget it, and then you have to learn it all
over again, which merely causes whatever in the hell the something is to seem new.

Connie was slow to get going. She continued to attend school
regularly. She now had for herself a job. That was understandable and a sure indication that wherever Felkin was he was in no
shape to send her money, if indeed he would bother. She was
working nights as a hat-check girl in a curious little restaurant
called the Bread and Wine, which hung on the east side of Telegraph Hill. A long flight of wooden stairs connected it to the
street. The food was excellent. The trade was more or less of the
carriage variety, and the bar did a thriving business until the
whole establishment, with admirable independence, closed
promptly at nine-thirty. There were candles on the tables, saw-
dust on the floor, and always a line of smart-looking cars parked
outside. It was one of those places, Kelsey thought; the kind
members of the force never quite felt up to, not when it was cus-
tomary to tip fifty cents for your hat. Connie had had the job for
just three weeks when the boy friend showed up. He was tall,
good-looking, and he drove a brand-new Studebaker. Kelsey was
not surprised. He was disappointed. It was where he came in.

Standing on the terrace outside the restaurant, he could see
Connie through the wide-paned window. She was dressed at-
tractively in black—damnit, she was always attractive—and the
candlelight seemed to turn her hair golden. There was not a
real check room, but merely a long rack opposite the bar on which
she set the hats and hung the men's coats. Connie stood before
it, and now she was smiling and sometimes laughing as she
handed out hats and said good night to the last departing guests.
She seemed to be enjoying herself, and Kelsey decided must
have pleased the proprietor, for she acted as a sort of hostess. She
talked with the customers while they waited for tables, took

reservations on the phone, and finally turned the diners over to the headwaiter.

"A smart tramp," Kelsey murmered to the night, "a very smart little tramp."

He waited for the last guest to leave the restaurant, then he watched the street below for a new Studebaker. When none came and Connie left the restaurant, he cut across the terrace and, without bothering to hurry, caught up with her at the foot of the long stairs.

"Fine night, isn't it, Connie," he said, coming easily to her side. She turned suddenly and Kelsey thought he saw fear in her eyes, then they went cool again and he was strangely pleased that there had not been the slightest hesitation in her steps. There was, he thought, one peculiar satisfaction in police work. In a case involving top people, everyone wanted in on the act. Top people, when they finally cracked, gave you the feeling you really knew your business. You got kind of proud of them.

"Yes, it is a nice night," she said. Kelsey knew she would say just that; he didn't know why she would, but before he had finished his own greeting he was sure he could quote her reply. They continued to walk easily up the hill to the summit of Union Street, and they might have been two people out for a pleasant stroll.

"Like your new job, Connie?"

"Very much. How did you know about it?"

Kelsey looked at her and pretended disgust. "Connie . . . *please*. I been in this business a long time. Ask me how you did on the English test in school and I'll tell you."

"I haven't seen you for so long, Kelsey," she said. "I've been feeling neglected and lonesome."

"Not so lonesome as you might be. How do you like the new Studebakers?" Was there a hesitation in her step just then? Kelsey was watching for it, but he wasn't sure.

"They're fine. Very comfortable." She bothered to turn her head, but her voice said only a statement of mechanical fact, nothing more.

"Who's the new boy friend, anybody I know?"

"I don't think so."

"You're getting co-operative, Connie. You don't say 'could be' any more."

". . . could be."

"Who is he, Connie?"

"None of your business."

"He looks like a Swede. Nice-looking young fellow."

"When did you see him—or do you hang by your knees from the trees all the time?"

Kelsey laughed softly. They turned the corner at Union Street and started down the steep hill.

"Going any special place, Connie? If you're not, I'll walk you home."

"I was just on my way to a ball, Mr. Kelsey, but for the pleasure of walking with you, I'll give it up." They walked along in silence for almost a full block, not hurrying because Connie was setting the pace as Kelsey wanted her to do.

"This new boy friend, Connie. He isn't much better than your last. Why can't you meet an honest man for a change?"

"Who said he wasn't?"

"I did."

"Are you ever wrong?"

"Once in a while, but it so happens this young fellow is quite a liar."

"So?"

"Or maybe he is just forgetful or has amnesia or he's been drinking at the fountain of youth. When he put the down payment on that new car he took out the registration in the name of Henry Mullins." Kelsey watched her lips. There should be some sign of surprise there, but her lips remained together. Kel-

sey told himself that some day, just for the hell of it, he was going to inform Connie that Canada had declared war on the
United States just to see if he could create the slightest flicker of
interest in her eyes.

"What if he did?" she asked after they had walked almost to
the corner of Grant Avenue.

"Well Connie, it so happens Henry Mullins is sixty-four years
old."

"He never said the car was his. I guess he just bought it for
another man. I don't know him very well."

"When Henry Mullins took out his driver's license three
years ago, he gave his occupation as a scavenger. He was going to
drive a refuse truck but he never did, according to their records.
I can't seem to dig up any scavenger by that name in San Francisco, Connie."

"I should think a busy man like you could dig up almost
anything."

"There was a Henry Mullins on Skid Row once. A fellow they
called Corky. But he sobered up one day and hasn't been heard
from since. Missing Persons can't seem to get a line on him . . .
yet."

"Don't bring me your troubles, Kelsey. Remember, I'm not
on your side. You won't let me be."

They were at her apartment steps now and Connie stopped to
look up at the sky. "You were saying, Kelsey, that it's a nice
night. Are you coming up or can I go do my homework in
peace?"

"No, Connie, I want to see you head your class. But I'd like to
meet your new friend some time. I'm always interested in your
future."

"Tell you what, Kelsey. Bring your wife and we'll make up a
double date. I can't imagine anything more fun. Now, so long."
She went quickly up the steps and was unlocking the door when
Kelsey called after her.

"Heard anything from Bruno lately, Connie?" She looked back over her shoulder at him and the street light fell across her face in such a way Kelsey could have sworn she was grinning although he was sure she was not.

"Sure. He calls every day. Long distance . . . from the moon." She let herself through the door and slammed it without looking back. Kelsey watched her legs disappear up the hall stairs and it occurred to him once more that a man's interest in such things remains long after his ability to do really enough about them has faded. "But I would honestly like to see her head the class," Kelsey thought, "so help me God, I honestly would." Jingling the change in his pocket, he turned down Chestnut Street. Though it was downhill again, he walked very slowly, for some meditation was in order before he reached the place where he had parked his car at Fisherman's Wharf. It might be a crazy, useless, lead, but Missing Persons knew very well where this Corky Mullins was. And perhaps by now he would be in from the sea.

Connie turned on the light in the living room and the bedroom. She moved back and forth in front of the window facing the street several times, then turned off the living room light and watched the street below. There was no sign of Kelsey. The street was deserted. She put on her hat again and went quickly down the apartment steps.

At the street door she searched the corner once more and then started up Grant Avenue. She was late, a good twenty minutes late because of Kelsey and his curiosity; another time—before Bruno—it might have been fun to see how long Carl would wait, or if he would. Now things were considerably different.

At first, seeing Carl had been like seeing Bruno. And that was satisfying. Now there was a new feeling too—a slightly guilty feeling. After that first night Carl had decided to behave himself. He seemed a different person, one worth knowing. He had a curious way of commanding and asking at the same time.

When he said "Meet me at La Bohème, ten o'clock sharp" . . . well, the urge to be with him and to be on time was strangely powerful. It might have something to do with the way Carl had of laughing at himself, and at everything else for that matter. After Bruno, who cared so desperately about everything and laughed—let's see, when did Bruno ever laugh? Never. He couldn't laugh. He never knew how to begin. Things were never any fun for Bruno and it was a little hard on whoever shared his time. Perhaps that accounted somewhat for the guilty feeling. Being with Carl for only a few minutes was always easy. It was possible to stop wanting and to think that whatever you had was fun.

On her way to the Bohème Connie was careful to look behind her at every street intersection.

The Bohème was a combination bar and restaurant with a juke box that played nothing but operatic tunes. It specialized in an Italian drink called *Cappucino,* steaming hot chocolate and brandy. The Bohème, Connie thought, was the kind of a place only a relaxed man like Carl would choose. Bruno would call it a dump—nothing but the very best for Bruno, no matter what he had to do to get it.

Carl was sitting at one of the tables beyond the bar. He made a broad lazy sweep with his hand as Connie came through the door. He was leaning back in his chair, a *Cappucino* already before him, and he didn't seem to care how long he had waited. Still breathless from her fast walk, Connie slipped into the chair beside him.

"I'm late and I'm sorry," she said.

"Who's been chasing you?"

"No one. I made sure. But Kelsey knows about you, or at least that you have a car."

"Everybody's got a car. And who's Kelsey?"

Connie hesitated. Now why had she taken it for granted that Carl knew everything about her, and always had? How could he make it seem the two of you had been together a hundred times, instead of only four or five? Leaning far back in his chair now, confident, so sure of himself, yet knocking any idea of conceit away because any minute he would find something to kid himself about . . . it just seemed like he had a right to ask you anything.

"Kelsey is a policeman."

The smile left Carl's face, but he only tipped back farther in his chair.

"How come you know him?" he asked casually.

"A friend of mine is in trouble. Kelsey thinks I could tell him something about it."

"Can you?"

"No."

"Would your friend be Bruno?"

The waiter came just then with Connie's *Cappucino*. She put the steaming hot glass to her lips quickly.

"Oh! It's hot . . . and so good."

"I asked you a question."

"Yes. It's Bruno."

"I was afraid it was me. I'm getting so I don't like being Bruno's delivery boy. It's damned dangerous. If he didn't pay off so well—"

"I wish you'd never done it."

"Why?"

"It does things to you, and they'll catch you."

"I'm going to quit before that. Any day now."

"That's what Bruno always said. Carl, why did you tell me that car was yours? You don't have to impress people that way."

Carl finished the drink in his glass and ordered another. When the waiter left he shook his head and seemed to be laughing very quietly inside.

"I guess you're right, Connie, now that I come to think it over your way. I don't know why, but I do want to impress people. A big car makes me feel big . . . a shot. But it's really my car, except what I still owe the finance company."

"Then why isn't it in your name?"

Carl came forward with his chair. He wasn't quite so relaxed now. His big hands came up on the table and then he returned them to his pockets.

"You know too much for a girl with blonde hair, Connie. But it so happens I made a wrong guess not so long ago. I swiped a car . . . just for the hell of it, plus the whisky in my belly, plus the girl in my head at the moment. I woke up on probation. So the car has to be in another guy's name. What did you tell your friend Kelsey?"

"Nothing. But he'll find out. He won't stop until he finds out."

"There's nothing he can do. Officially the car isn't mine. And they can't hang you for driving without a license."

"He could find out about Bruno."

"To hell with Bruno. He made a monkey out of me when I should have been big enough to break him in two."

"They might find out about you."

"Does it make any difference to you?"

"Yes. I like you, Carl."

"Don't like me too much. Your boy friend plays rough."

"Is he all right?"

"I didn't ask him."

"Didn't he tell you to call me?"

"No. It was my own idea, this time. And now that we're at it, just what kind of trouble is Bruno in?"

Connie studied her glass a moment. What had happened to the laughs they had enjoyed together? Bruno might just as well have been sitting with them now. He could be in either one of the vacant chairs, sitting there tense and serious, tight and ready to spring—a little like Kelsey said, like a wild animal. If Bruno hadn't done so much without asking, if he didn't need someone

so badly, it would be very easy to hate him. Or at least the idea of
him. There was no getting away from Bruno. If he hadn't killed
a man, why didn't he come? It was so hard to keep believing
without some explanation.

"Why don't you ask Bruno yourself?"

"He's against questions."

"Then so am I, Carl." He looked at her a long time before
he reached out and took her hand. Even then Carl sat silently,
as if waiting for her to say something else. Finally he examined
her fingers very carefully, letting them fall slowly to the table
one by one.

"I like your not telling me," he said, and his easy smile returned. "Yeah . . . I like that, Connie. But something ought to
be done. You're much too solid a girl for Bruno . . . something ought to be done."

THE BOAT "WAYFARER" AND THE BOAT "FRED Holmes," working together, found the year's first real run of salmon eight miles below Pedro Point. As a result of their discovery, their radios were busy most of the day spreading the news to the fleet. Other vessels called them constantly for bearings, for the weather, the state of the sea, and the size and number of the salmon. They willingly reported the sea as calm and of a color ideal for salmon—reddish brown. There were many birds working, they said, and a school of whales was exploring the area. There were ample indications that the waters were rich with feed. When Hamil Linder called the *Fred Holmes,* a man he addressed as Pablo came cheerfully back to him.

"The *Fred Holmes* back to the *Taage.* Well, well, Hamil, long time no see. Good to hear your voice again. You still fishin' black cod? Come back."

"No . . . no, vee are right after you, Pablo. Vee all rigged for salmon now. Maybe the *Taage* come down to help you. So many fish for yust two little boats is bad. You get too rich, maybe?" Hamil laughed into the microphone and after a pause the laugh was returned.

"The *Fred Holmes* back to the *Taage*. Yeah, Hamil. You might want to get in on this while it lasts. We took about thirty aboard the last two hours—some pretty nice slugs—run about twenty-five or thirty pounds. But a lot of jellyfish too. So I guess you can't have things easy. Where are you, Hamil?"

"The *Taage* back to the *Fred Holmes*. Vell, vee come out some little after midnight and have been vorking towards the Farallones, but only picking up small stuff now and again. Yust for the pot, no real market fish. I think vee come down your vay now if you give me a short count please. Over."

"The *Fred Holmes* back. All right, Hamil, here goes. One . . . two . . . three . . . four . . ." as the voice intoned the numbers, Hamil slowly turned the handle on the loop direction finder. At a certain point in his turning, the voice faded, and then as Hamil passed the point it increased again. Hamil sought a division on the loop compass card where the voice would have the least strength. The aural null would indicate the exact direction over the horizon of the counting voice and Hamil could transpose it to his chart.

". . . twenty-one . . . twenty-two . . . twenty-three. Did you get my count all right, Hamil? Come back."

Hamil studied the loop direction card a moment and then picked up his microphone.

"Ya, Pablo. I make you bearing sou-sou'east of us, maybe vun quarter east. Vee come down that vay now and pick you up by and by. Thank you very much, Pablo, and good fishing."

"The *Fred Holmes* back to the *Taage*. Okay, Hamil! We'll be seein' you. Say, you usin' bow poles this year? Come back."

"No. I took them off. Maybe I regret it, but I took them off. The *Taage* clear with the boat *Fred Holmes*." Hamil switched off the dynamotor and turned to Bruno, who had been watching him. He smiled.

"Now maybe you see a little more action, Bruno . . . pretty soon. At last somebody find the fish. Maybe we make an honest dollar today." Bruno shook his head.

"I don't get it," he said. "I don't get it at all. That guy's in the fish isn't he? He's on to a good thing? Why should he split with everyone else? It don't make sense. There must be fifty boats listenin' to him."

"That's so, Bruno. And they vill all come running and maybe break up the school pretty quick. But in this business vee got to help each other. Maybe by and by the *Taage* find the fish, so vee tell everybody too. Either you vork together or you become a outlaw. And then maybe you starve. That's the vay it is. You have to share. Now let me ask you something, Bruno. Can you handle a gun?" Hamil was puzzled at the expression on Bruno's face. He turned his head so quickly, and almost spit the cigarette out of his mouth.

"A gun?" His mouth relaxed as suddenly as it had tightened. "What for, we goin' huntin', or fishin'?"

"There be alvays a lot of sea lions off Pedro Point, Bruno. Yust ven you are bringing up a nice salmon a sea lion vill svim along and bite him right in half. Vee have to shoot them or they steal you crazy. If the school is vorking pretty hot, Carl and I be very busy and you could most help by shootin' the sea lions now and again."

"Oh. Sure, I guess I could handle that."

"There is a rifle under the mattress on my bunk and a box of shells yust by the head. You look it over now."

Hamil changed the *Taage*'s course, making the turn wide so the salmon lines would not tangle, and then he left the wheelhouse to stand on the foredeck for a time. There were a lot of things he wanted to think about, and as long as Carl was back in the trolling pit watching the lines, this was a good time to plan for the next few days. There was the ice in the *Taage*'s hold to be thought of—it was already four days old, and since he had only taken a ton to begin with, it was doubtful if it would last out the week. Therefore it would be best to make port on Friday, unload whatever catch there was, ice up once more with perhaps two or three tons this time, and really hit the fish during the following week.

Now this was already Wednesday and the *Taage* would have at best one more day to complete the catch. It was impossible to tell, but unless their luck improved the total aboard would probably be less than a ton; nothing for Hamil Linder to hold his head very high about.

Year after year, it seemed, the salmon were coming along in fewer numbers. It was easy to remember when a man could poke his bow out the Golden Gate and be sure to come back with a ton a day. But the price then was so low—was it seven or eight cents a pound?—so low that a fisherman had an almost hopeless struggle making a living. There were no radios then, and no mechanical gurdies for hauling up the fish by machinery. In those days, two months before the start of the season, a man soaked his hands in brine an hour or so every day, toughening them against the punishment they would surely take. Then, hauling all day long, a man's muscles alone were matched against the salmon. Hand over hand they had to be brought to gaff, and there were times at the end of a day when the fisherman's hands were so cramped in position they became torn claws, and it was only with the greatest suffering that they could be straightened to their natural position again.

These days things were easier, although the voyages themselves were longer, and so perhaps in certain ways the hardships balanced out. Now, on each side of the trolling pit there were six metal drums, driven by the *Taage's* engine. They could be individually controlled by pushing and pulling levers, and on each drum there was at least a hundred and fifty fathoms of steel wire. The wires led over spools hanging from stern davits and then through porcelain insulators attached to the stout thirty-foot trolling poles by heavier wires.

Hamil turned and leaned against the pilothouse, studying the *Taage's* gear. It was extremely important that it be exactly right, or when the salmon really began to hit there would be snags and headaches enough. As the *Taage* moved very slowly through the water, the wires stringing back from the poles formed a delicate webbing which brushed back and forth across the blue sky. The poles were set into the *Taage*'s bulwarks at an angle, so that no matter how she rolled, the tips would never dip in the sea. The extreme ends of the poles were some fifteen feet above the water and from them the tag lines stretched far back beyond the *Taage*'s wake. Hamil watched the water action of the Montara bags, the inflated rubber floats which held the tag lines free of entanglement with the others, and decided they were still too close to the boat.

"Carl," he called, "give your tag lines another three or four fathoms!" In the trolling pit, Carl waved his hand and threw the gurdy levers. The drums turned and the Montara bags dropped back until Carl locked the levers again. Carl made a question with his fingers and Hamil nodded approval.

It was a funny thing about Carl, Hamil decided. You could never be sure of his behavior. He could take a licking with good grace. It took something to come back, apparently in good humor, after losing a fight to a smaller man. The boy had one very valuable thing. He had never taken himself too seriously. Of course that could be a weakness too. A careless man seldom accomplished very much. Watching Carl and Bruno together, it was hard to believe the fight had ever happened. The very next day at the shipyard, they had worked together. They had even joked about their cuts and bruises, and it seemed, if that was what he wanted, Bruno had succeeded in more ways than one. In all ways, Carl was easier to handle than before. He appeared to take a new interest in the *Taage,* and what was still more surprising, in his father. For the first time since Carl came out of the army, it was possible to look upon him as a companion. How long it might last was something else again.

It would be unfair to ask Bruno to leave the *Taage* now, not when he seemed so anxious to stay aboard. Because salmon fishing was really a two-man operation there was no sensible reason for him to be aboard, but he had worked hard and had done his very best to be helpful in many ways. You couldn't put ashore a man who so naturally took to the sea and everything about it. Bruno was fast becoming a good hand in his own right. He was clever, that Bruno, as clever a man as Hamil had ever met. You couldn't leave him standing on the dock when he fought for you—when he openly asked nothing more than to be with you. He was a puzzle, this Bruno, and whatever kind of business he had was very difficult to understand. But then there were a lot of mysterious men in the fishing fleet. Their backgrounds were never explained because it was against custom to ask, and they didn't talk about themselves. Many of them were fine fishermen. If Bruno didn't care to talk about himself, then the best thing to do was to take him as he stood.

Hamil searched the horizon for signs of life. There were no birds, no whales, not even another boat to be seen. There were no porpoises flashing back and forth across the *Taage*'s bow. The ocean was dead. He sighed and watched the metal shock springs on the trolling poles. They were motionless, and had been so for too long a time. If things were happening in the depths, any one or all of the shock springs would jerk. At the other end of the wire, some fifty fathoms below the surface, a salmon would have taken the hook.

Hamil scratched the stubble on his chin. Something was very wrong. Thirty-six brass spoons flashed behind the *Taage*. Carl and Bruno had carefully polished each one of them before dawn and so far only five salmon had bothered to notice them. Maybe, Hamil thought, he had made the nylon leaders too long this year or the small knots and clips attaching the leaders to the wire were not just right. Or the weights should be changed—say put a fifty-pound lead on the main lines instead of a forty-pounder so the lines would hang down just a little straighter. Sometimes a

very insignificant thing, hooks not set from the spoon properly,
leaders a few inches long or too short, one spoon out of so many
twisted around the wire and causing an unnatural wildness as it
passed through the water—there were always a hundred little
things which could cause a boat not to fish. Two boats working
along within hailing distance of each other, sliding over the same
school of fish, could have such a vast difference in their catch it
was almost unbelievable. At the end of the day, one boat might
have two hundred fish while the other had barely scratched up
ten or twenty—and the difference could lie in the size of the
swivels which, when held in the hand, varied hardly an eighth of
an inch.

"Hey, Pop!" Carl yelled, and Hamil thought he heard a new
note in his voice again, a friendliness such as he had not heard
for a long time. "You're one hell of a fisherman, Pop! Every
boat in the fleet is hauling 'em aboard and look at us. You drag
the whole Pacific Ocean and we haven't got enough to make a
good cioppino! How about trying more speed?" Hamil nodded
his head. Maybe Carl was right, you never could be sure. One
day the salmon liked a fast boat, one day they liked a slow boat;
in fact when things were hot, it was always a good idea to vary
the speed every few minutes. Sometimes salmon would follow
along just a few inches behind the spoons, as if trying to make
up their minds, and then if the spoons were suddenly dragged
away from them, they would strike.

"All right, Carl. You maybe try a little more throttle."

Hamil walked slowly aft, studying the lines and then the sea.
There was feed in the water, not shrimp, which would have
been the best, but a plankton of some kind, and it should have
drawn salmon. Hamil watched the *Taage*'s wake for a while,
searching through his experience for an explanation, trying to
envision what was going on in the half-darkness of fifty fathoms.
The spoons would be twinkling like stars there, twisting along
in an inviting ladder, one above the other. Each spoon would

be a fathom apart, so that every reasonable depth was covered. The *Taage's* course was good. She was headed directly into the late morning sun and neither side would cast a shadow below. And yet—nothing.

"When you polished the spoons this morning, Carl, were any of them nicked?" Just a scratch could make a difference. Hamil had seen it happen.

"No, Pop. We used just the brand new ones. And Bruno, he kept his fingers off 'em like you said. We were both careful as hell."

Hamil took out his knife and slit the belly of the salmon at his feet. He examined the stomach and entrails carefully and shook his head.

"They are not full of feed . . . not so much as a shrimp or a sardine. They are yust not feeding, but they should be hungry. I can't figure it." He pushed the salmon into the shade of the hatch and sat down on the bulwark. He chuckled quietly and ran his fingers through his hair.

"I guess you say something true, Carl. I be vun hell of a bum fisherman this day. By and by, though, vee make some kind of magic. Ven this happens, you got plenty of time to think how you do wrong." Carl moved across the trolling pit until he stood near his father.

"I been doing some thinkin' too, Pop. Don't expect me to change my ideas about this lousy business, but I been waitin' to say something. This is as good a time as any . . . while Bruno isn't here." Hamil looked at Carl, but he said nothing. He waited, still thinking of the fish. "I was wrong to hit you, Pop."

Hamil looked away from Carl and then became absorbed in wiping his knife on his boot. He cleaned it with great care, and as he leaned forward to lay it on the hatch, their eyes met for barely a second. Just then Hamil wanted to reach out and put his arms around Carl. He wanted, this instant, some touch of his own. And yet he knew it would be the wrong thing to do.

Carl would break away, angrily perhaps, and if what he had just said was finally a thread of understanding between them, then it was best to leave it alone.

He looked away at the sun, and then down at his heavy fingers because they were the easiest things to look at. A hundred words raced through his mind. He had a sick feeling that if he lost this moment it might never return, and yet his mouth only worked soundlessly. Carl had given a little, and it must have taken a great deal to do that. The chance was rushing away, as a following sea might overtake and pass a boat, and still he could find nothing to say. Father of Christ! Could a man admit, and still make his voice sound true, that there was really anything to forgive in his son?

Just as Hamil found a few words, because wrong or right something had to be said, Bruno came on deck with the rifle.

"What goes on?" Bruno asked. "What's the picture? Where are all these salmon I hear so much about?" He threw a beer bottle high in the air, put the rifle to his shoulder, and the bottle barely hit the water before he fired and broke it. He raised his eyebrows in mock surprise and the corner of his mouth twisted into a smile. "Strictly a Daniel Boone," he said.

Now this was better, Hamil thought. He could find his full voice again. He slapped the bulwark triumphantly.

"Vare you learn to shoot like that, Bruno?" he laughed. "By golly! I bet you never do it again!"

"I guess it's sort of a natural talent, but in the real estate business we got lots of gophers and ground hogs, Hamil. You keep in practice or they overrun your property."

"I thought maybe it vas during the var . . . maybe in the army," Hamil said. Bruno looked at the rifle and then scanned the horizon as if looking for another target.

"No. During the war I was close enough to guns . . . but I served in a sort of non-combat capacity. Say, where are all these fish?"

"In the ocean where they're damn well going to stay," Carl said. "Pop went and lost his touch. Maybe you and me, Bruno, ought to go get on a good boat."

"Yust a *minute!*" Hamil held up his finger. He wanted to laugh louder than he had for years. He wanted to dance on the deck. He wanted to take his son and this Bruno who had become almost a son, and wrestle with them—let the good feeling of this little time when they were closer than they ever had been explode within him. He wanted to yell, to move violently, to show the sun and the sea that this wetness in his eyes was only happiness. "Yust a *minute!*" . . . Standing straight in the sunlight, he spread his arms wide as if to gather in their smiles.

"You think the old man forget the fish, ha? You think I don't know vat happens in the salmon's brain? You think I yust been sitting here vaiting for the fish to yump on board . . . asleep in my head. So?" He smacked his belly with his fist. This was wonderful. The moment was wonderful because the three of them were so warm together. Only the *Taage* was failing this moment, and suddenly Hamil was certain he knew the reason.

Craftily, making sure of their attention, Hamil lowered himself to the deck. He lay flat and with elaborate cunning placed his ear against the deck. He closed his eyes while he listened and then opened them again to be sure Carl and Bruno were still watching. He nodded his head and then pushed himself quickly to his feet. "So?" he said mysteriously. "So?"

"So . . . what?" said Carl.

"So I have two ignoramuses for a crew. So vun day before vee leave the shipyard I tell them to grease the propeller shaft bearings. And so they are so busy knocking each other's block heads off and thinkin' of everything else in the vorld but fishing, they forget to do like I say! And so the propeller turns and the shaft goes squeak-squeak-squeak, pound-pound-pound all the day long and the salmon say who is that damn fool that is so crazy to think vee can't hear? So he sends out varnings verever he goes, scaring

us to some other parts of the ocean before vee ever get a taste of
his hooks. They vant to know who is that damn fool who don't
know yust vun little sound you can hardly hear on the surface
is fifty times louder down below. And they think the damn
fool's name be Hamil Linder and they be right!"

"What a hell of a way to run a navy," Bruno said. Still laughing, Hamil reached out and ruffled Bruno's hair.

"Admiral Felkin," Hamil said, "go get the grease gun. Carl,
come. Vee move the hatch and by and by the *Taage* be in business again!"

It took almost an hour to prove Hamil's point. After the shaft
was greased and the hatch replaced there were still no salmon
for a while. Then they came, one, and then another, and finally
the gurdies to the bowlines, the main lines, and the tag lines
were all busy raising and lowering the spoons. Hamil worked the
port side and Carl the starboard while Bruno cleaned the salmon as they came aboard. By nightfall the *Taage*'s decks were
slippery with blood and scales and the sea gulls screamed with
delight overhead. For they had landed almost a ton.

"Maybe," said Hamil as he stood red-faced and smiling in the
clear evening, "maybe, Carl, your old man be not so dumb after
all, ya?" His fists were on his hips and his long legs spread to
catch the *Taage*'s roll. This was almost as happy a moment as
the one that had come earlier in the day.

Bruno handed a salmon down to Carl, who was icing them in
the hold.

"What do you say, Carl?" Bruno said. "We going to let him
get away with that kind of bragging—or is that just our pop?"

Corky Mullins regarded his situation as fat. He could reach
into the pockets of his dungarees and find more than two dollars in change, and he could reach into his mind and find a
friend. Both were strange and wonderful luxuries. Carl Linder
had given him a twenty-dollar bill for the mere use of his old

driver's license, and in so doing had torpedoed the best-laid plans of Johnnie Mae Swanson. Now there would be no more nonsense about marrying her just to keep the *Thunder Mug*. For Corky Mullins there was going to be a change of scenery.

He had hoarded Carl's twenty dollars until he considered the season just right. Then he filled the *Thunder Mug*'s rusty tanks with thirteen dollars' worth of gasoline, stocked her larder with four dollars' worth of rice, flour, beans, and coffee; and now there were still three dollars left over for future emergencies. Anyone could see that Corky Mullins was over the hump. He needed only a little luck with the salmon, even thirty or forty fish would do, and he would at last become a fisherman of means.

As he pumped the *Thunder Mug*'s bilge he envisioned it full of glistening, silvery salmon. He saw himself exhausted from hauling them aboard. He saw himself jumping on the salmon to pack them in the bilge; there were so many he would not have to care if he bruised a few. And he saw the *Thunder Mug* wallowing up to Paladini's dock at Point Reyes, almost awash with the burden of her fish. At each stroke of the pump Corky gathered strength, for he was not really pumping; he was handing up salmon to the scales. They were heavy slugs, every one of them—and finally the buyer on the dock was alternately peeling off five-dollar bills and patting Corky on the back, congratulating him on being such a fine fisherman.

After the load was delivered, the first thing to do was write a letter to Johnnie Mae Swanson. "Dear Johnnie Mae," the letter would begin, very formal. "Due to the fact I have caught so many fish I enclose a money order for umpteen dollars which pays off what I owe you on the vessel *Thunder Mug*. I do not intend to return to San Francisco ever, come hell or high water, and so you had better send me a receipt in care of this here place. Also, you may as well know I would not marry you for any reason whatsoever . . . so the hell with you." Resting at the pump a moment, Corky contemplated the ending of his letter and decided against a postscript. He would just sign it, "Yours very truly, C. Henry Mullins," and that would be enough.

He would take the letter to the dock, being careful not to brag too much as he passed through the crowds of admiring fishermen, and he would mail it right away. Then he would buy two cans of paint and go to work on the *Thunder Mug*. Blue would be a good color, or maybe white like Hamil Linder's *Taage*. Perhaps he would catch so many fish he could afford to run all the way up to Fort Bragg and there have the *Thunder Mug* hauled. Her bottom could be caulked and there would be no more pumping. A radio would be nice too. Probably there wouldn't be enough money left to buy a transmitter, but one of them little sets that had a fish band and also played music would be fine company on the nights when the *Thunder Mug* lay anchored in some quiet cove. Then Simon Lee, if he lay nearby with his *Alert*, could row over and they could listen to the music and jaw for hours about this and that—Simon Lee, the professor, was smart enough to enjoy a good gab—and the cabin would no longer be such a lonely place. Oh, it was going to be a fine summer thanks to Carl Linder's initial twenty dollars and of course the discovery of Simon Lee.

All his life Corky had been looking for a friend like Simon. The wonder was that they had never come together before, except to nod once in a while as they passed each other on the wharf or wave a hand as the *Alert* set out through the Golden Gate. But the very day Corky decided to spend his twenty dollars, their paths crossed in the grocery store where they were both buying supplies. There was a whole bag of potatoes on the floor and the man said that if they would buy the bag together and so take the whole thing away before the contents sprouted any longer roots, they could have it for half price. They instantly pooled their money, returned to the wharf, and divided the potatoes. In the process they fell to talking of their boats and fish, which was natural enough, but Simon's dog Tunie chose this time to chase a sea gull down the dock and fall in the bay. Before Simon could take off his boots and jacket, Corky dived into the cold filthy water beneath the pier. He came up gasping, his face smeared with oil. He seized the dog's neck with one hand and struck out for the nearest iron ladder. Finally he placed the shivering dog at his master's feet.

"A courageous rescue, for which thanks," Simon said. "But the little wretch doesn't deserve it."

"He never would've made it up them iron ladders," Corky said. Then as Simon wiped some of the water from the dog, Corky was glad he had made the plunge. He saw an expression in Simon's eyes he had almost forgotten. Gratitude. Corky Mullins had been able to do something for another person and that had not happened for a long time.

"It's fine company to have a dog," Corky said, kneeling. "By God, if I'm not goin' to pick me up a little mutt soon as I get enough fish to feed him."

"I'll admit there are times when even this animal is better than human company," Simon said. "But come on the *Alert* and dry out before you catch your death. We'll take the stove fuel cost out of Tunie's pay."

From the moment he stepped aboard the *Alert* Corky sensed their new friendship. Simon chewed on his pipe and listened while Corky talked through the rest of the afternoon. And when they grew hungry, Simon stuffed the belly of a ling cod with onions and bread crumbs. He poured some wine over it, placed a bay leaf on top, and baked it in the *Alert*'s tiny oven. And while they waited he allowed Corky to talk some more. At last all the loneliness left Corky, and when he had said everything he could think of to say, then Simon talked, and it was evident to Corky that Simon was also starved for things stronger than food.

Now as the *Thunder Mug* heaved drunkenly against the first dark swell beyond the Golden Gate, Corky was extremely happy. When the pumping was done he could think of the long afternoon and evening he had been with Simon and of the meeting they had planned for the following week in Drake's Bay. From then on they would fish together. The *Thunder Mug* and the *Alert* would be companion boats, running together during the day and anchoring side by side at night. If one broke down the other could always furnish a spare part, or at least a tow, and if one boat failed to find the fish, the other was bound to do so. Yet the important part, Corky thought happily, would be the nights, when there would be someone to talk to.

Fueled and victualed at last, the *Thunder Mug* had finally made her escape. She was off to sea in the night and the best of Johnnie Mae's lawyers could not attach her. Only one person knew the destination of Corky Mullins when he slipped his moorings. One man, a man who had thrown the lines on deck and called down softly, "So long, Corky . . . see you." The man was Simon Lee—friend.

Her old make-and-break engine fussed the *Thunder Mug* out and beyond the sweeping light on Bonita Point. The ocean accepted the little boat and the man within her reeling cabin. Corky was so happy to feel living water beneath the deck, so busy thinking and planning, he ignored the full Pacific. There was only darkness beyond the spray on the cabin windows, and a man of sixty-four who could still think of the future, a man who had a friend, had no need of darkness. To hell with the rising wind!

CHAPTER — — — — — — — — — — — *II*

T HE "CAPELLA" LAY STRAINING AT HER AN-
chor beneath the black cliffs at Drake's Bay. Barney Schriona
stood in the darkness on the foredeck studying the angle of his
anchor chain and measuring the placement of the shore lights
against the *Capella*'s rigging. A smart northwest wind had come
with the night and Barney was uneasy. Sometimes he was fairly
sure the lights were moving, which would mean the *Capella* was
dragging anchor, and then again he was certain the lights remained fixed. The *Capella* had the best anchor money could
buy, but then no one could ever be too careful about anchors.
Anchors had given seamen sleepless nights for thousands of
years, and though there were always new and guaranteed types
—guaranteed to keep a boat or a battleship where it ought to be
no matter what the wind—just the same too many vessels wound
up on the beach every year.

Barney hunched his back against the wind and watched the
black water hiss along the *Capella*'s hull. Thanks to the cliffs,
there was very little motion in Drake's Bay despite the wind.
The *Capella* hardly moved and Barney was grateful he was not
at sea. It was not a real storm, nothing dangerous for a good

boat, just a rotten wind that would make dragging the bottom an uncomfortable waste of time in the morning. Barney tried to light his cigar, but after the wind doused two matches he gave up in disgust. Then he looked at the anchor chain again, trying to take some real interest in it though he knew very well the angle was perfect. It was not, he finally admitted, the wind that had forced him to the deck in the first place. It was Rosanna's damned chapel.

She should have known it might be used by a man like Hamil Linder who would have some very strong ideas about what he should say to God, and that such a man would say a lot of things in a voice that could be heard all too clearly through the thin bulkhead between the galley and the chapel. Rosanna should have known that listening to another man pray could be a very embarrassing experience. It was like looking into his open heart. And if he was a deeply troubled man, one you loved, then hearing him was all the worse. No man with any honesty could sit in the warm galley and pretend he could not hear. So the cold deck was a better place, at least until Hamil finished—or was he going to be in there all night?

As the wind began to rise in the late afternoon, Hamil had brought his *Taage* into Drake's Bay and anchored within hailing distance of the *Capella*. After a while he rowed over in the *Taage's* skiff. They made coffee and talked as they always had talked. But now, thinking back on it, Barney realized Hamil had come for more than a talk with him. When they had sat down in the galley, the silences between them had been longer than usual and Hamil had kept pounding one fist into the palm of his other hand almost continuously, as if the motion would help him to speak.

"What the hell is the matter with you?" Barney finally had asked. "You're worse nervous than some old woman."

"I be in a little trouble, Barney . . ." Hamil had said, so lightly that at first it was impossible to believe he was serious.

"If it's money, get off my ship. I ain't got none." It was a silly thing to say, of course. Hamil Linder could have anything in the world of Barney's on demand. It wasn't money he was after. It was something even harder to find.

"I have tried to think some things out and I don't get anyvare at all," Hamil had gone on. "You know I am not a Catholic."

"So what? Lots of people ain't Catholics. You ain't going to get religion on me?"

"No. It be much too late for that, but there are some things to be said, things I vant to say, that vill be much clearer if I come right out and say them. . . ."

"You don't make no sense. What the hell you beatin' around the bushes about?"

"Vell . . ." Hamil had taken a long breath then and kept his eyes on the deck. He had looked only at the deck and his coffee cup. "Vell . . . Barney Schriona . . . if you please . . . I vould like to use Rosanna's chapel for a little time. . . ."

"Go right ahead. No charge."

"Not being a Catholic, like I say, I'm not sure how to begin."

"If Rosanna was here she'd take you through all the devotions step by step and love it. But not me. I forget most of the stuff anyway. Go on in and kneel on the little bench in front of the altar and run your own show."

"You sure it's all right?"

"Why not? Us Catholics don't own God. I haven't been in there for so long I'm afraid to go now. A thunderbolt might sink the boat if I did. But I'll wait right here for you." That had been a mistake, planning to wait in the galley, for Hamil did his praying in a heavy voice that was better suited to fighting the wind. Just rattling coffee cups could be carried on only so long.

Hamil first had said a rough version of the Lord's Prayer; very rough, Barney thought, with strange lapses into Scandahoovian silence. Then he had opened his heart and Barney had heard more than he wanted to hear before he had had the good sense to escape.

". . . now yesterday," Hamil had said, ". . . it happened my son vas close to me, like he has never been since he vas a small boy. Sir, he be the same as he vas the time his mother lived . . . and it make a vunderful feeling I think for both of us. Sir, I like to keep this feeling and I am afraid every minute I vill do something to drive it away . . . because I am the father and I must teach him . . . and I must love him . . . and I must never be veek . . . alvays strong . . . so? Because vat reason is there for my living if I cannot do this vun thing? Sir, it has to be said that I lost Carl a long time ago and now if there is some chance to get him back . . . I do not vant to make the same mistakes. Now I think you vill understand all this even if I don't say it yust right . . . because Sir, you vere a father and . . ."

The salt in his eyes, Barney had thought, was not coming from the Pacific Ocean and the unlighted cigar in his mouth had suddenly tasted rotten. The hard brush of the wind against the galley windows he had welcomed, because it had been a perfect excuse to go on deck. You never could tell about an anchor.

Now, though the wind had penetrated his heavy shirt and chilled him for minutes, he waited until he saw Hamil return to the galley. Then he walked casually along the deck and stepped in the door. He paused just inside to light his cigar and when it flared he sat down as close to the stove as he could get.

"It's blowin' pretty good now," Barney said. "I hope you've got plenty of scope on the *Taage*'s hook."

"Ya, plenty of scope and Carl be vatching."

"He gettin' along all right with the salmon?"

"Sure. Maybe you don't believe it, but he really be a fine fisherman, Barney."

"Why shouldn't I believe it?"

"Vell sometimes . . . I thought . . . maybe people get the wrong idea. Carl . . . he seem to change a lot lately."

"How about that other guy? You still got him with you?"

"Ya. Bruno. He be a fine fellow too."

"You goin' to keep him on? You don't really need him, do you?"

"Not yust for fishing—no. But I think I leave him stay for so long as he vants. Now I say good night, Barney." Hamil buttoned the collar of his shirt and turned to leave. Barney thought he stood a little straighter than when he first came on board. He seemed completely at ease and there was new life in his eyes. Rosanna would have to be told about Hamil. After all, the chapel was her idea and she would be pleased to know it was being used again.

Barney held the skiff's painter as Hamil lowered himself over the *Capella's* side.

"You picked a hell of a night for a row," Barney yelled. Sitting in the bouncing skiff, Hamil looked up at him and smiled.

"Good vind, Barney. It makes me feel good. Cast avay!"

"You . . ." said Kelsey, crooking a finger at General Ball. "You come here." General Ball left the dock committee and shuffled reluctantly toward the car in which Kelsey was sitting. Though the car was his own and certainly displayed no marks of authority, Kelsey knew that General Ball knew, or at least guessed, his identity. Men like General Ball were possessed of a hidden warning system. Drunk or sober, it functioned with remarkable efficiency, and enabled them to spot official trouble almost before it happened. Behind General Ball, Kelsey was not in the least surprised to see his comrades rise from the timber on which they had been sitting, stretch themselves, yawn, and then move away in separate directions, until suddenly they were all gone. Kelsey understood perfectly why they had found it unnecessary to exchange a single farewell.

"Your name's Ball, isn't it?"

"Agreed," the General said. His dirty fingers fumbled with the collar of his shirt and then fluttered vaguely upward to straighten his hat. He sniffed in open suspicion, and his red eyes searched Kelsey's face and body anxiously for more certain identification.

"Maybe you can do something for me," Kelsey said.

"I was just leavin' . . . in a hurry to get home."

"You haven't got a home."

"I was just this very minute going to an appointment. Friend of mine is waiting to give me a job." General Ball started away suddenly. Kelsey allowed him two steps.

"Come back here." The General stopped and returned to stand before Kelsey, displaying his best persecution face. Kelsey ignored it. He had seen such faces a thousand times before. There was no need to show a badge. General Ball's face was indication enough that he knew Kelsey had a badge to show. "How much money do you have in your pocket, Ball?"

"I just this minute loaned my last ten dollars."

"Nuts. You haven't seen ten dollars altogether in ten years. How long since you been locked up on a vag charge, General?"

General Ball hesitated.

"I never—"

Kelsey pulled a scrap of paper from his coat pocket.

"How does January twelfth sound? Vagrancy-drunk-disorderly-disturbing the peace?"

"Maybe it was my brother. He looks almost like me. He's a problem, that fellow. Why—"

"I understand." Kelsey nodded his head sympathetically. "Now there's just one thing more I'd like to know, Ball. And unless you want a few nights in the tank, you'd better give me a straight answer. You've spent the best part of your life standing on this wharf. Who is this fellow Henry Mullins? I hear they call him Corky."

"Corky Mullins?" An expression of surprise and then one of great relief chased each other across the General's face. "He's a fisherman—that is, he has a boat."

"I know that. Where is he?"

"Down at the end of the wharf where he always ties up."

"You know damn well he isn't. Remember your financial condition and the tank, Ball. You know everything that goes on around here."

"Come to think of it, he has gone. First time in a long time."

"When and where?"

"It must have been night before last. I took my regular look around yesterday morning and he was gone all right."

"Where did he go?"

"Now listen, I ain't a swami."

"Start being one and find out by tonight. Have you seen his car?"

"He ain't got a car."

"No? Why not?"

"Corky couldn't have, bein' broke. He's always broke. His boat don't even belong to him."

"Who does it belong to?"

"Some woman. She's sweet on Corky. A regular sireen."

"Did she buy Corky a new Studebaker?"

"It don't sound reasonable. It couldn't've happened without me knowin' about it."

"Are you and Corky Mullins friends?"

"No. Corky don't drink so he ain't got no friends. Wait a minute . . ." General Ball snapped his fingers. "He's got one friend. Just one. Him and that professor fellow, Simon Lee, been together a lot lately."

"Where's this man Lee?"

"On his boat. She's the *Alert*. Next wharf over. Too rough outside for ling cod, the waters has got to be clear green, you know—so he's been layin' in. He's smart, that fella. Used to be a regular professor."

Kelsey put his car in gear.

"You find out where Corky went," Kelsey said. "I'll be back to see you." He eased the car ahead a few feet, then stopped it.

Reaching in his pocket for a cigar, he held it out the window without looking back at General Ball. Almost instantly he felt the cigar being pulled from his hand.

"Thank you very much, Chief!"

"Smoke slow, General. It'll last longer." Kelsey released the clutch and the car moved ahead. He turned toward the street and parked two blocks down near the union headquarters. He got out of the car, rolled up the windows, and locked it carefully. Two years in Auto Theft had convinced him no one could look quite so foolish as a cop illegally deprived of his own. He walked through the wooden gate and then along the line of Italian crab boats that had been pulled out of the water for painting. He passed a group of older men who were sitting in the sun outside union headquarters. They were speaking only Italian so he went on. He paused a moment at the bridge connecting the finger wharves with the land. Then, jingling the change in his pants pocket, he walked thoughtfully between the boxes and nets and barrels scattered along the pier until he came to the *Alert*. He breathed deeply of the smells around him and hoped he was not completely wasting his time.

A man was working in the trolling pit of the *Alert*. Kelsey noticed that a rooster and a small black dog followed the man's every movement. He was winding steel wire off one spool and transferring it to another on the opposite side of the boat. At regular intervals he would stop the wire, take up a ball hammer, and carefully pound a small piece of brass around the wire. Then he would move the wire a little farther and pound on another. He was sucking furiously at his pipe and seemed completely absorbed in his work.

"Mind telling me what those brass lugs are for?" Kelsey asked.

"Not at all." Simon Lee kept his head bent to his work. "They're called line stops. Very ingenious."

"What do they do?" Still without looking at the dock, Simon held up a piece of black rubber cord about twelve inches long.

There was a large metal snap at one end, something like a safety pin, Kelsey thought, and from the other end a long leader led to a brass spoon.

"The stops keep the spoons where they ought to be on the line when we're trolling," Simon said. "I carry them about a fathom apart. As the wire goes down you just snap them on between each pair of line stops. When they come up with the fish, you just unsnap them. It took years to develop although it's really very simple."

Kelsey waited until Simon had pounded on a few more of the line stops. Then, when he paused to refill his pipe, Kelsey sat down on the dock.

"You happen to know a fellow named Corky Mullins?"

"Yes, I do. As a matter of fact I was going for salmon with him." Simon hesitated in his puffing and then looked up at Kelsey for the first time.

"Why do you want to know about Corky? Are you a friend of his?"

"No. I'm just trying to save him some trouble." Simon Lee looked Kelsey over very carefully.

"If you're thinking of putting a plaster on his boat, I'd suggest you forget about it. Corky's gone—to a South Sea Island."

Kelsey laughed. "They always do. What's the name of the island this time?" Simon Lee spit in the water and turned angrily back to his work.

"Fiddler's Green!"

"Just where is that?"

Simon sucked so violently on his pipe Kelsey could hardly understand him. "Look it up. It's right on your chart, Sheriff—if you have the proper chart. You can tell Johnnie Mae Swanson that Corky will no doubt write her from there!"

Kelsey stood up and sighed. Was he looking for a debt-ridden fisherman named Corky Mullins or a smart operator named Bruno Felkin? It had become an effort to stay anywhere near

Bruno's track—if there was a track. Missing Persons must have made a mistake. They had the wrong Mullins, and even if they had the right one, by what stretch of circumstance could this Mullins have anything to do with Bruno Felkin? Maybe it was Felkin who had gone to this "Fiddler's Green"—wherever in the hell that could be. It was a pain to have your leg pulled, when you knew damn well you deserved it.

His head bent, still jingling the coins in his pocket, Kelsey walked slowly back to his car. He took his time driving home and was so deep in thought he narrowly avoided two accidents. He put his car in the garage, forgot to lock it, and trudged up the narrow back stairs of his house. He walked through the kitchen until he came to the dining room and, passing through it, was rather surprised to find himself sitting down in his easy chair without bothering to pick up the newspaper.

His wife came into the room, smiled, and started toward him. Then she stopped and looked at him quizzically.

"What ails you?" Kelsey asked.

"What's the matter with you? Cold in the head?" Kelsey reached for his head vaguely and found that he still wore his hat. He removed it and put it beside the chair as if he was ashamed of it.

"I guess I'm going crazy all right," he said. "I wish I was Charlie Chan." He sighed heavily.

"What's gone wrong?" his wife asked.

"This Addleheim case. I get nowhere and it's important right now that I do get somewhere, if we ever expect to get the appointment to the attorney's office."

"If it's so bad you wear your hat in the house and don't know it, let's forget it. We want a pension, not ulcers—or have you changed your mind?"

"I haven't too much mind left. No mail from the state, I suppose?"

"No. I'm sorry."

"So am I." Kelsey rubbed his eyes and then looked at his wife with a new interest.

"I wish you wouldn't look at me like that," she said.

"Why not?"

"You make me nervous. Please forget about Mr. Addleheim while you're home, darling. You always have before."

"I know. But it's really a man named Felkin I'm thinking about. Let me ask you something . . . I'm at a point where I'll take a lead from anything. What's the minimum time a woman can be faithful to a man?"

"Darling! You are tired. Such a silly question."

"What would you say the time was? Come on now." Kelsey was astonished at the annoyance in his voice.

"I couldn't possibly tell you—nor could anyone else. It would depend on the man and the woman. It might be forever or it might be only a few hours. For heaven's sake, whatever got you off on such a subject?"

"A girl named Connie Thatcher. If I could account for her behavior I'd know whether Bruno Felkin was alive or dead, and if he was alive I think I could find him, and if I could find him I think I could know who killed Sam Addleheim."

"If you're depending on a woman's behavior, dear, you'd better try something else. You should know better."

"I do know better. But it's the only thing I have left. If Felkin just ran away and left her I don't think she'd act the way she does. And if he was dead, I just have a hunch she'd take off herself, or behave differently somehow . . . not take up with another man right away. She isn't the kind. Anyway, that's what I keep telling myself. So what's left? From the way she acts I'd be willing to bet Bruno Felkin is right close at hand somewhere. It's just a hunch, but I could swear to it. I wouldn't be surprised if he knew all about this other fellow. Like she said, probably he's watching her from the moon."

Kelsey's wife turned away from him suddenly and started off toward the kitchen.

"Where are you going?"

"To get you a cold beer. They say it calms the insane and is good for ulcers . . . and if I have to follow you through a woman's emotions with all the whys and wherefores, I'll need one."

Kelsey unbuttoned his vest and bent wearily to unlace his shoes. "You'd better get two then."

CHAPTER — — — — — — — — — — — *12*

THROUGH JUNE AND JULY, THE "TAAGE"
fished for salmon. As the fish moved north Hamil followed
them, first to Point Arena and then as far as Fort Bragg. When
they were in port Bruno did his best to remain inconspicuous,
but as the season wore on he found it increasingly difficult. The
wariness with which he should have regarded everything and
everyone was collapsing.

When the northwest wind was blowing too hard outside and
the fleet stayed in a quiet harbor, the boats tied four and five together, like shoes along a threshold. Then the men who manned
them became a company instead of individual units. They clambered over each other's boats to reach the shore. They borrowed
tools from each other, and gear. They exchanged advice and
woes and cursed the fish buyers, gathering first on one boat and
then another to do so. They laughed a good deal and slept
when they were in the mood, not caring for the time of day, and
in the evening the smoke from their galley stoves laced the thick-
ets of masts and outrigger poles together. There were other
new men in the fleet besides Bruno, and gradually each man became a part of the company.

Bruno knew that he was liked. It was hard to remain cautious when other men greeted you in the morning with open enthusiasm. At first it was hard to believe—this feeling of belonging. Somehow it relaxed the mind, perhaps dangerously, but there was nothing to be done about it. Here in Fort Bragg, a good two hundred miles above San Francisco, escape could simply be arranged by walking off the *Taage.* The town was small and the local police probably couldn't catch a cold. For the mere price of a plane ticket a man could go north to Seattle and then to Canada, or New York, or Mexico, or anywhere in the world. And in most of the world they were not actively looking for the man who killed Sam Addleheim. They would have other things to think about. Then Connie could be sent for if she wanted to come—or if she didn't there could always be someone else.

Yet the desire to escape was mixed up with a lot of other things. There was Hamil. There was the *Taage,* and there was the sea. It was an all-around screwy feeling—like being stuck in the mud. It was wake up every morning determined to get going, and then find at the end of the day you hadn't done a thing about going. For why? Here was a wide-open door and you weren't running through it. Delay, delay . . . and procrastinate some more. For why? Except the idea of being alone, really alone again, running and hiding, was harder and harder to think about. You were kidding yourself that all this was good for you. It could get you the gas chamber.

Except for one little flare-up from Carl, even the Western Sales Company presented no real problems. The idea of Carl having trouble with his teeth had worked out first-class. Regardless of the *Taage*'s location along the coast, he now had to make regular visits to a dentist in San Francisco. Carl didn't seem to mind too much although he had started a little rhubarb in the beginning. But you straightened him out in a hurry with a few neat words.

"Do exactly like I've told you, or you'll *really* have some trouble with your teeth. I'd hate to muss up that pretty face again. Now you make your deliveries just like you always done, make sure Connie is all right, and then get back here with your pop. Keep your mouth shut and don't flash any money around. By the way, what are you doing with your dough?"

"I manage to get rid of it. That's a sweet racket you got, Bruno. Don't think you're foolin' anybody. When are you going to do some work on it yourself?"

"I'm taking a vacation and I told you not to ask questions."

"Have it your way—but if that's the way it's going to be, you don't pay your help enough."

"If you're tryin' for a little squeeze, Carl, forget it. I been squeezed by experts. Now grow up. When I feel like giving you a raise, you'll get one. In the meantime let me congratulate you for one thing. Lately you been treatin' your old man somewheres like he deserves. See that you keep it up."

"For a little guy, you give a lot of orders, Bruno."

"You got a lot to learn."

That's all there was to it. Carl did just like he was supposed to after that. He kept on laughing like he didn't give a damn, but he wasn't fooling Bruno Felkin.

The times Carl was away in San Francisco were the most satisfactory days and nights a man could ask for. Being alone with Hamil on the *Taage* was really something. Going to sea, just the two of you, working from dark to dark, seemed to knock all sense of time out of your head. It seemed like you had fished ever since you could remember, and Sam Addleheim, even Connie, became hard-to-remember people. At night, when the salmon were cleaned and iced down, you were the one who did the cooking. Not good. Not bad either, by God.

"You come to be quite a cook," Hamil said that one swell night you were sitting outside on the bulwark, smoking and having coffee.

"It's all in the good book . . . I'm just one lesson ahead of the stove," you told him. Then Hamil put his head back and laughed and you noticed again how massive his features were— the big nose, the heavy gray eyebrows, the mouth that almost always said something worth listening to. It was a moment to remember, and if just then Hamil had said, "Give up all your plans and stay here with me . . ." well, that would have been it. Being with Hamil was getting to be more and more like having a father, and for Bruno Felkin that was a lot.

"The albacore vill be showing up any day now, Bruno, and so vee be ready for them," Hamil said. "Ya, I think vee go south to San Francisco tomorrow. That kind of fishing I think you like very much."

"What's so good about it?"

"It is more excitement and I think you like excitement, Bruno Felkin. But it is not so very comfortable."

"I forgot what it's like to be comfortable. If I sat in a real chair I think I would fall out of it. What's so rough about going for albacore?"

"Vee stay at sea for maybe eight or ten days—fifty, a hundred miles off shore. In little boats like the *Taage,* if the vind comes and you are caught out there, it is not so nice. You must be very careful about the weather or you have a long svim."

"If you're going, I want to go."

"What about your business? You be avay a long time now." It was the first time Hamil had ever mentioned your business directly and even in the half-light it was easy to see there was more than curiosity in his eyes. "I think you must have a very funny business, Bruno."

"It don't give me any bother right now. I got things fixed so it sort of runs itself."

Hamil's big hands caressed the *Taage*'s bulwark cap. He seemed about to say something and then for a long time there was only the slosh of the waves against the hull.

"I think maybe you be in some trouble, Bruno Felkin," he finally said. "Maybe you vould like to tell me about it."

Tell Hamil about Sam Addleheim? You not only wanted to tell him about Sam, but about everything since you was a kid in South St. Paul. It would have been like taking a bath to tell Hamil, to explain to him what it was like to be kicked around a lifetime, to tell him about the long days and nights when your old lady and your old man were drunk—sitting in the kitchen with a line of stinking home-brew bottles in front of them and never caring a damn about what went on until they ran out of brew and money.

It would be like taking a physic to tell Hamil what it was like to beg bones from the stockyard polacks, gnaw what meat there was left on them, and then take the bones back to that kitchen and make your own soup . . . while your old man and old lady thought it was the funniest thing they ever saw. And later when they fought as they always wound up doing, and either the neighbors or the police came around to quiet things down, Hamil should know what it was like to be nine years old and hold your old lady's head while she puked all over the back porch.

Hamil should know what it was like to be ninety when you were really nine, to be sick and have nobody hear your crying because there was so much singing and hollering going on in the kitchen nobody could hear anything as far as the next room—and wouldn't give a damn if they did. To tell Hamil what it was like to have the other kids sing-song verses they made up about your old man brushing his teeth in beer, which was almost true, and how your mother was called a witch-bitch because her hair was always falling in her eyes, would be a great relief.

To tell Hamil how you ran away to sleep under the railroad bridge just outside South St. Paul and only come home when they brought you home to see what was left of your old man and old lady after they got just too drunk one night and swiped a car supposedly to look for you . . . and hit a streetcar before they'd gone three blocks—those were things to tell Hamil about.

You didn't cry then, and you'd never cried since because all the tears were permanently dried up long before. Hamil should hear about that, and finally the county home and the industrial school, and he would finally understand about the business and Sam Addleheim.

But he wasn't going to hear. It should never be forgotten, no matter how close you felt to him, that Hamil was, and always had been, on the other side of a wall. He didn't hear it that night and he never would.

"No. I never been in any trouble," you told him. "Whatever give you that idea?"

"Your face. I think you look much older than you be. Your mouth twist sometimes like a man who be afraid he say the wrong things. You are fighting all the time."

"Who isn't? You don't fight and the world walks all over you. You fight the fish buyers, the weather, and the sea . . . so what the hell's the difference?"

"I can vin, Bruno Felkin. So I am not afraid." You thought that over, but the moment of wanting to tell Hamil everything, the moment of weakness, was suddenly over. The urge to slip was gone—and a good thing, too. This pause away from everything was just a little section of a life that was really going to amount to something. It would pay to stick around just a little while longer and then take off. Why louse up a good thing—as you had almost done once before—just because you happened to like an old fisherman? Treat him like Connie. Never let him get inside the real Bruno and things would click along all right.

"What you need is a cup of coffee," you told him then. "I'll go down and whip one up for you. You Scandahoovians get to thinkin' crazy without your coffee."

After that Hamil never asked any questions, not even on the long run down the coast to San Francisco.

By anchoring overnight in Drake's Bay, Hamil broke the long run from Fort Bragg. Barney Schriona was in from his

day's dragging and when you went aboard the *Capella* he
showed you something his net had brought up from the sea.

"I was making a tow in forty fathoms last week," Barney said.
"Just inside of Spanish Shoals, where I been a thousand times
and it's all good bottom. All at once I hit a hell of a snag. I can
tell it's a big one and I think the cable is going to break to say
nothing of the net tore all to hell. I'll tell you this bottom
fishin' for the prices they pay is the most heartbreakin' fishin'
a man could do. Anyhow, I swing around, work the cable in
slow, and finally the net gets free of whatever it is. It ain't tore
too bad and I'm feelin' pretty good when one of the boys finds
this jammed in the net. It's all wound up in a ball."

Barney held out that wrinkled cap that had once been white.
Both you and Hamil had a good look.

"Look on the inside," Barney said. Hamil turned the cap over
in his hand and at first there was nothing special to see. Then
you both made out two roughly drawn letters, but they were
so faded it was impossible to be sure of them. "Don't that look
like a C and a M to you, Hamil?"

"Ya . . . it does a little look that vay."

"I never thought much about it till I run into Simon Lee in
San Francisco. He says to me that fella Corky Mullins took off
one night in that tub of his and ain't been heard from since."

"How long ago vas that?"

"About a month . . . maybe six weeks. Simon, he looked at
the cap a long time chewin' on his pipe and when he finally
come to make up his mind it was a C and a M I never seen a man
so low. Was they special friends?"

"I don't know. They both be funny fellows—all the time
alone. Sometimes they come on board the *Taage* yust to talk."

"Of course he could be sittin' in some quiet harbor. The wind
could just have blowed it off his head." Hamil put the cap down
on the galley table.

"Vas there anything else in the net?"

"No. But there was that big heavy snag that could have been his boat. I marked my chart 'wreck' right where I hit, anyway."

It was Corky's cap, all right. You should have been glad to see it like it was, because it sure eliminated a guy who was inclined to be over-curious. But somehow, these days, you weren't glad to see it. In the next life, if there was one that would allow some spare time, you might think about devoting some of the Felkin talents to this whole fish business. It could stand some straightening out. Some geniusing of the brain for poor suckers like Corky. Once you got the picture it made you sick.

The *Taage* lay at Fisherman's Wharf in San Francisco. Her engine had barely cooled before the radio that had announced only discouraging reports for so long took on a new tone. The voices of the men at sea were full of suppressed excitement as they talked of a flash run of salmon outside.

"It be too late," Hamil said cautiously, ". . . too late to amount for very much and they are excited about really nothing. Some fellows, they catch saloon fish, you know, and ven they get maybe five or ten on board something happens to their eyes and their heads. They hope so bad those five or ten fish turn into fifty or a hundred they really think they see them. It is alvays that vay with fishermen."

Yet as he listened, Hamil grew restless. Bruno watched him pace the deck. He would sit on the bulwark for a few minutes, pretending to ignore the radio, then he would climb up on the dock to look toward the Golden Gate; then he would come down to the *Taage* again and apparently lose himself in a study of her rigging. The radio chattered continuously. Hamil went into the deckhouse and turned the volume down. He came out again, circled the hatch slowly, and then made another circle at a slightly faster pace.

"Talk, talk—all the time talk!" he said. "By golly, how can

they be catching so many fish if they talk so much?" Laughing within himself, certain he knew what Hamil would eventually do, Bruno lay on the hatch in the sun and followed Hamil's nervous movements with his eyes.

"If it's just so much talk, why not turn the radio off?"

Hamil stopped in his tracks. He stared unhappily at the sky. "Vell . . . vell, maybe . . . maybe vee miss something."

"Ah."

"I yust listen a little more, then I turn the damn thing off."

"Quit kidding yourself. You just listen a little more and we go to sea. I'm beginning to know." Hamil leaned over Bruno. There was a smile in his eyes as he pointed an accusing finger at him.

"You begin to get too smart, Bruno Felkin. I think you begin to understand fishermen."

"It's worse than that. It's getting so I'm feeling the same way." Hamil scratched his chin as he looked up and down the dock.

"If Carl vas here I might be tempted to go. He should show up by now."

"Dentists take a long time these days. You can't always get an appointment. Will you for the love of God sit down and relax?" Hamil sat down obediently, but only for a moment. A distant voice came through on the radio and he almost ran into the cabin to turn the volume up again. The voice spoke of whales and birds working.

"Of course vee could go vithout Carl," Hamil said. ". . .yust for a few days . . . long enough to prove vee are foolish to leave the dock."

"Ah."

Hamil looked across the water at the ice dock. A huge green trailer was parked just above a boat. Just ahead of the trailer was the truck which carried the ice-crushing machine. The men on the truck were dragging three-hundred-pound blocks to the crusher. The high-speed metal teeth seized the ice block and in a matter of seconds pulverized the ice and shot it under pressure down a long rubber hose into the boat's hatch. The noise of the crusher was tremendous and even at a distance the shouts of the men handling the ice and the hose could not be heard. As block after block roared down the hose the frantic energy of the machine seemed to increase.

"Of course it vould be necessary to take on some ice," Hamil said thoughtfully. "A ton, anyvay, maybe two."

Bruno sat up. "Look," he said. "Let's get the ice and go to sea before you drive us both nuts."

"Maybe vee make yust one more salmon trip before vee rig for albacore. I think you got a good idea there, Bruno."

"Don't blame me for it. You were going to do it anyway."

Hamil moved the *Taage* over to the ice dock as fast as he could get the engine started and Bruno could free the lines. He ordered two tons and the very demand seemed to renew his energy. Bruno put on boots, rubber pants, and gloves, and lowered himself into the *Taage*'s hold. It was familiar, pleasant work now. He removed some of the bin boards and Hamil passed down the heavy black hose to him. The truck men started the crusher and as the ice shot down Bruno directed the thick stream of flying ice equally into the bins, stamping it down occasionally with his boots. On deck Hamil maneuvered the hose so that Bruno could more easily swing the end fore and aft. The hose shuddered and whipped against Bruno's body like an angry python and only the loudest shouts could be heard above the noise.

As Bruno moved the hose from the midship bins to the after bins, there was a pause in the flow of ice as the men on the truck moved a new line of blocks to the crusher. Resting the hose on his knee, Bruno was reaching in his shirt pocket for a cigarette when he saw something on the dock that stopped his hand dead still. Carl was on the dock, and he was talking to a man in a gray suit. There was something about the man, an air, the way he bulged in certain places, the way he stood, the way his gray hat sat so exactly level on his head; for a moment Bruno could not explain what he saw in the man that was so unusual. but he instantly ducked down in the hold and turned his back. Jesus Christ! He was twenty feet from a cop. And a good one too. Bruno knew it as surely as he knew Carl had made some kind of a mistake. The man's face was as much a giveaway as if he wore a badge on his nose.

Bruno turned his head just far enough for a quick look. Their mouths were moving, all right, but the damned ice crusher drowned out their words. The man's hand came out of his pocket. He fondled a coin, then put it back in his pocket. Just as he looked toward Bruno the ice started down again. Thank God. Bruno bent low over the hose. His mind raced with the sound of the crusher and his heart seemed to match the pulsating hose. How come? How *come*? How did that flatfoot ever wind up down here? What gave him a lead? Jesus! Even Connie didn't know for sure where Bruno Felkin was except Carl said he had told her about a boat. That loud, stupid Carl!

As the ice shot out ahead of him a dank smell rose from the after hold. It was the same as the smell of a prison. McNeil Island. Jesus, Bruno, you should have beat it when you had the chance!

When the crusher ground to a stop, Bruno took his time pushing the hose back up to Hamil. He kept his face turned away from the dock, and once Hamil held all of the hose he ducked back quickly into the after bin. He whipped off his gloves and his hand searched his face. Was there enough change? The two-day beard, the heavy sunburn, the long hair might help. But not enough to fool a really smart cop—just not enough.

He managed to get a bin board stuck in its slot so that he could take a long time freeing it. Then he crawled back on the ice, pounding it down with his hands—anything to take more time.

"Bruno! You goin' to stay down there all day?" It was Hamil calling to him and he had used his name. "Carl is here. Vee go now!"

"I got another stuck board. Just a second."

Bruno heard the engine start. If he could only delay just a little longer. He moved forward along the bins until he could just see the wharf over the hatch combing. His breathing slowed. The man was gone. Carl, still dressed in his shore suit, was letting go the lines and Hamil was at the wheel.

Bruno ducked back to the after bins again and leaned against the boards. It hadn't happened. The old Bruno Felkin luck was still holding, but it would take quite a while to stop this shaking.

As the *Taage* headed out into the bay and turned for the Golden Gate, Bruno replaced the hatch boards and stowed the tarpaulin cover. He took off his rubber boots and pants and hung them on the after side of the wheelhouse. He lit a cigarette and waited for Carl. He fought down the urge to follow Carl into the cabin. To do so would mean passing Hamil at the wheel—and he didn't want to see Hamil just now if it could be helped. This was a time to genius the brain again, get back in the groove without any peculiar outside influences.

When Carl came on deck after changing his clothes, Bruno was calm again. He told himself that Felkin was back in business. A close one like that cop could sure change a man's thinking in a hurry.

"Carl. Come 'ere."

"Hello, stranger." Carl was smiling. He was jaunty, the ironhead. He'd just had himself a hell of a fine time on shore. "Pop says you two had a good trip down."

"Never mind. Who was that guy on the dock?"

"What guy?"

"The one you were talking to when we were taking ice."

"I dunno. Some joker. He wanted to sell me some insurance."

"Insurance?"

"Yeah. What about it? What you so het up about?"

"What kind of insurance, wise guy?"

"Car insurance. Anything wrong with that?"

"Since when you got a car?"

"I bought one. I guess I forgot to tell you."

"I guess you did. How did you manage to get a car?"

"I paid for it. With money I got for runnin' your racket. Now mind your own damned business. I don't want any more part of it anyway."

"How could you register a car when you're on probation? Ain't the laws workin' in this state any more?"

"It's in Corky Mullins' name. He was willing for a small consideration."

"He don't need it no more, but maybe that's all to the good. So you register the car in another guy's name and this fellow on the dock tries to sell you insurance. How come?"

"He saw me drive up and park it in the lot behind the union hall. He said he always keeps his eye open for drivers of new cars. It's smart business."

"You bet it's smart. So you got a new car and you drive it around wherever you feel like. I suppose it's a Cadillac."

"No. Studebaker convertible. I been wantin' a car like that ever since I can remember. There's no reason to tell Pop, though. He might get mad and tell the judge, and with my year not up I'd be in a hell of a fix."

"You're *in* a hell of a fix. So this fellow just walks up to you and says he's an insurance salesman and you are a big shot and don't tell him the car really don't belong to you."

"I don't see where it makes any difference. I didn't buy any insurance from him. I told him I already got some, what the state requires. What the hell do you care anyway? Or have you heard from Connie and it's eatin' you?"

"What's Connie got to do with it?"

"I been takin' her out a little. I like her . . . and I think she likes me."

"You been takin' *Connie* out in that car?"

"Yeah."

There it was! The whole damned thing. It was always the things you never dreamed would happen that did happen, and that's why working alone was the only way to be sure of anything. Nobody else ever thought. This bird-brain who don't know Connie is sure being watched for another reason takes her for a spin in his new toy. So sixteen cops that got nothing better to do open their eyes and follow right along for the ride. They want to know who is this guy with Felkin's girl and how come. Great. Things were going to start happening and they would have to happen fast. It was just a question of how much they knew already.

"This insurance salesman ask you many questions?"

"No. He just said he's around the wharf quite a bit and if I needed another policy he'd be glad to take care of it for me."

"What did he say his name was?"

"He didn't say."

"So. An insurance salesman who don't introduce himself and hand you a card right off. Great! And you fall for it. It so happens your insurance friend is a cop."

"What makes you think so?"

"I got a nose and I can smell. I don't think—I know he's a cop."

THERE WERE TWO WAYS TO HANDLE THE thing, Bruno decided, the easy way and the hard. But if you were con-wise, if you had been around and were not a tinhorn, a little figuring and foresight plainly showed that what appeared to be the easy way was really worthless. The pens were full of men who had tried the easy way, who thought that all you had to do if you were in trouble was to beat it to some other part of the country and keep quiet for a while until you were forgotten about. Sure. If it happened in the South, go North. If it happened in the West, go East. The old urge to get moving because it happened to be a big country. So what gives—in the real?

You're sitting there in some room one day, maybe reading a paper, or taking a bath, or making a pass at some tomato, and you're all surprised when they walk in without even bothering to knock. They snap on the cuffs, and you're what they call "en route" as of immediately. It never occurs to a tinhorn that he gets more famous than a movie star in no time at all. His picture really gets distribution, every post office and bank has it, bridges, railroads, bus lines, taxi companies. Profile and full face, height,

weight, the color of your eyes and your hair. If you got a mole
under your left armpit, they tell about that too. The teletype
machines start clicking off the rest of your story and you can't
run fast enough even by plane to beat the electricity. Sooner or
later somebody, it may be only your landlady, sees that face of
yours, and you've had it. Tinhorns always underestimate the
enforcement agencies. Which is why they are tinhorns. Which is
why they are always winding up in the pen.

Smart operators lined things up carefully, using their heads
and making sure there was absolutely nothing, no matter how
small, that could go wrong. Then they hired a lawyer who
really knew his business, set a bonus for acquittal, and stood
their ground. Like in this case here.

Although they probably knew all about the Western Sales
Company, it really didn't matter. They would want to hang
you for a bigger thing—specifically the elimination of one Sam
Addleheim. In the first degree. Actually you had done them and
the whole world a favor, but they weren't going to look at it
that way. They were only trying to run a business too; they had
a quota to make, and to be sharp, you had to be sympathetic
and understand that to keep their jobs they had to bring in
enough convictions to prove they were doing something besides
sitting on their ass. When the conviction business got slack,
as it was bound to every once in a while, they got rough and
filled their quota no matter what. It helped elections. You
wound up as a number on their conviction record for the year—
with a number on your back.

Take Connie now. She was going to have to be a little
mixed up in this, but just to testify and it really wouldn't hurt
her none. Carl was different. He wouldn't take the gas because
the evidence would be all circumstantial, but he would probably
cool for a few years and that might do him good. Give him time
to grow up if he was ever going to. It was too bad to do a thing
like this to Hamil, but things were getting out of control in a

way you hadn't expected, and Hamil would just have to sweat it out. Anyway, you had to stop thinking about Hamil. Don't even let him in your mind because when that happened you thought soft, and that would be the end of Bruno Felkin. Someday maybe you could make it up to him, buy him a new boat or something, but right now you had to survive. The only way to do it was the hard way. You're alone in this world, Felkin, you always been and you always will be. Even Connie might sell you out if you told her too much. Be smart. Use your heart for pumping blood only, and you'll get a long ways.

From where he stood on a hill overlooking Sausalito, Bruno could observe the shipyard where Hamil had docked the *Taage*. It was the same shipyard where he had fought Carl— that was a stupid damn thing to do if there ever was one—and he could see part of the *Taage*'s graceful hull outlined beneath the light on the dock. Hamil had given up the salmon after three days' fishing. They returned with only sixty fish and went at once to the shipyard to rig for albacore. The lay-up couldn't have come at a better time. For the next few days there was going to be a lot to do on shore. Strictly in the Felkin fashion.

The hill was high and very steep. The houses with their lighted windows tumbled downward to the water almost from Bruno's feet. He could see the whole bay. The almost full moon made a metallic sheet of Raccoon Strait and cut a black outline of the hills beyond Oakland. The lights of San Francisco seemed to hang in the air on the far side of the bay, but because of the moon, neither the lights nor the stars had any sparkle. Bruno waited in the shadow of some trees. He watched the road that twisted down the hill and reviewed the instructions he had given Carl that afternoon.

"What time did you say Connie gets through work?"

"Nine-thirty."

"Okay. Now that new car of yours needs some romance.

You're going to pick Connie up at nine-thirty like you probably done before. Make sure you laugh and have a good time when you drive away from that restaurant. Head for the Golden Gate Bridge and drive slow. Put your arm around Connie once in a while, but not enough so you get pinched. Drive slow, understand? I checked the tide table and it says there's going to be a big moon tonight. Point the moon out to Connie every once in a while. When you stop to pay toll on the bridge, lean over and give Connie a little kiss on the cheek or something. Let the bridge guard see you, the guy who takes your fifty cents. Remember he's a copper too. Then start over the bridge as if you had all the time in the world, understand?"

Carl opened his mouth just once. "I don't—"

"Shut up! You do exactly as I say or you're going to jail for peddling narcotics, falsely registering a car, violating probation, and plenty more. Now get this. You're just out to show your girl the moon. When you come across the bridge take a good look in your rear-vision mirror. There won't be hardly any cars on the bridge by then—it should be just around ten. Anyway, everybody speeds up on the bridge, and you're going to be slow, see? Don't forget that. Not over twenty-five miles an hour, and not under. The bridge gives you a good straight look in your mirror all the way across, nearly. Watch that mirror. If there's a car behind you going as slow as you are, stay on the highway until you get through the tunnel, then keep going until you get to that drive-in joint near the Larkspur turn-off. Stop and have a hamburger, look at the moon a while, then take Connie back to her apartment. When you've dropped her off, come back to the shipyard, park your damn car, and go to bed on the *Taage* and see me in the morning for more instructions. It ought to be all over by eleven-thirty and don't think I won't be laying in my bunk waiting for you."

"I don't get this, Bruno. You might as well know the last time I tried to kiss Connie she really hung one on me."

"Good. But not like I'm going to if you make a mistake. You tell Connie I said for her to be all smiles no matter what you do. Now listen. If there is *not* a car going as slow as you are across the bridge, turn off at the Sausalito fork. Drive through town the same way—slow. Then see that street that winds up the hill. You take that street, and when you get to the top, stop your car and look at the moon a while. Turn off everything but your parking lights. I'll be watching you and the whole road all the way down the hill. After you been there about ten minutes take a hike for yourself. Don't go too far, but don't come back till Connie blows the horn."

"Am I supposed to tell Connie she's going to see you?"

"Why not?"

"She might not come."

"Carl. You don't know women like Connie. When a guy has a little trouble, they'll always come."

"All right, this once I'll do like you say. But this is the last time. Get yourself another boy, Bruno. I told you I'm quitting and I mean it."

"You're doin' *what?*"

"Quitting. I've had enough."

"You're quittin' nothing. Not until I say you can go—or maybe you're tired of living?"

"You're a son of a bitch, Bruno."

"Correct in every way."

That punk. Thinking he could walk out on Felkin! Well, after that conversation he knew better. There hadn't been a peep out of him since.

Bruno congratulated himself on his choice of location. It had been a real vacation going to sea. A tired mind would not have thought things out so well. He was protected from every angle. To follow Carl up the hill, twisting with the road, a car would have to stay very close, and with his commanding view of the road, not even a car that hung back could approach without

Bruno seeing it. Waiting beneath the trees was also a natural. Tonight things were off to a good start.

Gears whining, a car came up the hill a few minutes before ten o'clock. It passed on beyond the crest and disappeared beyond the turn to the north. It was a sedan and a man was alone in it. For a moment Bruno wondered if Carl had gone to the police with the whole plan. If that punk had shot off his mouth! No. You're sure getting jumpy, Felkin. Coppers don't operate that way. They might pick out an ordinary-looking sedan but it would not be driven alone by a man who smoked a pipe. It was times like this when experience and appreciation of detail paid off. A tinhorn might have got really panicky right then. And so maybe made his first mistake. A tinhorn wouldn't calm down fast and remember very, very few cops smoked pipes. For some reason they just didn't. Maybe they were too easy to get shoved down your throat.

Shortly afterward another car came up the hill. It turned over to the side of the road, stopped, and the lights went off. Without actually seeing their faces, Bruno knew that Carl and Connie were sitting in the front seat. He waited impatiently for Carl to leave, wishing he could see Connie's face. It had been a long time. Jesus, he had almost forgotten what a woman smelled like, what one felt like. How about just climbing in the car and driving off with Connie . . . east somewhere toward the mountains? Shack up in a tourist camp for a few nights anyway and the two of you renew old acquaintance? Connie had other things besides the kind of a mind that understood yours. Bruno laughed softly. Connie—she had imagination.

That's right, Felkin, you just get to thinking like all the other tinhorns and drive off with a babe in a car that was hotter than if it had been boosted the regular way. You'd have her all right—if you hurried. But it would be many years before you'd get a chance at a second one. Maybe never. You'd be too old when you got out. Keep your mind on your business now, think straight and fast, and in six months you and Connie can have yourselves a time.

When Carl was gone, Bruno left the shadow of the trees and crossed the road quickly. He slipped in the front seat beside Connie and took her in his arms without a word. Her lips were warm and moist. A little whimper of surprise came from her as his mouth covered hers. He held her tightly until he could feel the heat of her. For a moment he was lost in her. Then he pushed her away, slowly—very tenderly.

"What you do to me!" he whispered.

Her hands were shaking as she sought in her purse for a cigarette. They could hear each other breathing as Bruno held a light for her. Then they made a sound between them that was like laughing but so subdued neither of them realized they had made a sound.

"You're so thin, Bruno . . . and hard."

"I been working for a living."

"You look wonderful."

"So do you."

"When Carl told me I was going to see you, I had dizzy spells. I'm still whirling. I guess I was afraid."

"Why?"

"I don't know, Bruno. I'm not sure about anything lately."

"You been behavin' yourself?"

"Too much, I guess. When are you coming back?"

"Never."

Her hand reached out to him and passed slowly down his cheek. "Why, Bruno? Once you said we needed each other. But since you left I've been wondering if you ever needed anyone. The whole world isn't against you, Bruno."

"The hell it isn't."

"I'm not."

"I thought we were never going to go in for that sort of stuff. We talked that all over when we first met."

"Haven't you changed your mind . . . even a little?"

"Yeah—I have. We ought to be together permanently and I'm working on it. But we got to swing a deal first. It won't be easy for either one of us."

"Sam Addleheim?"

"Who told you?"

"The police. They've been in my hair ever since you left. Oh Bruno, I begged you not to carry that gun."

"Well I did—and the bastard deserved what he got. As long as I had to make a mistake business-wise, I'm glad it was him."

"Can't you run away?"

"Me? Alone?"

"Yes."

"What is this? You runnin' out on me?" Bruno's hand tightened on her arm. She caught her breath and twisted in pain.

"I didn't mean it that way, Bruno, I just thought you could move so much faster alone."

"Well, have another think. I'd never get away with it. Running is for punks. The numbers just don't add up in your favor . . . not when there's one of you and a hundred thousand of them. There's only one sure way and you got to help me work it out."

"I'll do almost anything, Bruno."

"Cut out the almost. It don't sound like you. Now what movie did you go to that night?"

"The . . . Bella Union."

"What were they showing?"

"I . . . I can't remember the name . . . some foreign picture."

"Think. You got to remember."

"I could get a back newspaper and look it up."

"No good. I got to know now. This is important."

"Wait a minute . . ." Connie closed her eyes. "It was taken in Italy. . . .What's Italian for friend?"

"*Paisano*—God knows I been with enough paisanos lately."

"That's it, *Paisan*. That was the name of it."

"What else was on the program? I'm looking 'way ahead on this, to some questions that are going to be asked maybe six weeks from now, and I got to give the right answers."

"There was a cartoon and a scenic about skiing in the Alps."

"Good enough. Anybody specially notice you go in the show?"

"I don't think so."

"It don't make too much difference anyway. I could fix that if I had to. You went straight back to your apartment, didn't you? Didn't stop off nowhere for a soda or something?"

"No. I went straight back and waited for you."

"When we're on the boat goin' to Europe first class and got nothin' whatsoever to do I'll tell you about what happened from then—how Bruno Felkin got into the fishing business. Jesus, this making an honest living is the straight road to starvation. But never mind now, we got more important things to set up. First thing in the morning you call up some newspaper and ask for the movie department. Ask if they can tell you who made this picture, that is, who's got the film now. If they can't tell you, look up the film companies in the classified section of the phone book and keep after them until you hit one that can tell you. Then when you find who has the film, call them up and say you're the secretary of Mr. Mulroy. You got that name right? Mulroy. Mr. Mulroy is in town for only one day and he wants to arrange a private showing of this here picture. In their office if it has to be that way, anywhere, just so he sees it. And he don't care what it costs—cash on the line even if they have to hire the biggest theater in San Francisco. He wants to see this picture at three o'clock tomorrow afternoon, understand? Don't take any excuses—it's got to be done." Bruno reached in his pocket and pulled out a slip of paper.

"Here's the number of the Foster and Keim shipyard where

I'll be at one-thirty, standing right by the phone on the wall. You call me exactly then and tell me where this showing is going to be. Do all your calling from a pay station. When you're through, go about your business until you hear from me. Now have you got all that straight?"

"Yes. But I don't see—"

"How could I knock off Sam Addleheim when I was at the movies with you? And can prove it. Also, when they ask, you're goin' to swear to it. The exact time Sam got it is on the police record although I never thought it would come in so handy in just this way. To lock things up tight I'm goin' to give the Homicide boys a break by fingering the guy who really did it. A little smoke screen to get them confused, but they'll have enough evidence to keep them busy for months. I'll be taken in for questioning on some general charge, but the bail will be all set before I sign the book. If things go wrong and we have to jump it, well, that's why it pays to save your money. That's the time to run fast."

"Bruno . . ." She drew her hand away from his. "I don't like this."

"You got to. Or was that just a lot of talk about us needin' each other?"

"You know it wasn't just talk." Her hand returned to his and clutched it.

"Then you got to take the bad with the good. Do you need any money?"

"No. Bruno, who . . . will it be?"

"The less you know, Connie, the better off you'll be. Now good night."

"You aren't going. Not for a little while. Please, Bruno. There's so much I've been wanting to say."

"I love the way you talk since you been to that school. All correct, with almost no slips. But save it until we get out of this jam. It will sound even better when we're lying back on some bed not giving a damn about anything. Don't think about now. Think about a year or so from now. That's how I manage to wait. Don't think about anything for this moment, Connie. . . ." He pulled her to him and again he could feel her whole body.

"Please, Bruno . . . I don't want—"

"Shut up."

"Please . . . Bruno."

Afterward, he kissed her eyes and her lips lightly and then slipped out of the car.

"One question," he said, smiling. "What's with you and Carl?"

"Nothing . . . I guess. Oh, Bruno, can't you find some other way . . . take a plane to Canada—"

"We'll go together when the right time comes. We'll have a real life together, understand? Do just exactly like I told you. I'm trusting you with our life. Now blow the horn—and so long." He turned away quickly and slipped down the hill.

Connie put her head back against the car seat and closed her eyes. For a moment she was sure she was going to be sick. She felt for the purse beside her and found a handkerchief. She wiped her mouth hard, until it hurt. She wanted to cry, but when Carl came to her she was laughing instead, a dry laugh that sounded as if it came from another person.

"You didn't blow the horn," Carl said. "I waited as long as I was going to." He was leaning across the door, looking at her in the moonlight. "What's so funny?"

"Nothing . . . nothing at all. I just knew all along it wouldn't work. It never does for me—nothing ever does."

"What did he say to you?" She stopped her laughing and wiped her mouth again and then her eyes.

"Get in the car, Carl. Take me home. No, take me to the Bohème. I want to get drunk."

Carl slipped behind the wheel and they drove down the hill

in silence. As they approached the bridge he reached to turn on the radio but she pushed his hand from the knob almost angrily.

"What's the matter with you?" he asked.

"Nothing. I just don't want to hear music."

"I thought you wanted to go to the Bohème."

"I feel more like taking a bath . . . I feel dirty, Carl. I changed my mind again. Take me home."

"Whatever he said to you I don't like the effects. When I have you home I'm going to the police and tell them where Bruno Felkin is. My guess is they'd be interested."

Connie started to laugh again, but the laugh turned into something else.

"No, you're not, Carl. Don't you see? Bruno has everything planned so if you went to them you'd only hurt yourself. He always figures everything out. He couldn't do things any other way if he tried. He couldn't think any other way because that's how he's always had to think. He's twisted . . . two persons, twisted . . . just like Kelsey said . . . and he's wound around and around like a tight rope. He'll never break. He's a devil, Carl . . . and yet I've seen him when he seems like half a saint."

"What's he up to now?"

"I don't know . . . I wish I was dead."

"Don't talk that way."

"I'd be better dead. I've been in trouble ever since I can remember. It looks like I'll always be in trouble."

"Whatever it is now, I want to fix it for you. Tell me and it's done." Connie looked at his face. He was driving slowly but all his attention was on the road. It was the first time, Connie thought, she had ever seen him tense—without even a suggestion of a smile. He was a new Carl, a deeply angry man. She wanted to slide closer to him on the seat, but instead she moved farther away. She reached quickly for a cigarette and by the time it was lighted some of the choking sensation in her throat

had gone. Connie Thatcher . . . hash slinger first class. Crazy
enough to hope something would work out. Bruno called it.
You're the tinhorn.

"Carl . . . would you want to help a tramp?"

"Yeah. Seeing it's you. I would."

GENERAL BALL PREENED HIMSELF IN THE noonday sun. He walked from the barber shop inhaling the delightful aroma of lilac powder and bay rum that enveloped his newly shaven face and his fresh-cut hair. As he marched briskly down Columbus Avenue, he moved his right hand from time to time as though it swung a cane. He whistled.

On the way to Fisherman's Wharf he interrupted his progress frequently to pause in front of a store window and examine his appearance. The new green hat, the new brown suit, tan shirt, and flowing purple tie, all of which he had selected with the greatest care, would make people along the wharf sit up and take notice. People would say, "Well, I guess Ball really struck it," or, "Ball always had it in him," or, "Now you take that fellow Ball, he's the quiet kind that always has some big deal marking time in his head and you never know just when one is going to pop. . . ." People would say things like that.

As he passed a bar on the corner of Union Street his pace slowed. The odor of the necessary became a tangible wall and his feet suddenly became very difficult to lift from the pavement.

He leaned forward slightly, his whistling became more anxious, and then he passed through the wall. He did not look back at the bar, though God knows the remaining eleven dollars in his pocket would not be seriously damaged if he had just one little whisky. No. He would be resolute. He would be stone sober as per agreement. And besides, he had an immense amount of thinking and supervising to do.

For one thing the albacore season was at hand. The frenzied activity at Fisherman's Wharf kept him busy from morning until night. With the exception of Little Bat, who drank far too much, in Ball's opinion, every member of the dock committee was also busy. Their timber was deserted half the time as Mr. Fancy, Spade-face, and Hoolihan shuttled between this wharf and that, stumbling on and off boats, lifting, pulling, handing things down, giving advice, criticism, and spreading reports.

The wharf was full of strangers, men who had come down from as far as Seattle, Bellingham, Astoria, Newport, and Eureka. Not understanding the function of the dock committee, these strangers were the first to threaten a member who was only trying to help. Their objections varied between a shove in the face and just a plain "get the hell outa here!" It happened every year. The strangers were frugal about giving blessings. If you told a man where he could buy tuna hooks at a slight discount, or held a skein of tuna line while he stretched it, or spent a whole afternoon cleaning somebody's stinking bilge, or just sat on your duff unraveling new tuna line you had managed to tangle, the strangers were coldly unappreciative. They obviously placed slight value on your reports as to the exact location of the tuna outside. They performed their own errands.

The local boys knew better. The minute you hove in sight they tossed a dime or sometimes even a quarter your way and they laughed instead of calling names.

Hoolihan had gone commercial. He was going up and down the dock every morning with a wooden cigar box, giving a spiel.

"Pencils! . . . Shoelaces! . . . Razors! . . . Post cards!" He should have known better; studied his clientele with greater care. Fishermen either couldn't or wouldn't write; they used one razor for a month; and right now with the salmon season a dud, most of them were broke. Yes, indeed! Hoolihan would be astonished and envious when he saw a genuine negotiator, and he would come mewing around with the others for a go at the bottle of number-one whisky which would be available this very night. General Ball was deep in a deal.

Nodding with condescension to the young Italians who stood outside the fish grottos on Powell Street, Ball turned the corner at Sabella's Restaurant and walked straight for the oil dock at Pier 43. The oil dock was next to but not a part of Fisherman's Wharf. It was used principally to unload tankers, and a railroad track ended on it. As now, there was usually a line of freight cars along the dock. When they remained on the track for any length of time and some thoughtless switchman did not haul them away in the middle of the night, the cars often served as a refuge for those members of the dock committee who were not too drunk to find them. General Ball walked along the line of cars as he had been instructed and was not surprised when a voice called to him.

"Okay. Right here."

General Ball turned between two cars.

Bruno Felkin waited on the other side of the coupling. "You smell like a pink rose, but why take all morning?"

"I had to wait in the barber shop. There was a gentleman ahead of me."

"First, let's have my change?" Bruno held out his hand.

"You give me forty, didn't you?" General Ball searched hesitantly in his pocket. "I was very conservative. All in all, coverin' everything, you get three dollars back."

Bruno reached across the coupling and seized his wrist. "How would you like a broken arm? Give with the rest."

General Ball found another two dollars. Bruno slapped him so hard his eyes watered.

"You shouldn' done that to a man my age."

"Give me the rest, damnit! Empty your pockets." Wilting, General Ball gave Bruno the balance of his eleven dollars. "I just don't want you to get in any bad habits . . . quite yet. Have you had a drink?"

"No. Absolutely not." Bruno recoiled as the General blew out his breath.

"Okay, okay. See you don't until you get this job done or you'll find yourself in the bay with an anchor around your neck. Now you've had two hours to forget everything I told you. Let's see how much of it you can remember."

"You're goin' to give me twenty bucks more if I get them papers for you by six o'clock tonight."

"Is that all you can remember—the twenty bucks? Come on."

"I go to a place on Mission Street and say I'm a printer."

"What place, for Christ's sake!"

"The Marvel Coin Machine Company."

"What's the address?"

General Ball considered the question. This fellow had told him the address all right, he was sure of that, and there was once a day when he could remember numbers. But numbers were hard to remember now, along with a lot of other things. A good mind needed some kind of a stimulant or it wore itself out just working so hard. For instance a good stiff drink of number-one whisky. It must be already past noon. The General's lips worked as he considered several possible addresses.

"Now I think . . . was it twenty-five Mission?"

"You're crazy as hell. It's five eighty-three Mission. Look. I'm writing it down for you. Put it in your pocket, and when you find the place throw this slip of paper away."

"Yeah, it'll be better if you write it all out."

"Now what do you say when you get there?"

"I tell 'em I'm a printer and I want to see some of their stationery and in . . . ?"

"Invoices."

" . . . invoices. And I say they look pretty good, but I think I can do a better job."

"Then what?"

"I ask them how much do they pay for their printin' of this stationery, and say I can do it at half whatever price they are already paying."

"You're doing better. Go on."

"I say, how about my making up a few samples of my work and can I have the papers . . ."

"With no obligation involved."

" . . . with no obligation involved, and can I make a few samples and have the papers they show me to sort of work from. No matter what happens I put those papers in my pocket and walk out of the joint."

"Or you don't get your twenty bucks."

" . . . or I don't get my twenty bucks. Then I bring them to you right here tonight." General Ball smiled. Obviously his memory was as dependable as ever. It was as accurate as one of them Chinese abacus in a laundry. "What you want these papers so bad for anyway, mister? You look like a fisherman to me."

"I want to build a fire. Now think hard, General, and tell me what day this is?"

"Could it be . . . Saturday?" General Ball hoped it was Saturday. Planning things ahead, there was nothing like a few drinks on a Saturday.

"It's Tuesday, damnit. Now I got another job for you, and if you can remember to do it on schedule there's another ten spot in it for you. But you don't get the ten until I find out for sure you done it, understand?"

"Sure, sure. Busy as I am, you can depend on me."

"Day after tomorrow you go to a pay telephone and call Sutter 1-2020. I'll write it out for you. Ask for Homicide. When you get it, say you're a friend of Sam Addleheim's. Tell them you know who gave it to Sam, see? If they will cover a new Studebaker parked behind the union hall until the driver shows up, they'll have what they're looking for. Don't say anything else. Hang up right away and beat it. Go have yourself some good drinks. Now that's Thursday you make this call . . . day after tomorrow, understand? Stop blinking your damned eyes like you're goin' to sleep!"

"I was just thinking."

"Don't think. Just do like I told you."

Heavy with fuel and supplies, the *Taage* left Fisherman's Wharf just after dark. She had a long way to go and Hamil was particularly careful that everything aboard was properly stowed and secured. It was too early in the year for any big winds, but the Pacific Coast had a way of being unpredictable, and a boat bound to sea for albacore was more likely to return if extra precautions were taken. The northwest trade winds were deceptive in their regularity. Sometimes the winds swung around to the southeast or the southwest, and every year a few boats manned by men who trusted the Pacific sailed over the horizon and were never seen again. Even so, fishing for albacore, the long-finned, big-eyed species of tuna, was sometimes known as "gentleman" fishing—but only because the gear was relatively simple and the fish were iced down without the mess of cleaning them.

The albacore began to run off the coast of Mexico in early June. As the season progressed they worked northward along the whole Pacific Coast, generally following the Japanese Current. They were a speedy, highly temperamental fish. Though their magnificent gold-green, silver, and jet-black coloring faded soon after they hit the deck, their power to excite professional fishermen was far greater than any other fish. Going for cod was hard, monotonous work. Salmon were at least fairly predictable, and the slow pace of fishing for them in the brown waters close in always subtracted from their interest. The pursuit of albacore called the ocean hunter. They were the climax of the fisherman's year. The thought of them lured him far to sea, fifty, a hundred, two hundred miles—until he found the blue-green water of perfect clarity. Then he set his lines. Then, if there was any love of fishing left in a man who regarded it as a livelihood, then the madness that could draw him to such an occupation became temporarily understandable.

Since he had first come to San Francisco, Hamil had done a good deal of thinking about albacore. There were years when he resolved never to go after them again, when he swore he would stay with the salmon, and not be tempted away. Albacore were such a high gamble. It was possible to cruise for a week without landing one. Even if a few boats were lucky every year, albacore made no sense financially. Trolling for them was done at full cruising speed, sometimes with bursts of full power, and so the fuel cost was high. A man could take on a load, perhaps three or four tons, and return to port exhausted from days and nights of knocking against the open Pacific, only to find the bottom had fallen out of the market. The price actually paid would be half what it was the day of sailing.

The *Taage* passed the sweeping finger of light on the main Farallone island shortly after two in the morning. Hamil stepped out on deck to watch the light and the stars. It was almost time to wake Bruno, who would relieve him on watch, but he would allow him to sleep a little longer. This night with the *Taage* plowing faithfully west, leaving all the entanglements of the land so far behind her, was a night to be appreciated. Out here the air was sharp. It promised. As the *Taage* went on a multitude of phosphorescent stars appeared in the water—more stars than there were in the sky. They glowed, ran wildly together, swirled aft and joined the *Taage*'s electric green wake. There they chased each other away in a trail of cold fire.

Hamil put one foot on the bulwark and braced himself against the cabin. Other men could have their mountains. They could have their plains and their forests. They could have their city streets. This was his. If only Carl could be made to see it as Bruno did. There was now no doubt about Bruno's feelings. As they rigged for albacore he had gone ashore several times—saying he had some things to do about his business. He always returned with that pinched look about his eyes and mouth. But this very night, as the *Taage* threw the first channel spray over her bows, Bruno had changed. He smiled again. His black eyes sparkled when you pulled down the chart and explained that in the morning the *Taage* would be over the Pioneer Sea Mount, and it might be there, in the vicinity of this submarine hill, that the first albacore would be taken. The rise of the hill was shown on the chart's fathom-contour lines circling to a peak. Far below them other lines were drawn on the chart to indicate the Monterey sea valley, a deep canyon really, where it would also pay to explore.

Bruno studied the chart for more than an hour before he went to sleep. He seemed fascinated. He said that to really understand it, he would have to turn his mind inside out and imagine what the country would be like if all the water was suddenly drained out of the ocean. It was really surprising how eager Bruno was to learn everything. He was constantly hungry for knowing. Sometime he must have been starved for it. His mind had been hurt, and it was just recovering. If only he would relax a little and perhaps speak of the things that so tightened him, it would be easier to help him. By golly, Bruno needed a man, an older man to share his troubles—like a father. Well, if he wanted one, he had one.

Hamil took a last look at the sea and the sky and turned into the wheelhouse. He felt his way surely down the dark cabin steps and switched on the light in Bruno's bunk. Bruno's face at rest looked so much different. His head moved very slightly on the pillow with the *Taage's* motion. For the moment he was at peace. His sleep was so easy and deep, Hamil hated to wake him. He looked so much younger, almost as young as Carl, who slept below him. Hamil tugged gently at Bruno's blanket.

"You like to sleep forever, maybe?" Bruno opened his eyes. When he saw Hamil a slow smile crept across his mouth. He looked at his watch hanging on a peg beside him and sat up quickly.

"Jeez, you let me sleep too long, Pop. You must be tired. You shouldna' done that."

"It be fine night and going for albacore alvays make me feel young. It make me a boy again." Hamil took off his pea jacket, cap, and boots. He rolled into his bunk with practiced ease. "Ya . . . it make no sense for a old man to go so far to sea in a small boat, but I guess I alvays do it . . . alvays so long as I can stand up and have plenty of really young fellas around."

"Right this minute I'm the one who feels like an old man," Bruno said, pulling a sweater over his head.

"You be pushing too hard, Bruno. By and by you vake up some day and you say to yourself, vat happened to all the years? It be something like a disease, Bruno. You catch it like a cold— and I think too many Americans are always sneezing from it. Ven I took out my first papers I promised myself I never do that. Push, push, alvays push, and run around in a hurry to be a big somebody."

"You're a fine one to talk. You never heard of the forty-hour week."

"That be different." Hamil closed his eyes and folded his hands across his chest. "I don't expect to be anybody, but I am proud of vat I do. I don't take a rest because somebody else says

I need it. I think you should rest ven you feel you deserve
it. . . ."

"Dope off, Pop. It'll be light in a couple of hours."

"Vake Carl yust before dawn and put down the trolling
poles."

"What's the course?"

"Sou-sou'west. She be all set. Vatch out for other ships. Now
vee are right in the steamer lane. Remember, red to red, sailor
bevare."

"I remember, Pop. Now sleep hard and fast. You deserve it."
Bruno carefully tucked the blanket around Hamil's shoulders
before he went up the steps.

In the wheelhouse Bruno turned on the radio and spun the
dial until he found an all-night music station. Satisfied, he
watched the gyrations of the compass card beneath the binnacle
light for a while and decided that the *Taage* was, like himself,
strictly on course. Maybe a little off here as the night seas swung
her, a little off there, but she always returned to average a single
course. When she swung off, the automatic pilot magically cor-
rected the wheel, and that was that. There must be some kind of
an automatic pilot inside Bruno Felkin—one not affected by
people or surroundings. And it had been functioning perfectly
the last few days, guiding surely when there was temptation to
swerve off course.

It had cost a mere hundred dollars to see *Paisan*. The distrib-
uting company had been glad to run it in their projection
room—and for a rock-bound alibi, that was cheap at twice the
price. Even better, the manager had volunteered the information that the picture had not run anywhere else in San Francisco since the night Connie saw it. Connie and you, don't forget. Great. Let them try to break that one down. They could ask
any detail about the picture they wanted, and Bruno Felkin,
who knew how to genius the brain, could answer correctly. Be
a little vague, maybe, because you were supposed to have seen
it long ago, but you couldn't help being convincing. Now—

Now the part that didn't taste so good, but had to be done. Just remember you're really doing Hamil a favor. This was where the automatic pilot came in. Don't think. Steer straight and blind.

General Ball had turned out to be quite a printing salesman for a guy preserved in alcohol. He showed up with the papers and they were just the thing. One invoice, an envelope, and two sheets of stationery. Marvel Coin Machine Company—the blind Sam Addleheim had used for years. Christ, he didn't even know a coin machine from a steam shovel. But beneath the firm's title, Sam in his fatheaded vanity had always caused to be printed, "Sam Addleheim, Prop." Prop what? The jerk. He should have had it read President, like a real businessman. Anyway it was there, big enough to knock anyone's eyes out, and Carl would have one hell of a time explaining how they happened to be in the pocket of his best shore-going suit. Just saying he didn't know would never satisfy the prosecuting attorney. A thought—be careful to fold those papers tight, then rub them awhile, with a pair of gloves on, of course, until they looked like they had been in the pocket for some time.

Don't forget the gloves, either, when you transferred the gun from your seabag to Carl's. The gun that had given Sam Addleheim a thirty-two-caliber nembutal and hadn't fired a shot since. The ballistics experts would have a field day shooting that gun into their damned wax. They could draw up charts and look through their damned microscopes all they wanted—and they would be just so right. Just mumbling he didn't know wasn't going to do Carl any good there either. And finally Mort Wolf, the best little unparticular lawyer in San Francisco, was all set. He would get a letter telling him to stand by in the morning. Mort Wolf, who could spring you out of any general charge—anything but income tax. Carl was the one who was going to need Mort Wolf, but he was already retained in this trifling matter by Bruno Felkin, who was right on course.

The few details left were insignificant. Connie to close the bank account, yourself down to the post office to empty the Western Sales Company's private warehouse so Carl wouldn't have a leg to stand on. Bail—there would be that probably—advance fee to Mort Wolf, clothes for you, for Connie, if she wanted to come—details, nothing important. Mexico City would be a good place to start a new business of some kind.

An hour after he took the watch, Bruno went out on deck. He walked back to the trolling pit for a pair of canvas gloves. He looked all around the horizon for any lights and, seeing none, returned to the wheelhouse. There was no sense in taking any chances at this point. He promised himself not to look at Hamil when he went below.

The steady beat of the *Taage*'s engine covered the sound of his movements as he let himself down the steps. He removed the gun from under his bunk mattress and placed it in Carl's sea bag. He stood rubbing the papers between his gloved fingers for several minutes, crinkling them slightly. Then he reached into Carl's locker and carefully inserted them in his coat pocket. Still keeping his promise, he took off the gloves and climbed back to the wheelhouse. What an automatic pilot! Nothing could drag it off course.

The affairs of a bookie who had been shot four times in the stomach kept Kelsey up all night. By the time he finished questioning the several witnesses, all of whom were talented liars, and had seen them properly on the blotter as "en route to Sacramento," Kelsey found that he could turn out the light in his office. There was sufficient light from the window now to show that the results of his night's work consisted mainly of his own penciled doodles on the note pads scattered over his desk. He was hungry, and though he knew that eating breakfast would cancel any desire to go home and sleep, he went across the street and had breakfast anyway. When he finished eating it was four-thirty. He bought a morning paper with the idea of going home, taking off his shoes, and reading it. Such sessions always allowed the gears in his mind to slow down gradually, and daytime sleep was therefore more easily attained. It was, he concluded, one hell of an hour to be conscious.

There was almost no traffic on the streets and yet Kelsey took his time driving to Fisherman's Wharf. The area was not on his regular route home, but the moment he turned on the ignition he knew that he would at least drive past the wharf. The place was getting to be a habit. Occasionally he would stop, but most of the time he would simply slow down and wonder what possible attraction the wharf had for him. Since a man named Corky Mullins had chosen such an inconvenient time to drown himself, there wasn't much left to go on. There was a lad who was driving a new car which didn't belong to him, and he had been seen with Connie Thatcher. The relationship was interesting, but so far completely unproductive. And furthermore, just because a case refused to show a crack after a lot of hard work was no sign it had priority over more recent developments. Since the death of Sam Addleheim—a blessing to everyone's peace of mind—there had been four other killings. The taxpayers of San Francisco had not seen fit to provide Homicide with unlimited personnel and so it was necessary to take things as they came along and not be forever going back to cases which refused to progress. There was just so much time per man, per case, and that time had to be intelligently assigned. There could be no blind reliance on a personal hunch, which was the only thing that involved Bruno Felkin with the Addleheim shooting in the first place. Felkin left town apparently the same night. That was about all there was to say about him. His record as a three-time loser made him a candidate for suspicion. As an ex-con, the law said he could draw up to five years for merely being in possession of a weapon—so what? Addleheim had more enemies than a snake. Several of them had been hauled in for

questioning. They offered stone-cold alibis and there was no
reason to believe Bruno Felkin could not do the same.

And yet here was the wharf again. Perhaps, Kelsey told himself, he had just developed a fondness for the smell of fish.
There was no other explanation for parking the car on such an
unseasonably cold and windy morning and going for a walk
around the docks. There was nothing specific to look for, no
leads, no nothing. If he was going sight-seeing on his own time,
why not choose Golden Gate Park, where there were flowers and
trees?

At least there was activity along the wharf. Kelsey almost forgot the hour as he strolled slowly along the line of boats. Perhaps it was the wind which seemed to set everything around the
wharves in motion, but certainly the fishermen seemed unusually active this morning. They were working with their rigging, yelling to each other, washing coffeepots, dumping the remains of breakfast overside, and moving their boats back and
forth for reasons Kelsey could not analyze. He searched halfheartedly for a boat called the *Alert*. Though the fisherman who
owned her was certainly not the most co-operative conversation-
alist, he was at least a point of focus—some excuse, Kelsey
thought, for being where he was. But the *Alert* was not to be
found. She had apparently gone to sea.

Kelsey was momentarily intrigued by the constant chatter of
the radios on the boats. Every boat, it seemed, had a remote
speaker which could be heard on deck. The speakers rattled continuously with an almost unintelligible chatter, now and again
interspersed with howls, squeaks, and screeches. Watching the
fishermen, Kelsey concluded that if they heard or understood
the babel they must do so with a third ear, for they seldom appeared to listen. He paused on the dock just above one of the
larger boats. Two young men stood in the trolling pit attaching
bright feathered jigs to wire leaders. Like the other boats, it had
a radio speaker on the after side of the deck-house which crackled

a constant jibberish. After he had been standing there for a while Kelsey found he could understand a little of it. Somewhere, he knew, two boats were talking.

". . . I get a bearing on you sou'west by south about, but it's not so good a bearing. Tell me . . . have you found any good water yet? Over."

". . . Ya . . . I yust took the temperature a few minutes ago and vee in fifty-eight-degree vater now . . . good blue, too . . . something commence pretty soon now. . . . I think ve yust about over the Pioneer Sea Mount . . . maybe a little to the north yet. How's the weather up Point Reyes, Barney? Over."

"The *Capella* back. Fine . . . fine, Hamil. But I didn't pick up the weather report last night . . . the *Ginger* did, though, and he come by a while ago to say he ain't goin' out because it's supposed to blow tonight and tomorrow . . . varnings at . . . anyhow, I . . ."

There was a crash of static, obliterating both voices. Kelsey thought he heard the words "thirty to forty . . ." then some compass directions. After a few moments the voices cleared.

". . . I can't pick you up very well, Barney . . . I guess vee be too far away. Vee try it later . . . afternoon maybe. . . . Over!"

"Yeah . . . not good . . . take up any more time on the air . . . good fishing to you . . . same to Bruno and Carl. . . . *Capella*. . . ." As the voice faded entirely Kelsey suddenly stopped jingling the change in his pockets. He was dreaming. He should go home to bed if his mind was that tired, if it was beginning to hear things. And yet the name Bruno had been spoken. Kelsey was certain of it. That wasn't a common name—or was it in the fishing fleet? Bruno could be Italian. It could be Slav. It could be just plain American. Kelsey called down to the young men in the trolling pit.

"Hey, are you men listening to that radio?" Without stopping the deft movement of his hands, one of them looked up.

"Yeah, once in a while, but you listen too much and it'll drive you crazy."

"Did you hear the name Bruno mentioned just a minute ago?"

The young man scratched his ear with the pliers he was holding. "The truth is I wasn't listenin' very careful. Reception is lousy this morning. Probably there's a storm off somewhere. . . ."

The other young man thoughtfully smoothed the feathers of the jig he held in his hand.

"I think I heard somebody say the name. But I wouldn't want to say for sure."

"Who was that talking?"

"One of the boats was the *Capella*. She's a dragger. I dunno who the other one was."

"Do you know anybody named Bruno on any of the boats?" The young men looked at each other, shrugged their shoulders, and then turned their faces up to Kelsey again.

"No. We're from up north. We know a lot of the boys but not any Bruno. Still, they come and they go, you know."

"Could you call that boat? The one that was talking?"

"Not from here, the way reception is. Anyhow, he's way up beyond Point Reyes. We'd just waste juice."

"But you did hear the name mentioned, didn't you?" Kelsey was surprised at the anxiety in his own voice. He was almost pleading. He should be home in bed.

"Jesus, mister. I couldn't swear to it—I wasn't really payin' no attention."

"All right," Kelsey said hopelessly. "All right. Thanks."

A gust of wind snapped up the brim on Kelsey's hat. He pushed it down in place again and shivered. It was a cold wind and as he walked back along the dock he found it safer to hold on to his hat. The gusts of wind, he thought, were like the Addleheim case. One minute it was there, and the next minute it was not. Like the wind playing with a hat, you could worry a case too much. Until finally it blew your head off. You could

worry and fret, and lose a lot of good sleep following dry
hunches. Hearing the name Bruno over a fishing boat's radio was
more becoming to a very junior inspector, one who had yet to
learn that because you subconsciously realized a hunch was
based on nothing, your mind was likely to provide something
that would at least make the hunch hold a few drops of water.
An experienced man knew better, had the good sense to smile
at his own frailty. An experienced man had patience and didn't
hear voices in the early morning, not when the sun had yet to top
Telegraph Hill. An experienced man held on to his hat and
his hopes—and went home to a warm bed.

Connie left the school at noon. There was no use trying to stay
any longer. What the instructor said made no sense, he wasn't
talking about Bruno—or Carl. And though he was an educated
man it was unlikely he would appreciate the important difference between them.

She walked back to the apartment from school. It was a long
walk but the wind seemed to blow her up the hill. When she
reached the apartment she went at once to the bathroom to
brush the tangles out of her hair. The wind had really made a
mess of it, and in the bathroom there was no telephone. Avoiding the telephone had been a problem for two days. A twist of
the dial and then on the other end would be Kelsey.

When she was through brushing her hair she studied her
image in the mirror. Bruno Felkin had touched that image. The
face was still young, but it was tired. There was exhaustion
behind the eyes. The mouth could now produce only half a
smile—when it should, because of knowing Carl, really be
singing. It's getting late, Connie. The face says so.

Suddenly she turned away from the mirror and walked into
the bedroom. Just beside the telephone she hesitated, and then
reached out slowly and picked it up. She dialed the number that
had been engraved on her memory for two days.

"I want to talk to Lieutenant Kelsey." There was a brief silence and then a man answered.

"Homicide . . ."

"Lieutenant Kelsey?"

"He's out of the office."

"When will he be back?"

"Probably not until tomorrow morning. He was on duty all last night."

"I . . . I must talk to him."

"What does it pertain to?"

"Ah . . . couldn't I call him at home?"

"Not unless it's very important. Then I could try to contact him."

"Oh . . ."

"You want to leave some message?"

"Yes. Tell him to come by the Bread and Wine Restaurant tonight. Tell him to check his hat with Connie Thatcher. Tell him to come for sure. . . ."

She hung up the phone. She stood motionless for a moment, wanting to wipe her hands. Then she sank down on the bed and buried her face in her arms.

Seventy miles offshore the "taage" sped through the water, always farther and farther to the westward. Bruno had never seen the sea so clear or so blue—or so active. For the first time since he had been aboard, he saw the *Taage* in two ways. He saw her roll gracefully to the seas and in his memory he saw the smooth flow of her underwater lines and he appreciated her strength and ability. Standing in the trolling pit with Carl, he breathed deeply of the morning. When the *Taage* took a big wave over her counter and the spray hissed in all directions, sometimes splattering his face with droplets, he understood why Hamil liked to fish for albacore. This was a life!

Bruno had been on his feet since two o'clock in the morning. It had been too rough to make a decent breakfast; he was wet through with spray; and still he was neither tired nor sleepy. When he hauled in his first albacore under Hamil's direction, he yelled with delight.

"Remember," Hamil said, "the hooks have no barbs. Pull hard and even, never giving any slack, or you vill lose him. Put your back to it, son!"

"Son!" Hamil had said the word, and it set Bruno's mind racing. For a moment it was hard to concentrate on the albacore splashing along just on the surface behind the *Taage*.

"Don't be in too much excitement, but pull steady . . . so?"

Hand over hand Bruno pulled in the long cotton line, wanting with all his strength to do everything properly with Hamil watching. When he had dragged the albacore closer, until it rode foaming in the *Taage*'s wake, Hamil said, "Now ven you get him close, slide your hand down the length of the leader and bring him aboard in vun big heave. No slack . . . so? Never any slack."

Legs spread wide to brace himself, Bruno pulled. And when at last he heaved the fish high in the air, throwing him forward to the deck, and saw him at once bounce off the hook and set up a furious beating with his tail, he yelled in triumph. He knew he was laughing like a crazy man. His face and arms were splattered with the albacore's blood. Something had broken inside Bruno Felkin, and he didn't care. He didn't care for anything! Hamil laughed too and pounded him on the back.

"First vun of the season! Good! Good vork, Bruno Felkin!"

There were eleven lines stringing back from the *Taage*—five on each outrigger pole and one long line from the mainmast. At the ends of the lines were open hooks disguised in feathered jigs or artificial baits of various colors. The *Taage* carried over a hundred jigs which would be changed from time to time according to the whims of the albacore.

"Some days they like the feathers," Hamil explained, "and next day they go for little green squids . . . and next day they fancy red or white . . . you never know until you keep trying."

The lines were prepared in progressive lengths and weighted so they could be hauled inboard one above the other without snagging. Unlike the salmon rig, the weights were very light. The jigs were clearly visible trailing along just beneath the surface.

"The albacore be a fast fish," Hamil said, and Bruno thought he spoke with almost boyish enthusiasm. "He svim maybe thirty miles an hour and vee troll fast too in the *Taage* . . . maybe six or seven ourselves. It makes for a big bang ven they strike . . . so you vill see."

And Bruno did see. From the moment he caught the first fish, things began to happen so fast he had no time to do anything but pull and pull, heave, and throw back the hooks until his arms and back ached so painfully he almost wished they would lose the fish. He wanted to sit down and rest and smoke a cigarette and think about what had happened inside him. But no sooner did a jig hit the water and float away than its rubber snapper would be yanked almost to the breaking point, and the line would have to be hauled in again. There were no mechanical gurdies now. It was all back work—broken back, Bruno thought. And on his side of the trolling pit Carl was equally engaged. His powerful arms hauled tirelessly at the lines. No matter how hard Bruno worked he could not keep up with him.

Steering from the wheelhouse, Hamil circled around and around the school of albacore. From time to time he stepped out of the wheelhouse, shouting encouragment to Bruno and Carl.

"Get 'em now, boys! Haul fast! They von't stay here all day! Any minute they sound and then it is good bye forever!"

When the *Taage* ran downwind with the seas or even when she rolled with the sea abeam in the circles, it was not so bad; Bruno found he could use both hands for continuous hauling. But when Hamil turned the *Taage* back into the wind and the seas, then there was a scramble. The *Taage* would plunge down into a trough, her stern would rise up so rapidly it threw both Bruno and Carl off balance. Then they would have to grab for something—anything for support until the *Taage*'s bow rose to the next wave. Then at intervals the bow would meet a big one. There would be a crash forward as if someone had struck a huge piece of tin with a hammer, and spray would shower down upon the whole boat.

"It's those seventh waves get you!" Carl laughed and paused to wipe the water from his eyes. "Stand by to capsize!"

Bruno grunted as he yanked an albacore high out of the water. The fish glistened momentarily in the sunlight and then slammed down on the deck beside the others. "What . . . you mean . . . seventh wave?"

"I never believed it either, but you just watch . . . every couple of minutes a whopper will come along . . . one of 'em rolled me on the beach when I was a kid and scared me so I wanted no part of swimming ever since . . . it just works out to be almost every seventh. Don't ask me why."

"I got no time to count anything!" Bruno paid out his line as fast as his hands could move and then grabbed the tag line to one that was already loaded. He started hauling in again. "But . . . we got . . . to have a talk . . . me and you, Carl . . . make some changes . . . or is this going to go on much longer?"

"They'll sound any minute. Pop might get in too close to the school—or something else will scare 'em. Then for a while you'll wonder if there's any fish left in the ocean."

"Hey, you two old ladies!" Hamil was yelling from the wheel house. "Stop the gossip! I count only vun hundred and two fish. Vee got to do better!" Bruno glanced over his shoulder at Hamil. He looked so young standing there—forty at the most. His eyes sparkled with the same blue-green as the sea. The wind tore at his hair, making it whip wildly at his brow. Bruno found it almost impossible to look away from him. There was so much to be said now. He wanted to tell Hamil as quickly as he could, tell him that some kind of a control wire had broken inside the guy he knew as Bruno Felkin. There were a lot of things to be said to Hamil. Things that had been corked up for twenty years. Bruno waved his hand.

"Relax, Pop! We'll sink the boat for you!"

About noon the albacore vanished as suddenly as they had come. The lines that had been stiff and jerking a few moments before now were slack and lifeless. The school had sounded and even Carl was grateful. Hamil turned the *Taage* to run with the wind and the waves. As her motion eased Bruno and Carl crouched down out of the wind on the floor of the trolling pit. Their faces were covered with granules of salt and blobs of sweat. They wiped their faces on their sleeves and cupped their hands to light their cigarettes.

"How much you owe on that car?" Bruno finally said.

"Fifteen hundred and twenty bucks."

"Is that what you want worst? Do you want that car so bad you can taste it . . . like a friend of mine used to want things?"

"No, not any more."

"What happened?"

"I'm getting rid of it. It's too fancy for a fisherman."

"I had the idea you weren't goin' to be one."

"After knowing you . . . I'm considering a lot of changes. For one thing, you're getting off this boat and I'm stickin' with Pop for a while."

Bruno looked at Carl's eyes. This was a different Carl. The lazy smile wasn't there now. He meant what he said.

"Are you giving orders?"

"I am."

"Maybe you forgot about your probation. Maybe you want a rest cure in San Quentin. I can arrange that."

"You won't arrange anything. You're in enough trouble."

"Who gave you that idea? Connie?"

"Partly. The rest I figured out for myself. When we get back to port this time I'm going to give you two hours to disappear. I'm only allowing you that on account of Connie . . . and Pop. It won't do any good to make them feel sick."

Bruno smoked in silence, taking long puffs at his cigarette and inhaling deeply. This punk was telling Bruno Felkin! He was asking for another shellacking. But the urge to work him over was weak somehow—it barely existed. Felkin's automatic pilot had a short circuit somewheres. He was sitting back in the sun and thinking, thinking screwy ever since Hamil called out that one word, "Son!"

"I asked Connie what goes with you two. She said . . . nothing."

"I want to marry her."

"She's been livin' with me. You know that?"

"Yeah. I know it."

"What would your pop think, if he knew?"

"If I stayed with him, I guess he'd be happy."

"So you want to be an all-around sucker?"

"I told you. Two hours after we hit port, beat it."

Bruno closed his eyes. What went on here? You had everything all set. There was nothing to worry about, nothing that could go wrong; yet the fight had all leaked out of you somehow. You weren't even riled about Carl and Connie. Didn't even care if she had sold you out. You almost wanted to see them together, yes, by God! You were going crazy again, as crazy as if you'd been eatin' your own bindles, crazy from looking at yourself, crazy from the idea of having Hamil know everything wasn't level about you. It wasn't Carl. It wasn't Connie. It was Hamil and his damned wonderfulness. He was the first guy you ever knew cared about you. The thought of him was knocking Felkin completely off his trolley. The genius was only a little tinhorn.

Bruno flipped his cigarette into the air and it sailed instantly away on the wind. Then he found words coming from his mouth —words he could not believe.

"The Western Sales Company is going out of business, Carl. As of now."

"What's the catch?"

"No catch. You didn't quit your job. I fired you. And I don't want you to try for another one like it."

"I don't intend to."

"Like . . . Pop . . . says. By and by a man gets some sense. Okay. I'm going away. If we ever meet and have about fifteen hours to spare I'll tell you why I changed my mind."

"What about Connie?"

"That . . . we'll have to think about." Carl was looking beyond Bruno. Suddenly he raised his arm.

"You got a big slug on your tip line!" Before they could get on their feet Hamil was calling to them from the wheelhouse.

"Hey! Lazybones! You both asleep back there? You vant the fish to yump on board by himself?" Almost all the lines were alive again. Hamil had found another school.

Simon Lee would have liked to go for albacore, but now he was doubly glad he had decided against it.

"So we starve to death," he told the dog Tunie, "but at least we don't drown."

It might not be very exciting to bob up and down like a cork within spitting distance of the Farallone Islands, but there the Islands were, right within easy swimming distance, and from a boat as old and generally decrepit as the *Alert*, the sight of them was very comforting. The Pacific was really beginning to heave this afternoon. There was still only enough wind to mildly trouble the surface, but the swells, so easily measured against the island, were tremendous. And such swells, Simon thought, had some authority behind them. Their origin might be a thousand miles to the west, or it might be much closer to that limited area where the *Alert* bounced soggily up and down over the dens of the ling cod. Swells, like these, created in a sea that washed against China, were not going to stop until they smashed themselves against the coast of America. Not the way they were rolling.

Simon had not pulled a ling cod aboard for over an hour. In the early morning the water had been a clear green—ideal—but now it was riled and murky. Cod were cowards. When their liquid world began to push and pull, when the sea fans and weed swayed abnormally, they found a convenient rock and stayed under it until quieter times. Their timid ways were very discouraging.

Working his arm back and forth with the regularity of a machine, Simon tugged constantly at the wire line, bouncing the weight along the bottom. Tunie huddled wet and shivering in the trolling pit at his master's feet, and when a dash of spray peppered his face he licked the salt away from his chops and whimpered. His black eyes begged for sympathy.

"I'll thank you not to look at me in just that way, little mutt," Simon said. "If I stop fishing simply because it's getting choppy, the fish buyers can't make three-hundred-per-cent profit on what I catch, and we wouldn't want to do that to them, would we now? We must think of the poor fish buyers. How else can they keep in fifty-cent cigars?" Chewing angrily on his pipe, his arm never ceasing to tug the line, Simon watched a huge swell approach the north end of the nearest island. It hit with the rumble of thunder, exploded, and white water shot high in the air. Surprised, birds and sea lions together scrambled for shelter.

"Tunie, I'm not so sure. Perhaps your miserable little face is influencing my judgment, but I think we'll make just one more pass to the east here, and then work around to anchor in the lee. We'll just quit early. It might be a good idea. Hell, there's no fish anyway."

The *Capella* was dragging just a few miles off the Cordell Banks. Barney Schriona sat in her warm wheelhouse waiting for time to pass. It would be another thirty minutes before the net would be down long enough to produce a decent haul. Barney was beginning to wonder if he should wait. Certainly this would be the last drag of the day. To the north, over the area of the

Cordell Bank itself, the ocean was stippled with white. That was
nothing much to be concerned about, but the *Capella*'s windows
were beginning to rattle and it could not all be blamed on her
big Atlas Diesel. Besides the white water there were heavy
swells. When they raised the *Capella* the net seldom rose at the
same time and so the strain on the towing cable became a combination of the boat and the net itself. Cables broke very seldom,
but it did happen. Then not only were the net and otter boards
a total loss, but usually someone on deck was seriously injured.

Barney took a long look at the western horizon. In a very short
time the sun had changed color. It was a cold yellow now—and
there was something more, unless his eyes were tricking him.
The sharp line of the distant horizon was gone. In its place lay a
gray film, flat and still thin. But the curvature of the earth
would naturally reduce its thickness and there was no telling its
true depth beyond Barney's limited vision. Anyway, it was a
"bag of wind," the advance guard of a change in weather. Barney tapped the barometer with his finger and regarded it
angrily. Barometers were no damn good on the Pacific Coast.
They always changed after the weather arrived. Still looking, he
reached behind him and switched on the radio. His hand sought
the microphone, found it, and brought it to his lips.

"Calling the *Taage*. The *Capella* calling the *Taage*. Do you
pick me up, Hamil?" He waited. There was nothing but the
crackle of static. He tapped the microphone against the bulkhead to disturb the carbon particles. Maybe the *Capella*'s radio
wasn't putting out. "The *Capella* calling the *Taage*. Come in,
Hamil Linder!" Nothing again. Damn all modern inventions!
In the Adriatic you saved your yelling until you got into port.
He was about to return the microphone to its hook when a voice
broke through the static. It was clear and loud.

"The *Fred Holmes* standing by for you if you don't connect,
Barney."

"The *Capella* to the *Fred Holmes*. Well . . . hello, Pablo! I was thinking maybe my transmitter was busted. Have you heard the *Taage* recently?"

"The *Fred Holmes* back. No, Barney. I think he's 'way down south somewheres. I heard him early this morning but I guess he's too far away now. How's the draggin' going?"

"Pretty good . . . but I think we'll pick up now. We got white water all around and there's a bag of wind to the west. We're pretty close in . . . so we'll drop the hook behind Point Reyes tonight. Where are you and what are you up to? Over."

"We been chasin' the albacore around so much there's no tellin' where we are . . . but somewheres west by south of Point Reyes . . . maybe fifty miles. Anyhow, I don't like it, the way it's gettin' sloppy out here. Don't seem right for this time of year."

"How's the wind? Come back, Pablo."

"Not good, not bad. Maybe twenty miles an hour but it seems to be picking up and swinging to the southwest. We take a green sea aboard now and again."

"Will you drift tonight? Come back."

"The *Fred Holmes* back. No, Barney. I s'pose if we go in we'll be stuck there and our ice will melt, but this don't look good to me, so we're just about to turn for San Francisco. If it gets really bad, that'll give us a run for it. Want me to try callin' Hamil?"

"Yeah. Do that, please, Pablo. And thanks for the call. The *Capella* off with the *Fred Holmes* and good fishin' to you."

The children coming home from school knew what to do with the wind. As the bright yellow school bus came to a stop at the farms along the winding road to Point Reyes Lighthouse Station, the children would pop out of it, sometimes one at a time and again in groups of two or three. One boy invented the game and almost without exception the others imitated him. The moment the bus stopped and they were free of it, they spread their coats wide. Screaming, they sailed with the wind, scattering like leaves before it.

Those who left the bus last, those who lived on the Point itself, had the most wind to match their spirits.

After he took the direction-finder bearing on the Farallone Islands, Hamil braced his rump against the wheelhouse bulkhead and bent over the chart. He carefully slid his parallel rules from the nearest compass rose to the Islands station itself, and drew a faint line on the chart. He could have wished for a better bearing, one somewhat sharper, at least, but something was raising hell in the air, and the *Taage* was pitching heavily, and he had to be satisfied. At least the bearing generally agreed with the mental notations he had made all day, of course and distance covered. The *Taage* was west-southwest of the Islands—exactly how far was open to question. He had not been able to get any cross bearings; Pigeon Point was too weak, as always, and Bonita Point was half drowned in static. How far to sea had they chased the albacore?

He took the dividers from their place above the chart, opened them to six minutes of latitude, and walked them along the pencilled line of the bearing for the number of hours the *Taage* had been underway. Then he backtracked two hours, to allow for circling. That was reasonable. It was just a guess, of course, but to make plans it was only necessary to know the *Taage*'s approximate position.

He opened the dividers and placed one point on the cross he had drawn. The other he moved until it met the nearest land. Then he measured the space between the divider points on the chart's corresponding latitude scale. So? Seventy miles, more or less, to the nearest land—running time, a minimum of ten hours.

The *Taage* rolled far to starboard and Hamil was momentarily distracted as he tried to maintain his own balance and keep the dividers and rules from flying across the wheelhouse. A green sea thumped against the *Taage*'s hull. Heavy spray hissed over the wheelhouse with the sound of quickly escaping steam. The tin pots down in the galley clanged as they sought new positions. The engine slowed, then picked up its steady beat again. So?

Hamil looked aft to the trolling pit. The albacore were still coming aboard—only one or two now and then, but they added up. There would be better than three hundred aboard now. The deck was solid with their shining black bodies. Their long fins, pointing up like delicate sabers, fluttered in the wind. Though Carl and Bruno had put on oilskins, Hamil knew that underneath they were soaked to the skin. The sea was no longer blue. It was gray-green and covered with lacelike patterns of white froth. To the west there was one amber wound in the sky. But it was no more than a gash of light—weak and without warmth. As Hamil watched, the wound closed and immediately the entire sky seemed to descend. It appeared heavy, as if it intended to match the weight of the sea. The twilight that came from it set off Carl's and Bruno's yellow oilskins. Everything else lacked depth and shadow.

Hamil returned to the chart. A place called New Year's Island was the nearest shelter, but it was hardly more than an open roadstead and offered only poor holding ground at that. Furthermore, it was useless if the wind swung southwest, as it was apparently doing. It was just as far to the harbor at Monterey as it was to San Francisco. The Farallones were a possibility, but also poor shelter. Point Reyes was too far away to be considered. For the next ten hours, Hamil thought, all the harbors were too far away. That was the trouble with fishing the Pacific Coast. There were no real harbors where a small boat might run for shelter. As yet there was nothing to worry about, but it was going to be a rough night.

Wondering if there were any other boats near him, Hamil

turned on the radio and called the *Capella,* the *Wayfarer,* and the *Fred Holmes* in succession. He received no answer.

Just before dark, the cook on the Danish combination ship *Jespersen,* bound west out of San Francisco for Honolulu, stepped out on deck to cool himself and smoke a cigarette. It was custom with him, not only as a physical relief from the galley heat, but because years of estimating the weather enabled him to foretell with great accuracy the amount of dinner his passengers would consume. There were twelve of them, not including the officers. This would be their first night at sea. Unless they were unusually hardy, not more than six of the passengers would make an appearance in the dining saloon. The cook was certain of his calculation as soon as he stepped to the rail. The *Jespersen* was rolling a good twenty degrees already. The wind whipped at his white apron. He was glad he had left his chef's cap inside.

After a few puffs, he decided there was too much wind to make smoking on deck any pleasure. When the *Jespersen* shuddered along the top of a big swell and then rolled down with it, the cook·threw his cigarette toward the rail. It arched high and the wind threw it back almost at his feet. He caught it, rubbed out the fire against the metal scupper, and pushed it overboard. Straightening, he saw something on the sea just ahead. At the same time a blast from the *Jespersen*'s whistle startled him.

There was a small boat in the sea, dropping rapidly past as the *Jespersen* heaved on. Though it was the last light the cook could see her plainly when she crested a wave. Three men waved from her deck almost carelessly, as if their violent surroundings did not concern them. The little boat disappeared entirely for a moment in the valley of a swell. Then she reappeared, hovered uncertainly on a blossom of foam, and vanished again. Only her feeble little masthead light indicated she was still afloat. But in the moment of passing, the cook had seen enough. She was a fisherman. From the commanding height of the *Jespersen's* deck he had seen so many, all over the world—junks, sampans, sloops, Icelandic trawlers, and lateen-rigged Africans. They were always insanely far at sea. Wherever it happened to be, they were unquestionably manned by lunatics who were in God's particular disfavor.

When he left the cold deck and entered the *Jespersen's* bright, warm companionway, the cook was sorry there would be only six passengers for dinner.

Westbound at eight thousand feet, the navigator of a transocean airliner prepared to take his first drift sight of the flight. There was a large hole in the cloud deck below, and from the character of the dark sky ahead and the weather report folder on his table, it was obvious there would not be another chance to check the wind for several hours.

The navigator took a drift flare from the rack above his Loran box and, stepping across the flight deck, asked the radio operator to move his feet. Then, kneeling, he opened the small hatch in the floor beneath him. He dropped the flare and returned at once to bend over his drift sight. He adjusted the intensity of the luminous cross hairs in the eyepiece to suit him, and waited. When a pin point of light appeared in the void below, he turned the drift sight slowly until the pin point slid along parallel to the cross hairs. When the pin point vanished, he straightened and examined the calibrated scale on the front of the drift sight. Eight degrees. He made a notation on his log and, picking up the weather folder, went forward to the pilot. He turned his flashlight on the page of finely drawn swirls in the center of the folder.

"This front is a lot closer than they have it here," he said to the pilot. "We're getting eight degrees right draft already. That's three degrees more than forecast for this zone."

"What do you guess the wind?"

"Two hundred degrees. If we're lucky enough to get another big hole it might be a good idea to shoot a double drift for speed."

"All right. I'll let you know."

"The wind must be around sixty miles an hour at this altitude." The navigator leaned forward for a quick look at the night. Seeing no stars, he returned unhappily to his table.

On a Wednesday night the Bread and Wine Restaurant was usually filled to capacity. But on this night the customers arrived in driblets. As the men came through the door, Connie noticed that almost without exception there was a crease along their foreheads where their hats had been jammed down tightly. They rubbed their hands together vigorously and blew on them. They went at once to the bar, hardly waiting for their checks. The women, complaining that their hair was a mess, marched directly to the ladies' room and did not reappear for some time. When the door was opened the candles on the tables went out. The waiters were constantly relighting them.

When Kelsey came through the door, Connie saw instantly that he knew what was going to happen. It was in his eyes, all over his face, and in the quiet unhurried way he approached the hat-check stand. And, God bless him, he was making it look as if it was just any night, as if he had simply come by accident. He was trying to make it easy. He had brought a woman with him and there wasn't much doubt about her being his wife. The woman was plain and she fingered her purse nervously. She was embarrassed. She knows about you, Connie—Kelsey has told her.

On the way down to the Bread and Wine, or maybe before he took you away from your comfortable house, he has said that the hat-check girl is going to give him some information—just as he has been sure she would all along, if he waited long enough. Lady, you don't understand it, do you, turning on a man? I'm not sure I do either. You're the secure one, with a good hard set of rules to go by, lady. Some people have luck and some people haven't. You'd never understand me, or what I have to do, in a million years. You're not the one to be uncomfortable, lady.

"This is my wife, Connie," Kelsey said. "We're out on a little celebration tonight and I've always wanted to eat here."

"Anniversary?" Connie tried to smile at the woman, but smiling just at this minute wasn't easy. In exchange for Kelsey's hat she gave him the slip of paper.

"No, not our anniversary. New job. My appointment to the attorney general's office came through." The very fine pen Bruno had given you for school had written the words on the paper. It must have been the pen that wrote those words, not you.

"Oh . . . is that good?"

"We've been waiting for it a long time." The words on the paper told where Bruno Felkin was. The boat. The name Carl had mentioned so many times. The boat that concealed your Bruno, Connie.

"Congratulations, Mr. Kelsey." Kelsey would know what to do with the paper. He was putting it in his pocket now, casually . . . just a hat check.

"I won't be bothering you any more, Connie."

"Who will?"

"Probably no one . . . now. I'll try to fix that." He wouldn't read the paper until he had sat down, perhaps not until he finished eating. He didn't have to. Just throw it away afterwards, Kelsey, please.

"Thanks. Enjoy your dinner." Connie motioned to the headwaiter. "A nice table for two . . . by the window. These are friends of mine."

They went down the few steps to the restaurant without looking back, neither Kelsey nor his wife. Good. That was so much better. Kelsey didn't even have his hand in the pocket where he had put the paper. Oh, Mrs. Kelsey . . . if I can ever have what you have! How can two women have things so much different? Think about another kind of woman sometime, Mrs. Kelsey . . . my kind. Just to broaden your education.

Connie started to sit down in her chair. But the chair was so open and unprotected; she wanted to crawl under something or behind it, hide her face and her hands and the whole rotten person of Connie Thatcher. Suddenly she turned toward the bar.

The proprietor moved down the bar toward her, controlling the surprise on his face. "You want more than change for a dollar," he said dubiously.

"I'll have a brandy and water. The good brandy, Neil."

He hesitated, then said not unpleasantly, "I don't suppose you could stick by the rules and wait until after we close? We could have one together."

"No. I need it now . . . there aren't many customers. Please, Neil."

"Feeling rocky?" He selected a bottle on the shelf behind him and poured the drink.

"A little." She made a small toasting gesture with the glass and he watched her carefully as she held it to her lips.

"What's the trouble, Connie?" She made no answer. Oh, Bruno . . . I almost loved you. For one thing, because you taught me how to dream. But your dreams were no good. They turned into nightmares.

"I've stood behind this bar a long time," Neil said. "You get a free case of champagne for telling me something I haven't heard before. Now, when did he mistreat you?"

"That's just it. He never did."

"Another woman?"

"No. And I don't think he ever really had one. If I'm crying, Neil, it's just that in some ways I owe him a lot . . . for showing me what I didn't want. Would you be surprised if I told you what I really wanted was a house and kids?"

"On one drink? Yes, I would be surprised as hell."

"What's more, I think I've found the man."

"You don't have to lie to get the champagne, Connie." She finished her drink and set the glass down on the bar. Looking into the glass, she turned it very slowly.

"It's a funny thing, Neil, how I can remember almost everything he said—"

"Are you talking about the first man or this new one?"

"The first one. In a lot of ways he was wonderful. One of the things he always said was . . . you've got to be the very tops, Connie. You've always got to walk proud. . . ."

"So?"

"I'm going to do that, Neil. Even though I don't feel it. He would want me to."

"Alone?"

"I hope not, Neil."

His arm crooked around the mast stay, Hamil faced the wind. There were two kinds of wind, he thought, a hard wind and a soft wind. Sometimes, when they first began, the difference between them could only be appreciated in the memory and that was not always reliable. Many men who had been to sea all their lives were often frightened by soft winds, or tricked by hard winds.

A soft wind could bluster and cause discomfort. It sang in the rigging. It frequently came with rain, cumulus clouds, lightning —some display to support its false power. A hard wind needed nothing. Hamil remembered that it sometimes came on gradu-

ally out of an almost empty sky. It gave a seaman a chance, if he
was not too far from shore. Swells would precede a hard wind,
and finally when the wind itself arrived there was never any
question as to its ability. It lifted spume off the riled water, and
spat it horizontally, creating its own low, level rain. It moaned
in the rigging. Even though its actual velocity at first might not
exceed a soft wind, the difference could be felt on the cheeks. It
pressed them against a man's face and never relaxed the pressure. A hard wind, not needing squalls, drummed continuously
on a man's courage. There was never any escape from it. In time
it drew the strength from a man, leaving him either exhausted
or dead. It just depended. Hamil knew now that he faced a hard
wind. He was already afraid for Carl and Bruno—and for himself.

The night air was thick. Opening his mouth, Hamil could almost chew it. It pressed against his chest and belly and legs,
closing the oilskins about him as if he had been poured into
them. It sucked at his back, ballooning his coat, toying with it,
as if the heavy oilskin were the lightest of silk.

Hamil listened and watched, waiting for his eyes to adjust to
the darkness. He wanted to see the wind. It could be seen, if its
concussion, its relentless force, were looked at with all the
senses. Even when the *Taage* sank in the valley of a wave, it
stabbed at Hamil's eyes with a thousand tiny spears of water.
This wind overcame the sound of the *Taage*'s Diesel, replacing
the muffled exhaust with its own vibration. This wind would
allow no other sounds but those of its own manufacture. As the
Taage rose on the body of a wave, for the moment motionless,
almost suspended on the wind, Hamil would have a chance to
breathe. Then as the *Taage* reached the top of the wave, the
night exploded around him. According to how the *Taage* en-
countered each crest, he would be thrown first forward and then
to one side or the other. Not even his tight grip on the stay could

hold him in place. And frequently he would be buried to his calves in water.

Hamil watched the labors of his boat. This was not her first big wind; he trusted her design implicitly, but there were certain limitations for any boat. Improper handling in such seas could be disastrous. The waves, all out of proportion to the boat's size, could twist her like a chip of wood, and with the wind pressing against her superstructure, hold her so that she would be unable to meet the next wave fairly. Powerless to turn against the wind in time, she would be caught broadside in a trough. Then two things could happen, depending on the angle and velocity of the next descending wave. If she rolled the wrong way just as the crest broke, she could be deluged with several tons of water. Scuppers full, loggy, wallowing beneath the extra weight, she would be more and more at the mercy of each succeeding wave, until a roaring seventh came along and broke through somewhere—the wheelhouse windows, the fore hatch, or the wheelhouse door. Soon afterward she would founder. That was one way it could happen.

The second could be quicker. Rising to a wave, the *Taage* could approach the crest with too much speed. If she did, and if the wave was steep and sharp as these were, her bow, at the instant of meeting the crest, would project beyond it—completely out of the water. Just then the wind could blow her either way, to starboard or port, and she would crash down through the space of fifteen or twenty feet.

The *Taage*'s frames were of heavy oak spaced at four inches and her two-inch planking was the best Port Orford cedar. She could take a terrible blow and Hamil, having himself supervised her building, hardly gave a thought to her strength. But it would be the twist again. Slamming down, momentarily out of control, she could hit at a dangerous angle if the helmsman failed to anticipate. She could be swung completely around before the rudder could take effect. Her stern would be to the wind and the seas, lifted by each wave. She would be sent speeding wildly before it. Her bow would bury on the run and no helmsman could hold her exactly straight, especially at night. She would swerve in one of those fast runs, and the succeeding sea would catch her helpless. She would broach-to; be rolled completely over, and that would be the end.

Carl was doing a fine job at the helm, better, Hamil thought, than he could do himself. As the *Taage* climbed a wave he could feel Carl cut back the Diesel just before she met the crest. She would go over easily, taking the crest just off her bow, then her Diesel would take hold again. Carl was a seaman, that boy. This was his first real gale but he sensed perfectly what the *Taage* would do. He gave her help instantly when she needed it, yet did not overcontrol or prevent her from following her own lead when the chance occurred. But he had been standing at the wheel for three hours, and he was getting tired. He was also afraid, but then so was Bruno—and so are you, Hamil. The *Taage* was fighting, but she was in agony.

Hamil saw an enormous crest foam white against the black sky. It was unexpected, not in rhythm with the others. He bent his head and seized the stay with both hands. The crest broke with the sound of a hundred cannons. Hamil felt his feet torn off the deck; he was suspended gasping in cold rushing water. He fought with his legs, pumping them wildly to retain his feet, and though he could see nothing he knew the *Taage* was completely submerged. Only the stay assured him that he was not overboard. The *Taage*'s propeller came completely out of the water, the Diesel raced madly, and then there was a stunning impact as she smashed down on the back side of the wave. Father of Christ! As Hamil's boots found the deck he knew that even his *Taage* could not be expected to combat such power and win every time. Another would come and if it caught her just right she would never recover.

Hamil thought, as he had several times before, of the things that might be done should the *Taage* lose her fight. And as always the answers were empty of hope. The hopelessness was part of being a fisherman on any ocean—so many hundreds drowned every year and no one had ever been able to do anything about it. No boat was bigger than the weather except the largest steamers. And the most prosperous fisherman could afford only a small boat, small in relation to the element in which she must live. The *Taage*'s skiff was intended for making shore from an anchorage, or for visiting another boat. She would not last ten seconds in anything but calm seas.

There remained the life preservers. It might be a good idea to put them on now, but what was the use? Life preservers at this distance from shore were badly named. They were corpse preservers. They kept a body afloat indefinitely while the man inside lingered miserably at the edge of consciousness. They prolonged his dying from exposure. If there was any rescue near hand then the preservers might serve their purpose, but no one except other fishermen cared about the movements or location of a small fish boat. The Coast Guard would be willing to try— they always were, and many fishermen owed their lives to them —but even the Coast Guard was helpless without information. Presuming their own boats could proceed to sea against such a gale, they had to know where they were going. It took a long time to find three men's heads just above the surface of an ocean. A rescue boat could pass within a mile and never see a man. It helped to forewarn them, to send an approximate position on the radio, but Hamil had already tried that, just before darkness came. He could have saved his breath and batteries. Fishermen could no more afford expensive radios than expensive boats. When their antennas became soaked with flying spray, their already feeble power was reduced almost to nothing. And so there had been no answer from the Coast Guard. Hamil hadn't expected any.

There was a break in the black sky, a ragged tear no larger

than a man's hand. One star glittered in the hole. Seeing it, Hamil was grateful. There was something else besides the wind and the sea; something still, a thing revealing itself as indifferent to this struggle. It would be comforting to have the star remain, encouraging if it could be joined by others. But it was gone in an instant, jerked away as the hole passed on. The blackness that followed was thicker than ever.

Hamil hated to go back inside the wheelhouse. He preferred to face the wind directly, as he had on sailing boats in the earlier days. Outside a man was too uncomfortable, often too busy to fear. But that reeling, crazy wooden box required him. With the windows battened tight, it smelled now of hot Diesel, of damp clothes, spilled coffee, and tobacco. Every heave, twist, and pound the *Taage* made was exaggerated inside. The faint crying of her frames and deck beams would be just audible over the Diesel. The feeling of being trapped, of the *Taage*'s terribly inadequate size, would be undeniable. Inside, it was hard to say to yourself that of course her design and building was perfect, and she would survive.

Hamil waited his chance, and when the *Taage* shook herself free of a sea and started up to meet another, he let go the stay and threw himself at the wheelhouse door. He slid it open and stepped inside, closing the door immediately after him. Now he would have to forget his own feelings. He must be careful that Carl and Bruno did not see his doubts or sense his fear. As he came through the door their eyes appealed, asking about the night.

At the wheel, Carl bent his knees when the *Taage* fell off a crest and crashed down with nerve-shattering force. Every dish and pan in the galley clanged and clattered. The propeller came out of the water again and the Diesel whined. Spray slashed the windows, hissed along the top of the wheelhouse. Charts slid out of the racks overhead and the compass tipped insanely in its gimbals. Bruno and Hamil were thrown together against the chart table, their hands clutching futilely at the oddments of gear and tools and charts which littered it.

"I couldn't help that one, Pop! They seem to be getting bigger!" Carl said.

"Never mind, boy. You be doin' a fine job!" Carl's back straightened a little. His eyes lost some of their pleading. It was what he had needed, what he would need for hours and hours, until he asked for relief. He had to be told that in his hands the *Taage* would be all right, that it was possible for a man to guide a small boat through this night.

"Do you think . . . the wind is . . . dropping any, Pop?" Carl spoke between actions, a word or two and then a spin of the wheel, and then a few more words. His face, sharp-cut with shadows by the compass light, was stiff with concentration. It was a strong face, Hamil thought, very strong—but now it was desperate and afraid. If they lived through this night, Carl would know the meaning of going to sea. There was some comfort in thinking of that.

"Vell . . . ya . . . maybe it be dropping a little now. By and by she ease off and vee get some sleep." It wasn't easing. That was a straight lie. To see if it was, to hope, was the very reason Hamil had gone on deck. It was blowing harder than ever and it would be a long time before it would exhaust itself.

"This . . . I don't like!" Bruno said. He was braced in the corner of the wheelhouse and his face was white beneath his tangled black hair. "I don't like this one little damned bit!" And Hamil saw that he was afraid. He managed a smile and extended his hand to Bruno's shoulder.

"Vy, Bruno! I be surprised! I don't think you trust the little *Taage*. She vouldn't like that, Bruno."

"That's just the trouble—she's too damn little! I never realized how little she is before."

"If you are going to be a fisherman, you have sometimes yust to take the bad vith the good. No matter vat you do, it seems to be that vay. . . ."

"Well, I'm not goin' to be no fisherman." Bruno put a damp cigarette to his lips and his hands were shaking. "I made up my mind to that all of a sudden. This seems to be a day for making up my mind."

"This morning you be so happy as I have ever seen you."

"That was this morning . . . before God got mad."

The minutes of miserable confusion became hours. Nothing on the *Taage* was ever still. She seemed to have divided herself into parts, each bent on punishing the others; at times it was hard to be sure she was one vessel at all. The Diesel fought separately, the hull strained alone, and the wheelhouse was always a crazy box of loose articles constantly in motion.

Bruno had given up trying to stand. He sat on the floor beside Hamil, bracing himself against the after bulkhead. Only Carl, who had the wheel for support, could stand upright. Carl had been at the wheel for what Bruno thought must have been at least four hours, and as time passed obviously was becoming more certain of himself. There were times when barely audible shouts of triumph came from him—almost as if he were enjoying himself. He would sing out when the *Taage* emerged from a wave, the kind that Bruno was certain would be the last.

When Hamil took Carl's place at the wheel Bruno found it difficult to be sure they had changed places at all. Silhouetted against the binnacle light, with their backs to him, they looked exactly alike. The oilskins covered the difference in years in their figures, they were the same size, and they moved with the same certainty. They had the same way of bracing their shoulders and tossing their heads. Bruno thought that if his own father could have been in this wheelhouse tonight, he would have been crying. He would have been as afraid as his son was.

When Carl returned to the wheel he put his arm around

Hamil's waist and they stood there a moment, swaying together. A smile passed between them.

"Trying to get my job?" Carl asked.

"You must be tired, Carl. Take some rest."

"Nothin' doing. If I have time to think, I'll get scared. It's easier to let you do the worryin'!"

"I'm not vorried."

Carl gave his father's waist a hard squeeze and then took the wheel from him.

"Remember . . . vee with a dobble-yew, Pop. It's *worried*. But you just sit down and do it with any accent you like. Then we'll all feel better and a hell of a lot safer."

Balancing himself gingerly, Hamil slid his weight down the bulkhead until he sat next to Bruno. He sighed, but there was no exhaustion in his manner. Instead he was smiling, at first as if to himself, and then he turned his smile on Bruno.

"I have this to say, Bruno . . . and . . . if maybe vee go for a svim . . . I think you should know it. I have to say that you are a fine fellow."

"What all of a sudden give you that idea?"

"You began it . . . since a long time before the var I cannot remember how it is to have a son. Now I know again. Carl be vith me."

"I didn't have nothin' to do with it."

"So you say. But you can see it?"

"Yeah. I can see it."

"I vould like to have you as a son too, Bruno . . . for as long as you like to be. . . ."

Bruno pushed himself to his feet suddenly. He waited for the *Taage* to recover from a sharp roll and then looked down at Hamil.

"No, Pop . . . no, you wouldn't." He lunged across the wheelhouse and slipped quickly down the steps to the forecastle.

It was very dark below and Bruno stood for a moment in the blackness trying to steady his mind and his body. He hung on to the side of his bunk with both hands and finally he pressed his head against the bunk, allowing the board to cut his forehead until it hurt. And he remembered that he had stood in this position many times before—in his old cell at McNeil Island. He had occupied the upper bunk there too, and there were nights when he stood just this way, pressing his head as hard as he could, trying to clear his thinking—and cursing himself. Now, again he was crying! Bawling like a little crazy baby—with tears that kept coming and a body that wouldn't stop shaking. The sobbing, the sucking for air hurt as crazy much as the board did cutting your forehead. So why not give up, Felkin? Go on and make another mistake! You're a cheap little tinhorn and you always will be. You're afraid of your own shadow. If there's an automatic pilot inside you, Felkin, it's busted. You're only an almost genius and so you'll quit every time, get soft when you know softness will finish you. There was that smile of Hamil's, and his damn eyes; they were the only things you could see.

It wasn't going to work, taking Carl away from Hamil. It would break the old guy's heart, and you cared whether it did or not. He called you son! All the wind in the world wasn't going to blow that idea out of your soft head, and it didn't make any difference if you did go to the bottom tonight. No matter how you sliced it, no matter how you angled the thing, it always came out the same. Just as it had been doing for months. Your head is empty, Felkin, all screwed up . . . because an old dumb Scandahoovian gave you the only thing in the world you really wanted. All right. *All right!*

Feeling his way forward in the blackness, Bruno found Carl's locker. A sea thumped viciously against the hull, the blackness staggered and then fell out from under him. He picked himself up from the floor and made again for the locker door. He pulled it open quickly, hauled out Carl's sea bag, and took the gun from it. Then he replaced the bag and searched in the heaving darkness for Carl's shore suit. His fingers found the papers in the pocket, pulled them away. He was just turning around when he felt the *Taage* rise abruptly, straight up, it seemed. Then she fell with a deafening crash. She rolled far over and Bruno was thrown against the deck beams so hard it almost knocked the wind out of him. The Diesel screamed as the propeller came out of the water and for a moment he was certain the *Taage* would never recover. But slowly the blackness seemed to right itself; the pots and pans in the galley crashed intermittently back into place. Bruno found his feet and heard Hamil calling down to him.

"Bruno! Bruno! Topside—quick!"

As he moved aft toward the steps, Bruno felt a difference in the *Taage*'s motion. It was slower, soggy, as if all the life had gone from her. The Diesel was laboring heavily.

"Bruno!"

He made for the steps as fast as he could. There was no calm in Hamil's voice now. When he reached the wheelhouse, Hamil was at the wheel and his face was grave.

"Bruno! Go help Carl! Vee took a big vun. The hatch over the trolling pit is vashed avay. She filled aft vith a ton of vater! She don't steer right now. Much too heavy aft!"

"Won't the pump bail her?"

"No. Not time. She be so low every wave fills her again. Carl is getting canvas and nails. Vee got to cover that hatch. Right now. Maybe vee have only a few minutes. Take the hammer in the drawer."

Bruno bent to the drawer beneath the chart table and searched frantically among the scramble of pliers, tools, and assorted fishing gear. The crying had stopped but his body was still shaking.

"It ain't here! The damned hammer!"

"Use the gun then. Hurry!"

"The—?" Bruno saw that his hand still held the gun. For the love of God, he *was* going screwy! During all the tossing around below he had never let the gun go. He rose from the floor quickly and slid back the wheelhouse door.

"I follow you and steer from outside," Hamil shouted above the wind.

The two lights placed on a bar athwart the *Taage*'s mast illuminated her deck and the hissing confusion around her. In the light the *Taage* seemed smaller than ever and the seething, enormous activity of the ocean was no longer a remote force in the dark. It lashed at the boat and the men, spat and heaved, and with it the wind yelled.

Bruno saw Carl crouching aft by the trolling pit. He was struggling with a bundle of heavy canvas. The *Taage*'s stern was barely a foot above the water and the sight of it shocked Bruno. He was certain she was sinking. He had to force himself to leave the security of the handrail along the *Taage*'s wheelhouse. He thought that if Carl were not back there alone, nothing could have made him start down that deck.

Halfway to the main hatch, a wave engulfed him. He clawed at the main hatch cover with his free hand and finally emerged, spitting and gasping.

"Take this line vith you!" Hamil shouted. He threw a coil of heavy line, but the throw was foul. The next wave carried Bruno swiftly back until he hit the break in the deck beside Carl.

"Did you bring the hammer?"

"No! Use this!" He still clutched the gun.

"Hold the end down! We got to get one end down! Here's a nail!"

Lying on their bellies, trying to keep the wind out of the canvas, they fought for air and some little stability as they worked together. The trolling pit was completely full of water and with so much weight aft it was obvious the *Taage* would be almost unmanageable. The strength of the wind and seas had already impressed Bruno, but now the sea had removed a wooden hatch that must have weighed seventy pounds and the wind had taken it off into the night. Listening to the wind, feeling its pressure on his whole body, Bruno was strangely relieved to find he could think of nothing else. He was warm, but it was the sudden warmth of real fear, and it was like a fever. As Carl stretched the canvas ahead of him, he tried without success to concentrate on pounding the nails in the canvas.

Every small movement became a task that had to be planned. And when a sea came aboard and thundered down the deck to cover them completely it was always a few minutes before they could regain their breath and resume work. They moved together slowly around the border of the cockpit, setting the nails one by one; and when they came to the after side their legs hung over the stern and were constantly dipped in the sea. Bruno thought he heard Hamil shouting from the wheel, something about being careful and a line, but he could not be sure Hamil had made a sound. His ears and his mind were full of water and wind now. His entire attention was on the tremendous problem of holding a small nail so he could drive it home.

"Is that the best hammer . . . you could find?" Carl yelled.

"Yeah. Pop said hurry."

"We're getting it now!"

"We've had it! Looks to me . . . we could save ourselves the trouble!"

"No, the pump will catch up after a while."

"You really think we'll get out of this?"

"Sure. I got to think that way."

"You were right when you said this is a hell of a way to make a living. You were so right."

"It's better than—Watch it!" The rest of Carl's words were dissolved in water. A gigantic seventh wave roared out of the night and buried the *Taage*. Though he gripped the canvas with all his might, Bruno felt himself being torn away from it. The wave was not liquid, but solid. For one second he tried to recapture the gun—there were still a few nails—and then just holding on was all he could manage. He raised his head. He could see the *Taage*'s lights again and then, still choking, he looked for Carl. He was gone.

Now he distinctly heard Hamil shouting. He turned and saw Carl in the sea behind the *Taage*—still only a few yards away. Bruno saw his white face for only an instant and then his hand reaching out of the water. He could see his mouth open as if he was trying to say something and he was lashing out clumsily at the sea. In the flat left behind the seventh wave there was a moment in which both the sea and the wind seemed to pause, and Hamil's voice came to Bruno clearly.

"My Carl! . . . he never *svim*! . . . my boy!" His voice was a miserable broken cry. Bruno kicked off his boots and in an instant was swimming for Carl. It was the sound of Hamil's voice. Bruno thought only of reaching Carl while there was still time.

It wasn't a long swim, but it took forever. He came to Carl just as the *Taage*'s lights were beginning to fade. Carl was not wild, as Bruno had feared. Jesus, the man had guts. He was coughing, half drowned, yet he said "thanks."

"Don't try to swim! My arm now . . . under yours. Take it easy. We got to wait!"

They rose together on a wave and just before the crest broke over them Bruno saw the *Taage* far to the windward of them. He saw her two lights and Hamil working madly at the deckhouse wheel. Then the *Taage* sank out of sight behind a black mass and there was only a glow of light.

"Just take it easy . . . he'll come back. Are your boots off?"

"Yeah."

"Good. Try to float."

The next wave showed the *Taage* again. She looked farther away. What the hell! If Hamil didn't turn soon he would never

find them. Turn Hamil! Turn! Right back this way. Oh
Christ . . . please turn!

Bruno kept their backs to the wind as much as he could, but
they were still totally submerged in the breaking wave tops.
Each wave became an individual enemy. After the first shock,
Bruno hardly noticed the temperature of the water, but in a
few minutes, despite his exertions, the cold began to penetrate
his bones.

Carl helped considerably. While Bruno held him he managed
to slip off his rubber pants, and he kept his free arm going slowly
in the water exactly as Bruno told him to do.

"Keep your feet moving . . . tread water!" Bruno yelled in
his ear. "But not too hard. We got to save all our strength!"

It was not totally dark. Even when they sank in a trough and
had a moment to prepare themselves for the next wild tum-
bling, the shape of the oncoming wave could be seen. There
would be a white line high above them, foaming suddenly; the
hissing would become a roar, and then the whole crest would
leap upon them. Every time they rose, Bruno would try to see
beyond the few hundred feet that made his horizon. He lost all
sense of direction several times, and then regained it when a
chance came to feel the wind. Now they were both shaking
violently as the cold possessed them. And Bruno knew he was
becoming very tired. His eyes burned with salt and he opened
them only when they rose on a wave.

After a while, when he had lost all notion of the time they
had been in the sea, he was surprised to find he had also lost
interest in the *Taage*'s position. It was too late anyway. Hamil
could never return to the same position on a night like this,
and even if he did, how could he ever maneuver the *Taage* so
they would have a chance to get aboard? It was almost funny,
not stopping to figure this all out before jumping into the Pacific Ocean a hundred miles from land, jumping after a jerk who

couldn't swim across a pond—a half-baked jerk who had the nerve to try for your girl. Bruno Felkin, always the tinhorn.

It was Carl who first saw the *Taage*. All her lights had been turned off and she was approaching from down wind. She was a dark shape almost upon them. Carl tried to yell, but a wave choked him off and then the same wave hid the *Taage* once more.

"Did you see her?" Bruno gasped.

"Yeah! I'm sure!"

They began to yell together and when they rose again Bruno saw the *Taage* change direction slightly and he knew Hamil heard them. Now if he would only come closer, but not too close.

From the water the *Taage* looked enormous. She was rolling and pitching so far her bulwarks were almost even with the sea. When she dipped toward Bruno and Carl and then rolled away, half her hull below the water line came out of the water. Bruno wondered how they were ever going to board her.

The deck lights flashed on and Bruno saw Hamil leave the wheel. He held a life vest in one hand and a coil of line in the other. His arms flashed in the light and the life vest arced toward them. It landed only a few feet away. Towing Carl, Bruno floundered toward it with his last remaining strength. When he reached it he could only hang on to it.

"Put your arm through it, Carl . . . then I'll hang on to you!"

"Stay togedder!" Hamil yelled. "I make a lee—!" A crest broke over Bruno and Carl. It tumbled them, and for a moment Bruno thought the line would jerk his shoulders apart. But in the flat that followed he felt a new motion and saw that Hamil was slowly hauling them toward the *Taage*.

"We're in, Carl! We're practically aboard!" It was much easier now with the preserver supporting Carl. Just hang on to the line and wait. Little by little, a few feet at a time, they were getting closer to the *Taage*. Thank God for Hamil's strength! People talked about dying. They didn't know what it was like to drown every few seconds in the lonesomest damn ocean there ever was. People didn't know how hard you could want to live. For sure you didn't have any last thoughts, not when you were trying to keep alive so hard. This would be something to tell Connie about. Felkin, of all people, is a damned hero. How about that? Only a few more feet. Now don't get anxious and louse up the last part of the act. Let nobody ever say Felkin is a tinhorn.

"Take Carl first . . . he's about gone!"

"I t'row you another line!"

Bruno had to kick at the *Taage* to keep away from her. There was nothing he could do to help Hamil now. With each roll of the *Taage* he was hauling Carl a little farther up the side of her hull. Finally he caught Carl's belt. Bracing himself, he waited until the *Taage* started to roll up and then he heaved him aboard. Carl's limp figure disappeared beyond the bulwark and Hamil at once began to haul on Bruno's line.

"Put the line 'round your vaist—!" Bruno was just turning in the water to loop the line around him when he saw the *Taage* rise straight up as if lifted on an invisible elevator. A seventh wave. He saw the deck lights draw swiftly away, the line was jerked out of his hand, and he heard Hamil shout. Then everything came down on him. He kicked frantically trying to escape the tons of her weight. His flaying hands felt her slimy bottom, he fought the blackness, for an instant his aching lungs breathed only water, and then something exploded against his head.

GENERAL BALL EMERGED FROM THE OOZE surrounding his stupor and looked about him. He studied the peaceful faces of Hoolihan, Little Bat, Mister Fancy, and Spade-face, trying to remember where he had seen them before. Failing to do so, he belched twice. The action seemed to clear his memory, though he was so full of number-one whisky he seemed to gurgle when he moved. At last he found that he could place his companions, if not the events leading to their present condition. Somehow they had come to this room which was bare of any furniture save a sagging brass bed. None of his companions, however, was on the bed. They were on the floor as General Ball was himself, and at odd moments they snored angrily.

General Ball moved his tongue around his lips and attempted to swallow. He found it an extremely difficult process and remembering the bottle of number one began to search for it. That was it! There were two bottles of number-one whisky and these greedy bastids had horned in on the celebration. It had begun this morning, or was it yesterday morning? What the hell difference did it make anyway if the whisky was all gone? He searched in his pockets. All that money was gone too.

"The bastids robbed me!" He spoke not to his outstretched companions, but to the single electric light hanging from the ceiling. "The dirty ungrateful bastids! Wake up, you bastids!"

He kicked Hoolihan, who lay closest to him, without effect. He was about to reach over and shake him when a more subtle scheme fastened itself to his mind. Wake them? No. Out of the goodness of his heart he alone had provided the funds for this meeting of the entire dock committee. They had made many unanimous decisions, General Ball remembered, but what were they? It was because he was associating with men beneath him that he had forgotten. Forgotten everything. Not only were the bastids beneath his class—they were stupid and without ambition. So why do it again? There was more money to be had from that young fellow and there would be more bottles of number one. The thing to do was to escape these bastids who attached themselves to your whisky supply like so many pumps. Slipping out of the room now would be simple. Get away, and when the big pay-off came, Ball's whisky would be Ball's whisky.

General Ball half rose to his knees and then a thought struck him down again. He was supposed to call somebody? Who? He clawed at his memory. Who? Now who in the hell was it? He closed his eyes and tried to beat out the roman candles in his head with his fist. Who? Who did that fellow say to call? And when? But if you couldn't remember who it was supposed to be what difference did it make if you knew when? What difference did the whole thing make anyway when a man needed sleep so badly? More sleep. That was it. Don't go callin' up no one just because that fellow thought he was so tough. Why, you would break him in half the next time you saw him. Break him in three or four pieces. Spade-face would stand by you. So would Hoolihan and Mister Fancy, the bastids. All of them bastids. If they wanted whisky let *them* remember who you were supposed to call. Better than that, be independent. Wait. Yes, by God, make them call you! Start up a office! A re'ular damned office.

As soon as the scenery for General Ball's enterprise was erected in his mind, it fell down slowly and softly over his eyes. He could no longer see the light hanging from the ceiling. It was much easier to lay his head on Hoolihan's leg and sleep.

The wind eased with the coming of daylight. The waves lost their sharp crests and became merely interruptions on the faces of the enormous swells. And gradually, as the light increased, the Pacific lost her anger and instead became a sea of shooting green beauty. Barely moving through the water, the *Taage* rose easily to the top of each swell, seemed to pause momentarily, and then slid gracefully down into the following trough.

Carl sat on the mast's swaying crosstree, one foot hooked around the forestay for security. He was twenty feet above the deck and at that height he could now see more than three miles and the sound of the *Taage*'s Diesel would not cover any shout that might come from the water. He shivered in the dawn and his eyes were exhausted from searching the waves. There was no sign of Bruno.

On deck, Hamil steered the *Taage* in an endless circle which he attempted to enlarge slightly at each completion. But it was very hard to be sure of his location now. It was hopeless and he knew it. Too much time had passed since Bruno disappeared. He must have hit his head or slid along the hull until the propeller caught him. Hamil hated to think of that. He kept looking aloft, hoping for some signal from Carl. But there was no word—no wave of his hand.

As the sun rose the sea became an emerald green, and then the green was gradually dissolved in the reflected blue of the sky. The *Taage*'s bow wave, now small and leisurely, sparkled in the sun. A school of porpoises darted back and forth, missing the *Taage*'s cutwater by inches. They turned playfully on their backs and displayed their white bellies. They surfaced, driving themselves at full speed with their powerful tails, snorted, and then vanished in the depths. Both Hamil and Carl watched them, for there was no other living thing to see. At last Hamil called to Carl. His weary voice barely carried to the masthead.

"You come down now," he said. At first Carl remained still, then finally he swung down from the crosstree and descended the ratlines very slowly. At each step he paused and searched the sea again. When he reached the deck he went at once to the hatch and sat down, still staring at the water. Hamil came to sit beside him. He placed his hand on Carl's knee and for a long time there was silence between them.

Finally Hamil said, "You think vee should look any longer?"

"No."

"I think vee be near the same place all the time. So?"

"I guess so."

"I think Bruno never be a very happy fellow, maybe . . ." Hamil's voice trailed off as if he had forgotten what he started to say.

"He didn't want to drown," Carl said. "He had lots of plans. He would keep fighting as long as there was a chance."

"Vee look all day if you vant."

"No . . . it's over fourteen hours now. He was already tired . . . from saving me. I want to head in. I want to talk with his girl. I'm the one to tell her . . . and I think maybe she can explain some things to me." Carl put his hand on Hamil's. "Bruno thought one hell of a lot of you, Pop. He opened my eyes to a lot of things. Some bad, I guess, and some good. For a little while I want to forget I ever saw an ocean. Will you go see his girl with me?"

"Sure. But maybe I be in the vay—"

"No, Pop. One of the things Bruno finally got into my thick head was that you're a good man to have around when things aren't easy. I'm sure he'd like to have you go with me, Pop. I think that would make him feel better than anything . . . us being together more. It seemed to mean a lot to him."

Hamil stood up and without looking at either Carl or the sea he went into the wheelhouse. He pulled down the chart table and sought his parallel rules in the drawer beneath it. He made a mark at his approximate position and, moving the rules to the nearest compass rose, tried three times to set a course for San Francisco. But the first two times the numbers would not stay in his head. The third time he had difficulty even in reading the fine figures on the chart. And so finally he just put the *Taage* on a northeast course, at least the general direction of San Francisco. Later, when he could think better, when there was less of a mist between his eyes and the chart, he would figure the course more accurately.

There was not a paper on Kelsey's desk. He passed his hand across it, feeling its bareness affectionately, remembering the countless hours he had spent at it. The drawers were empty too, the little personal things were either in the wastebasket or already taken home. All packed up and ready to go, Kelsey thought, except for the final wind-up on the Addleheim mess.

Now someone else could sit at this desk, and some day, if they were lucky and kept their nose clean, they could wait the years out for a pension or a chance at the attorney's office. Well, whoever it was, they would learn a lot, and then they would unlearn a lot. Depending, they would end up not believing anything, or believing everything—when a certain kind of human being was involved.

Kelsey reached into his vest pocket and pulled out a small slip of paper. He unfolded it very carefully and laid it on the bare desk before him. He studied the nervous, almost illegible writing again. Not that he needed to officially; all of the information in the note had been acted upon.

Now it was a case of waiting and satisfying a certain personal
curiosity.

> I know nothing about what happened to Sam Addle-
> heim. I told the truth. But I finally had to make a
> decision. Bruno is on a boat called the *Taage*. It will
> be at Fisherman's Wharf in a few days. Boat owned
> by Hamil Linder. He and his son don't know any-
> thing about Bruno. You know I would never tell you
> this much if I didn't think it was important.

Think what was important, Connie? All of a sudden it
happens. What pressure caused a girl like Connie Thatcher to
squeal on the man who was supposed to be her lover?

Looking at the note again, Kelsey guessed it had been written
in a great hurry. Some powerful instinct had moved that hand.
Fear? Maybe. Fear for herself? Not likely, knowing the girl.
Revenge of some kind? No . . . this note had been written
with reluctance. She hated to write it, but felt she had to. The
words just ran that way. Asking Connie directly why she wrote
it would be a first-class waste of time. She wrote the note because she didn't want to talk, and making her talk had been
tried too many times before. You're very close to aiding and
abetting, Connie. If this desk wasn't so nice and clean and if I
didn't want to keep it that way until the transfer upstate, I
could ring you up on it. Ought to get five years for getting
tangled up with the wrong people, Connie. I warned you, but
we'll let it go by now. Only some day I'd like to know if my
guess is right just why you wrote this note. You wrote more
than you realized, and so I'm glad I made it easy for you.

There was a boat called the *Taage* all right, and it was owned
by a man named Hamil Linder. A check with the Chief Wharf-
inger and the Fishermen's Union had given a pretty good line
on the old man—highly respected, A-number-one character
references all around. The son—not so good. A rap for car

boosting almost a year ago, apparently a youth with an excess of misdirected energy. That seemed about all. On probation in his old man's custody. The same kid, Kelsey, who was driving the Studebaker, and so you weren't so far off the track after all. Was that luck or instinct?

For a moment Kelsey reflected on his numerous visits to Fisherman's Wharf and thought that in the future he would place more reliance on his hunches. It would be easier to be proud if the hunch was based on more than a probability. Presumably Felkin last headed for the wharf, because, thanks to San Francisco, it was the only direction left for him to go.

Now let's see, Connie. You fingered him, not because of a lovers' quarrel, not because of yourself. So my guess is, adding everything together, you and young Linder were beginning to split a fancy here and there. Bruno didn't like it and threatened? No . . . that's wrong. You wouldn't be the girl to put one man out of the way so you could have another one. But Bruno threatened something, somehow, and you had to put a stop to it. You got tired of playing with wild animals. That's my guess, Connie.

The phone rang and Kelsey reached for it quickly. It was about time. With everything else cleaned up, the call would probably be the one he had been waiting for. Now Bruno could come like a lamb, or come out shooting. The final result would be the same.

"Kelsey speaking."

"This is Lieutenant Elwaith, Coast Guard Intelligence."

"Good. What's new?"

"The boat you are waiting for will be at Fisherman's Wharf in approximately two hours. We just had a radio call from him."

"Fine. We'll get right on down there. Wait a second, how come they called you? Is that a regular thing?"

"Only when there's been an accident. It's regulation. They lost a man overboard. By the way, our bulletin board has carried a "wanted" flyer on a man named Bruno Felkin for over three months. Is that the same man you were looking for?"

"Yeah."

"He's the one they lost. There isn't much question about verifying the accident. We know the captain and he's thoroughly reliable. We had nine other boats in distress at approximately the same time. Winds were better than sixty miles an hour in the area. I'd be glad to send you an official weather report covering the period if you want."

"You're sure it was Felkin?"

"That was the name the captain gave. Of course he won't be declared officially dead for about thirty days. After the hearing. Do you want that weather report?"

"No . . . no, I won't need it now. Thanks, Lieutenant." Kelsey put the phone carefully back on its stand. He pulled a fresh cigar out of his pocket, snapped open his knife, and cut off the end. He put it in his mouth and held it between his teeth for some time without lighting it.

". . . won't be officially dead for thirty days. . . ." Why, in thirty days you'll have trouble remembering there ever was a Bruno Felkin! You'll be ex-lieutenant Kelsey . . . all settled down in a new house in Sacramento by that time. You'll have a new office with a new desk covered with papers and probably you'll have new headaches in proportion to the new salary.

Kelsey lit the cigar and puffed on it thoughtfully. He watched the smoke drift upward toward the ceiling that hadn't been painted since he walked into the office twelve years before. All right, Connie, I'm going to do you a little favor. It won't make any difference to anyone but you now, anyway. I'm not going to check up on the report of Bruno's death. That's Coast Guard business and we'll take their word for it. I'm not going near a boat called the *Taage* . . . and I'm going to forget you ever wrote a note. My guess is that would be a lot easier for you.

Kelsey took the note off the desk and blew smoke at it. Then he slowly crumpled it into a tight ball and tossed it in the wastebasket.

News—the theft of a salmon weight, the arrival of a new boat, the death of a relative, a price drop of a cent on bottom fish, the birth of a son, the discovery of a new school of albacore—these things spread rapidly on Fisherman's Wharf. And so Barney Schriona was not surprised when he saw Hamil walking slowly along the dock toward the *Capella*. He was expected, and had been for several days.

When Barney first saw the *Taage* at the dock and observed the inactivity about her, he wondered if her Diesel had broken down or perhaps Hamil was sick. Certainly she had no business lying so long in port during the height of a good albacore run, not when a million fish were reported outside. Hamil wasn't like so many of the others, not the kind to make one good catch and then celebrate ashore until all the money was gone. If there was a fish left in the ocean he would go right back out after him.

Barney had called down to the *Taage* repeatedly that first day although the look of the boat herself told him there would be no answer to his call. The door to her wheelhouse was shut and locked. Her tuna lines hung lifeless from the outrigger poles. She had the look of a boat hastily abandoned. Barney wanted to ask Hamil how he weathered the gale—it had blown hard enough even in the shelter of Drake's Bay—and he wanted to say that Hamil should do something about the *Taage*'s radio. It wasn't putting out the way it should—at least none of his calls had been answered. Then one of the dock committee told him about Bruno, and Barney understood why the *Taage* lay so quietly.

By tradition the loss of a man at sea was seldom considered the victim's fault. The circumstances of his loss were not important. The boat's commander, if he was a good one, assumed the blame. When it happened, as it must now and again, some men were known to sell their boats and leave the sea for years, sometimes forever. The boat became unlucky, her name was never mentioned in quite the same tone of voice as other boats. She was mistrusted. It was unreasonable, this feeling that had descended through a hundred generations of fishermen; it made no sense, but that's the way it was.

Hamil was wearing a dark blue suit. The brown hat Barney knew was almost never brought from its special box in the *Taage*'s forepeak sat exactly level on his head. He wore a tie and his freshly shaven face matched the neatness of his polished black shoes. The gold watch chain Hamil had once explained belonged to his father in Norway glistened across his vest.

As he waited for him to reach the *Capella*, Barney pretended to be interested in the minor damage to his net. The day before he had hung it up on a rock near the Farallones, a rock that shouldn't have been where it was. Actually he didn't care about the net, a few hours' work with the shuttle and twine would repair the tear, but it was something to look at besides the wheeling gulls, something to whistle over thoughtfully, while his friend found a way to speak his mind.

"Hullo, Barney Schriona," Hamil said quietly. Barney looked up from the net and smiled.

"Hamil. I been thinkin' when I would see you. Come aboard." Taking care not to soil his suit, Hamil let himself down to the deck very cautiously, and watching him, Barney thought he moved like a man who was much older than he remembered him from only a few weeks before. Of course it could have been the suit and the hat, or his perfectly clean hands, but when he spoke the vigor was gone from his voice and his smile was only a half-smile.

"Vell, I see you be loafin' again," Hamil said. "You cut that hole in your net vith a knife, so you can stay in port and eat Rosanna's good food, I bet."

"No, by God. This here hole come from believin' I know

everything and from bein' greedy. I made a drag about two years ago right over that same place and come up with some of the finest petrale you ever seen. I got it marked on my chart as clean bottom. Now I know it ain't."

Hamil looked up at the gulls and then down at the deck. "I guess you heard about Bruno," he said.

"Yeah. I heard."

"He vas saving Carl. . . ."

"Yeah."

"He be a fine fellow, that Bruno. Funny thing, I think about him yust like a son, you know."

"Yeah. How about let's have some coffee, Hamil." Barney took his arm and pushed him gently toward the *Capella*'s galley. "If you're goin' to be chasin' them albacore halfway to China all summer, we won't get much chance to talk."

While Barney started up the stove and made himself as busy as he could setting out the cups and measuring the contents of the pot, Hamil said, "Vell, Barney, for a while now I think I svallow the anchor. By golly I never thought I vould. Alvays it seemed to me a man should keep vorking until he vas yust too old for anything but sit in the sun, maybe . . . but I find out now that maybe you should slow things down little by little and maybe give some young fellows a chance—"

"You mean you're thinkin' of quittin' for the season with all them fish out there? Now listen, Hamil. I know you lost a man and that ain't good to think about, but it don't mean you have to stand on shore and cry about it forever. Maybe this was a little different and you probably feel you had no business bein' out there in that gale. . . ."

"It blow pretty hard all right."

"The weather report give sixty miles an hour."

"Ya. Maybe it vas all of that."

"When are you shovin' off again?"

Hamil moved closer to the stove and looked out the galley

window. His heavy fingers tapped a slow rhythm on the table
and for a time there was only the sound of the stove blower
whirring. Barney was uncomfortable. Damnit, he couldn't
think of a thing to say that would lead Hamil back to normal. It
would be much better if Rosanna were present. Women always
knew just what to say when there was nothing to say and how to
make a lot of little words sound important.

"You know, Barney," Hamil said without looking away from
the window, "I be a very happy man today. . . ."

"You don't look it."

"I guess I be like a boat that make a long sail . . . and by
and by come to port. I be tired now, Barney. Maybe I be tired
for a long time and be too stubborn to admit it. Vat you think
about that?"

"Hell, I'm tired too. Everybody in this business is tired. But
even you ain't so crazy as to quit fishin'. S'pose you tried that?
Off somewheres up in the mountains you go, and what happens
the second day you're there? You'll be down standing in some
stream trying to catch a trout—"

Hamil nodded his head slowly.

"By golly, Barney, I think I do yust that. I go up to the mountains next week and sit by some mountain stream and think how
lucky I be."

"So what happens to the *Taage*? She fouls her bottom at her
mooring? You let this thing about Bruno worry you too much.
The best thing for you to do is get the *Taage* to sea tomorrow.
There's a million fish out there."

"She going to sea tonight, Barney. It vill be funny feeling
to stand on the dock and vatch her go."

Barney was aghast. He went to the stove and anxiously examined the coffee to see if it was ready.

"You ain't gone and sold your boat?"

"Ya. I do that." Barney lost interest in the coffee. He slumped
down on the bench at the galley table and put his head in his

hands. He was stunned. Hamil, the rock, the always dependable Hamil. His face was already wearing the smile of an idiot.

"Oh God, Hamil! Why didn't you come see me first? I could have talked you out of that. I suppose you practically gave her away?"

"The fellow be a little short of cash, all right, but he vork it out by and by. He be a good man, Barney. You take a young man make a lot of mistakes maybe, but if he determined to vork hard and knows how, and if he have vun voman he like to show how strong a fellow he can be . . . you put those things to-gedder Barney, and they come out all right."

"Who bought her?"

"My son." Hamil's fingers no longer tapped the table. His whole body was still except for his eyes, which were more alive than Barney had ever seen them.

"But Carl . . . he don't like boats or fishin' or anything about this life. I'm a good enough friend of yours to say you don't have no right to push him into it. I got to say that, Hamil."

"I know how you think and used to be you are right. But now Carl come to me and say it is time for him to take over. I be vaitin' a long time for this, Barney."

"What gave Carl such a change of heart?"

"I don't know exactly. Funny thing, I think Bruno have a lot to do with it . . . and this girl whose name is Connie."

"Who is she?"

"A good girl, I think. I like her the first time I see her, and after vee talk about certain matters and spend some time to-gedder vith her and Carl, I have the hope that by and by I vill be in the vay. They take me two nights for a fine meal and on the second night they begin to laugh about little things togedder in a vay that is interesting. So last night vee are all togedder again and vee have some good vine to drink besides our food and that is ven Carl say he vant me to sell him the *Taage* if I be of such a mind."

"So what's the girl got to do with it?"

"Maybe I am seeing things that are not there. But now Carl is telling me yust how he vould do if he be captain of the *Taage*. He vould go south below Mexico and put a bait tank on her, and not be standing by so much in the vinter . . . so to make more money. I have the same idea for a long time but I be too old to care about it very much. But Carl is talking and making plans and drawing on the tablecloth vith a pencil and ven he forgets to say something about his plans it is this girl Connie who makes him go back and start all over again. So I can see he has talked vith her about his plans and she vould like to help him see them true."

"So you give away your boat?"

"I sell her. They are yust kids, you know, and to hear them fills you full of life again. So of course I like to help as I can."

"You better send that girl to speak with Rosanna so she will know what it's like to be a fisherman's wife. Then go have your head examined."

Barney rose quickly from the table. He hooked his calloused thumbs around his belt and rocked back and forth slowly, unconsciously balancing the *Capella*'s slight movement.

"I'm trying to figure out," he said uncertainly, "just who is crazy. You come to this country with nothin' . . . just like I done. You worked like a dog to build something and you done it, same as me. Now you want to give it all away. Just how are you gonna live? Take unemployment insurance like everybody else? Wait for an old-age pension? We didn't come over here for that."

"I vouldn't do a thing like that, Barney. I vill still have a small share in the *Taage* and I have saved a little. I don't need much. You vould do the same if you had a son."

Barney looked out past the wharf toward the Golden Gate and studied the water for a long time. Finally he sighed deeply and said, "Yeah . . . I guess I would."

"I'll send you down some trout," Hamil said. "And now, Barney, I vill have to ask you can I use the chapel?"

"Again? You're gettin' awful damn religious, Hamil Linder. Go ahead, but don't take too long. The coffee's almost ready."

Hamil stood up and walked to the galley door. The half-smile was still on his face. He turned to remove his hat and place it on the table. "It vill only take me a minute," he said.

Angered at the coffee's failure to boil, Barney turned the stove up full blast. He thought that if the blower would make enough racket he would probably miss a great deal of what Hamil would say in the chapel. His ears, he thought, were naked again, and he had heard enough. But Barney even heard the wood squeak as Hamil kneeled. Then Hamil's voice came clearly through the partition.

" . . . if I have lost a man, Sir," Hamil was saying, "then I have found another vun . . . and I come today to thank you for that. Now Carl, he go to sea . . . my son. Now he become a fisherman, as so many men who were close to your son be . . . and so there be times ven he needs you. Sir . . . I ask you kindly . . . bring him good fortune!"

Barney Schriona surprised himself. Bending over the coffee, he added a soft amen.